1998,

It had been two hundred years since the Battle of Twin Peaks was decided and the warriors of the Order of the White Rose had fought a long and grueling battle, losing over half their fighters against the Army of the Lord of Shadows.

The reason for the losses of these brave heroes was due to an evil dictator known as the Lord of Shadows. With his army, he descended upon the Scandinavian countryside to destroy all who stood in his way. Pillaging and selling the vanquished into slavery, he showed no mercy to his victims. He was defeated, however, not by the army, but by one man. That man was the leader of the Order of the White Rose, Master Eirik. He was a monk who had studied the ways of the warrior and had mastered Aikido and Stav fighting styles. He fought the Lord of Shadows near the evil one's temple and was able to seal the Lord of Shadows into an object using the forbidden technique of the Soul Seal.

It proved to be Master Eirik's last battle as he gave his life to seal in the evil one. The Lord of Shadows had now been safely imprisoned for two centuries. This left five keys with the five Masters of the White Rose, as when The Lord of Shadows became imprisoned inside a statue of a Norse god his power was dispersed among five keys. Only if those five keys were brought together within the temple would he regain his power. The Guardians were there to make sure that did not happen. To further protect the keys, the Guardians eventually spread out across the world. For generations, the keys had been passed down from master to student.

This is where our story begins.

Chapter 1: Bloody Beginnings

It is 1998 in Oslo, Norway. A young, blond-haired boy of about sixteen years runs to the bus stop. He is stopped dead as a slender woman in a white apron shouts from the doorway "Alexander, you've forgotten your lunch!"

The boy turned around, blushing, "Thanks, Mom." Grabbing the bag he turned and boarded the bus for school.

In the house, the mother walked into the kitchen. "Theodor, honey, you up?" The woman called up the stairs, directing her voice toward the master bedroom.

A tall man in his thirties with dark-black hair walked downstairs wearing a black suit and red tie. "Hey, honey, did you get Alexander off to school?"

The woman smiled kindly. "Yep. Do you want breakfast?" she asked as he leant across the table and kissed her.

Taking a seat at the table he replied, "Sure. I've still got an hour before heading into work."

"So when will you tell him about the test?" asked the mother.

"When he gets home, Rachael. I'll sit down with him and tell him all about the test to be a teacher at the dojo."

"Are you sure it's not too soon?" A tone of worry in her voice.

"Rachael, he's almost at my level already. In a few years with the self-training he does when he thinks we aren't looking, he'll surely surpass me. That's if he hasn't already."

"I know, but I don't want the position to go to his head. He is still young. Surely he needs some more time training the other students to ease him into it?"

"He's got a good head on his shoulders. Plus, I made it clear he's to get an education before I seriously consider giving him the rights to the dojo. After all, I had to make the same sacrifices with my training," said the father.

"I'm guessing I can't make you change your mind?" queried Rachael.

"I'll think on it at work and make a decision later today." Hearing the door in the foyer open, Theodor jerked his head around as a loud creek echoed from the foyer.

His eyebrows furrowed. "We aren't expecting anyone, are we?"

"Not that I'm aware of," Rachael said with confusion.

A strong odor came through the house. Getting up immediately, his chair falling to the floor from the sudden movement, Theodor turned, panic etched on his face. "I smell smoke. We have to leave the house. Now!"

Turning to run they found their exit blocked by assailants in black clothing. Their faces covered by white masks with a diagonal red slash. The two looked around unable to see an escape route.

"Run, call the police!" Theodor shouted as he punched the first assassin, the blow knocking his attacker unconscious to the ground. "They've picked the wrong house to rob!"

Rachael scrambled for the phone, grasping it as tightly as she could in her shaking hands. Theodor's eyes widened as his wife suddenly slumped forward, the phone falling from her fingers. The metallic glint of throwing stars shone from Rachael's back as blood ran from the wounds, staining the white apron a dark red. With a ferocious yell, he sprang towards the unknown enemy.

Avoiding the first punch, Theodor retaliated with a kick, the power sending the attacker off the floor, and into the wall. The sickening crunch enough to suggest a broken spine. Managing to raise his leg up and throwing his hands out, he blocked another attack. Grasping his clothing he tossed his enemy to the floor. One of the assassins had yet to attack, standing back from the fight, analyzing the fighting style Theodor used against his men. *He's using counters against our numbers.*

Making his way into the kitchen, Theodor grabbed a knife, hurling it at his closest attacker.

Grabbing a second knife, Theodor stabbed at the second assassin, puncturing his heart. He pulled the knife from the body causing it to fall to the ground. Turning around and kicking high the closest assassin was sent crashing into a glass display case as Theodor fought to survive. The remaining four attackers closed in.

The attacker that had until this point remained back finally saw an opening and rushed forward. With seemingly no alternative, Theodor threw the knife at one of the closest men, striking him through the right eye as the other three converged on him, their weapons drawn.

***

At Oslo High, Alexander Theodorson sat in class as he listened to the teacher drone on about some famous person. The red-haired boy next to him leant across and nudged him.

"Hey, Alexander, you want to go to the arcade?"

Alexander sighed. "No, Samuel, I have to head home. I've got practice."

The boy shrugged his shoulders. "Still practicing? Man, I know you can beat any of the students in the dojo. Only your father is stronger than you. You know you aren't too far off from his level."

"I need to keep practicing so I can improve my skill set. I hope I can take the Master's test soon. I know I'm ready. Besides, there's no such thing as being good enough. You can always learn more, even a Master."

Samuel stared at him and rolled his eyes. "You're kidding me, right? You have been practicing martial arts since you were six years old, studying at least one style *and* working on a sword style. You're more than ready."

Alexander shrugged his shoulders. "I haven't mastered real swords, only wooden ones. Father will tell me when I am ready."

Alexander tried to listen to the teacher, but still struggled to concentrate.

***

After his second class had concluded, Alexander found Samuel being thrown into a locker by a brown-haired jock in jeans. Samuel hit the locker and fell to the ground after the impact.

"Tom, didn't you learn your lesson last time?" asked Alexander, clearly annoyed.

"You got a lucky shot," said Tom with a scowl. "It won't happen again."

Alexander smirked, before replying, "I remember that, and I got a lucky kick and throw in last time we fought as well."

"Let's settle this after school. Same place," said Tom walking away as Alexander bent down and helped his friend up.

"You need to stand up for yourself, Samuel. I won't be there to bail you out every time."

The bell rang, signaling school was finished for another day. Alexander headed out of class and went straight to the spot behind the makeshift baseball field. A crowd had already started to form as Tom walked up with two of his buddies.

"Let us see how you do this time," said Tom.

"This is purely one-on-one, Tom. This is total crush - for you," Alexander stated, getting set into his stance. Despite his warning, the three boys attacked him as one, angry looks on their faces as they tried to overpower him.

Alexander blocked the first blow, then dropped, and swept the boy's feet from under him. A shout from behind him alerted him as he turned and grabbed a punch heading for his head.

"You're an idiot. When launching a surprise attack, keep your mouth shut!" Mocked Alexander as he span and tossed the boy away.

"Tom, there's no shame in backing out," Alexander said. "It's just me and you now."

Tom responded by charging and trying to hit the blond-haired teen, each sloppy punch he sent dodged calmly by Alexander.

"I'm done," Alexander stated with boredom before punching Tom in the stomach and knocking him down. Turning away he scoffed at the one-sided match. "Get better, Tom, before we do this again. That wasn't even a warm-up and you've made me miss the bus," said Alexander as walked away, the three downed bullies left writhing on the field.

Samuel and Alexander headed to their respective houses, chatting about the fight, until it was time to split up. "I'm heading to the arcade before home, Alexander, I'll see you later."

***

Fire trucks and police cars greeted Alexander as he turned the corner. Dropping his bag he sprinted towards his home, smoke billowing from the windows further evidence that something catastrophic had occurred. Police tape surrounded the house as crime officers wheeled two gurneys out of the front doorway toward the road.

"Mom, Dad!" he shouted as he ran up to a temporary barricade. The police Captain present reached out to prevent him running past.

"Who are you, son?" asked the Captain as Alexander struggled to get free.

"I live here. What happened?" asked the worried teen as his eyes darted from the Captain to the burning house.

The Captain sighed. "What's your name?"

"Alexander," he said and then asked again. "What's happened?"

"What is your relation to the deceased?"

"Deceased?" asked Alexander with a stutter. A feeling of dread crawled up his skin. "Who?"

"The couple who lived in this house."

"I am the son of the couple," said Alexander.

The Captain sighed again and pulled the young teen aside. "I hate my job sometimes. I'm sorry, son, but your parents are both dead. We found their bodies riddled with cuts and partially burned with most of the house. We got here only a few minutes after a neighbor called about a fire in the house."

Alexander turned in shock. *How could this have happened? Father should have been able to fight off any intruders,* he thought as he clenched his fist, nails digging into his palm. "Can you tell me how were they killed?"

The Captain noticed the tears welling up in the eyes of the teen. Glancing around and seeing no chance of anyone overhearing, the Captain replied, "We think it was murder due to the damage on the bodies."

Alexander dropped to his knees, his head in his hands as the Chief of Police approached.

"Captain!"

"Yes, Chief?"

"Have you find any clues?" the Chief asked.

"Yes, sir. We have found a used match by the gas line. We have also found a variety of weapons by the bodies," replied the Captain.

"Who is this?" asked the Chief.

"I am the son the deceased," said Alexander.

"Good. No harm in telling you what we found so far, then," said the Chief, turning his attention back to the Captain.

"What else did you discover?" asked the Chief.

"The lady was hit with what appears to be a multitude of some kind of throwing star from our initial investigation. The man appears to have been cut by a sharp object, some kind of blade, perhaps? We don't know what type," said the Captain.

Looking down at Alexander, the Captain did his best to console him, "Your parents put up quite a fight, son. We found five dead assailants littering the floor, one in the foyer and four more in the kitchen. We're doing our best to identify them, but they're pretty badly burned."

Alexander's eyes narrowed as he listened. His sadness began turning to rage and anger. "Did you recover anything of use?" He asked through his tear-stained face.

The two looked at each other. "Not yet," said the Captain. "After we complete our investigation you can enter your house and salvage anything you can find."

Alexander nodded his head. "I'll be by later then."

"You are a minor so you need to stay with a family," remarked the Captain.

"My friend's family will be fine," Alexander replied as he struggled to hold in his emotions.

"We'll wait for you to call your friend and have them pick you up."

Thirty minutes later, a blond-haired woman in a black dress used for office work arrived with Samuel. Rushing to Alexander, she hugged him. "I am sorry for your loss. When I heard what happened, I rushed over," she said with sorrow.

"Are you a friend?" asked the Captain.

"Yes. Well my son is." She opened her bag and pulled out her identification to show the Captian.

"Very well," the Captain replied before turning to Alexander and putting his hand on his shoulder. "We will find out who did this and you will get the justice you need, son."

Alexander nodded his head and turned from the scene of devastation, leaving with his school friend and his mother.

***

Alexander was called later that evening. He was accompanied down to the station so the officer could escort him to the remains of his family home. "I am sorry for your loss but we will find the ones responsible. You have my promise," the officer at the station told him as he left.

Getting to the house, the officer told Alexander he would be outside.

Walking in, Alexander looked around and saw a glimmering object in the cracked floorboard beneath him. Crouching down and pulling up the board, a box was revealed underneath. He quickly put it into his backpack and looked for anything else that might be intact. An hour went by, Alexander found nothing more that was salvageable.

Getting outside, he turned and took one last look at the home he had left his parents in earlier that morning. Wiping a tear from his eye he went with the officer and was taken back to Samuel's in the police car.

***

Alexander went straight upstairs and into the temporary bedroom Samuel's mother had prepared for him. Sitting down on the bed, he took the box from his backpack and opened it. Inside was a cubical item ornate with the carving of a rose, accompanied by a note.

He took out the note to read it.

If you're reading this, then you must be a descendent of Master Eirik or one of his Guardians. Inside this box is a key that when combined with four others will release the evil one known as the Lord of Shadows from his banishment.

Alexander folded the note and took a look at the key inside the box. It appeared have some kind of writing on it. *Is this why my parents were killed?* He asked himself as tears fell down his face. He balled up his fist, crumpling the paper in a rage. His parents were gone.

A few days later, a small funeral was held for the couple. The students of the dojo paid their respects as Alexander gave a speech, fighting to hold back his tears as he did so. He laid a flower on each coffin, turned and walked away.

School the day after the funeral went by in a daze as people gave their condolences to Alexander. The school counselor telling him to come to her if he ever just wanted to talk.

***

At the lawyer's office four days later, the man in charge of the will sighed sadly. "I was a friend of your father's, Alexander, and I am sorry for your loss." He shuffled the papers he held in his hand, before clearing his throat. "Alexander, I have here what I hope you will see as some better news. Your father has left you over two hundred thousand dollars. Your mother also has left you another two hundred thousand dollars from her will. The deed to the dojo is yours as well."

"I don't care about the damn money. It can't buy my parents' lives back!"

The lawyer rose and walked across, putting a hand on the boy's shoulder. As he spoke the sincerity was evident in his voice. "I know, Alexander. You're strong, but even the strong have limits. My advice is to get some counseling to help you to start to heal from this tragedy. It's how you move on from here that determines your state of mind."

***

In a stone temple on the top of a mountain in northern Norway, three men walked up to a statue. Around the statue were pillars containing indents of an unknown shape. They knelt in reverence.

"Did you find one of the keys?" asked a deep-voiced presence that seemed to emanate from the statue itself.

One of the men bowed forward, his forehead against the ground. "No, my Lord. It was too well hidden, but I did find the sword of the one who banished you." He rose and held out a jeweled sword towards the statue to prove his point.

The voice laughed, mirthlessly. "Yes, a good gift, but I don't tolerate failure! You didn't look hard enough. You have failed me!"

Lightning shot down hitting the man where he knelt. He screamed in agony as his body was wracked with spasms. His cries drifted away into silence as fire consumed him and he faded into ash.

The jeweled sword the man had been holding clanked to the ground. One of the other men stood, grabbed the sword, and put it on a pedestal in front of the statue where the voice was coming from. He then went back to his kneeling position.

"I might be only at one-fifth of my strength due to the seal, but I can still deal with any failures. Kira, you're in charge of these fools," said the deep voice. A young woman strode out of the shadows, her flaming hair accenting the forest green of her eyes. The sword strapped to her back sat perfectly over her short, striped coat. Her low sitting pants hugged her muscled legs, making them seem like they went on for miles.

The red-haired woman bowed down and asked, "What are your orders, my Lord?"

"According to the spies I have in the area, the son has retrieved a box from the shell of his house. I think that contains what I need. Take it from his lifeless corpse if you have to, but do not fail me," said the voice.

The woman bowed and responded, "Understood, my Lord."

Kira and the two men walked out of the temple. Joined as they left by another soldier who had appeared to take the place of the one who had most recently felt the Lord of Shadow's wrath.

***

Having struggled on his return to school, Alexander was absent the following week to allow him time to grieve. In a clearing near to Samuel's home, he was practicing with his wooden sword, fighting an invisible enemy. His reflection on the lake next to him as he went through various styles. *Why did this happen? What were you part of, Mother, Father?* Asked the teen to himself.

The previous two days, he had spent at the library to see if he could find anything about this Lord of Shadows mentioned in the note found inside the box.

His search came up empty despite his best efforts.

I suppose it wouldn't be public knowledge, thought the teen.

He was back in the present as a rustling came from the edge of the clearing. "Come out!" he demanded raising his wooden sword in a guard position.

Four people came out into the clearing. One of them was the red-haired woman, Kira. The other three were mere soldiers of the Lord of Shadows and decked in black tunics with cloths over their faces.

Stepping forward from the others, Kira said in a smooth voice, "Alexander, you've got something of my master's. It is a key, and your father had no rights to it. He stole it from my master. Bring it to me, and you will be rewarded. It's of no use to you."

Alexander's eyes narrowed. "Who is your master? Were you the one who murdered my parents?" He growled from his throat while slowly backing away.

"No, unfortunately I never got the pleasure of watching them burn," Kira said grinning maniacally. "If you do not bring us the key you have discovered, then we will have to destroy you. Will you be sensible and take us to it?"

"I don't know what you are talking about. I do not have any key," he lied; he had the box safely hidden in his room at Samuel's house.

The woman smirked. "Nice try. However, you will not be alive long enough to protect it" she replied.

Alexander tensed.

"Then, we will find out where you have been living and kill all those in that house, too. Now will you take us to it or not?"

Alexander shook his head, still brandishing his wooden sword and gripping the handle in preparation of the coming fight. He couldn't trust these people. He knew the key must be very important. "*How can I protect Samuel and his family from these thugs?* He thought.

"Kill him," ordered the red-haired woman as she stepped back.

The three charged Alexander with their weapons as the woman looked on, a cruel smirk etched on her face. The first man swung wildly with his duel short sword but missed his target and was kicked in the back by Alexander.

The other two charged forward as Alexander managed to block a wooden staff with his sword. He struggled to push back against the larger of the two men and fell to one knee. The man continue to force Alexander down and kicked the teen in the chest, knocking him flat.

The larger man raised his blunt weapon, ready to deliver the killing blow, when he was sent back by a strong kick from an unseen assailant. The woman's attention was caught as she glanced up and saw an elderly man of Asian descent. Wearing a blue robe with the symbol of a white rose on his back, he had his long white hair pulled back in a ponytail.

"...Who the hell are you?" she demanded, somewhat weakly. The sheer power radiating from this man had made her hesitate slightly. Foreboding and dread shaking her to her core.

"My name is not important to the dishonorable. You strike a downed warrior. This I cannot allow. You are a disgrace to warriors everywhere." He pulled out a dagger and beckoned the attackers forward. "Come."

The large man sprang to his feet and snarled at the newcomer, he then charged forward bringing his weapon down towards the old man. Quicker than anyone present thought possible, the large man was spewing blood from his jugular vein as the old man slashed across his neck with the dagger.

Kira wasn't used to feeling immense fear. Her body could not stop shaking in this newcomer's presence. He was dangerous. That much was certain.

The old man glanced at the large man's body. Seeing their comrade fall caused the other assailants to pause in shock. However, only for a moment, before they gathered up their courage and charged. With little movement both thugs were mortally wounded: one was stabbed quickly in the chest, the other cut across his throat, a wound matching the warrior's former comrade.

Turning around, the elderly fighter spoke to Kira, "How about you, young lady?"

Kira backed away with fear in her eyes. She looked at Alexander and said, "You got lucky, boy, but I'll be back." Turning on her heels she fled to safety, abandoning her fallen companions as they lay lifeless on the ground.

The old man looked at the teen, who was breathing hard and frowned. *He has already seen death, and yet he's so young. What brought him to this?* Turning the old man shuffled slowly away, the speed and agility he had shown a moment ago no longer present.

Alexander looked after him as he moved further and further away before he decided to follow him.

Chapter 2: The Master

Alexander continued to follow the man until he reached a medium-sized cottage. He had believed he had remained unseen to the elderly man, but a voice soon proved him wrong.

"I know you're there, young man. Why not come out?"

Alexander walked out of his hiding place and approached the man, readying to defend himself even though he knew he had no hope of winning in his current state.

"Would you like some tea or maybe a soda?" asked the man, walking into the cottage and motioning Alexander to follow.

The cottage was sparsely furnished. Through the gloom Alexander could make out the back wall and a wooden shelf holding various trophies and medals. On that same shelf were two pictures. One was of a young boy with an older looking man both wearing purple GI's.

The second picture was the same adult again, though this time he was joined by a blond woman in a wedding dress. The woman was being carried bridle-style in front of the camera. The picture was black and white, showing its obvious age.

Alexander sat down, "Soda's fine. I want to thank you for saving my life," said the teen.

Taking a soda from the aging, faded-white refrigerator in the corner, the man passed it to Alexander before pouring some tea for himself. "You're lucky I came by when I did," said the old man taking a sip.

Alexander bowed and said "Thank you. Um, I don't know your name."

The old man chuckled. "Yes, that would be a good thing, introductions. You can call me Master Luray, and you're Alexander, according to the identification in your wallet," Luray said.

"Your name sounds familiar. I know that name," said Alexander, struggling to recall just where he had heard the Master's name previously. "I know now, you trained my father. But he never completed his studies, did he?"

"Your father? Ah, yes Theodor," Luray replied, a faraway look in his eye. "He was a great student, but he had his school to deal with, so he could not complete his training even though he was so close. Though I believe he studied other forms and styles from another dojo, eventually attaining a master level? I was sad to see him study in another dojo, but I gave him my blessing. I am very sorry to hear of the fate of your parents. Do you know the warriors that attacked you before and why they wanted to kill you?"

"No, I did not know them," said Alexander bending the truth slightly. "They wanted something that was left to me. That's all I know."

"I see, what're you going to do now, young man?" asked the Master.

Alexander sighed and replied, "I don't know. I'm lost as to what to do." Thinking for a moment an idea struck him, he stood up from his seat and lowered himself down onto his hands and knees, asking, "Can you train me, Master Luray, like you did my father?"

"Why do you want to learn under me?" asked the Master. His eyes seemed to pierce

Alexander, bearing deep into his soul, as though trying to decipher the teen's intent.

"I did, at first, want to avenge my parents, but I realize this would tarnish their memory. They would never want that. I want to make it so I can defend myself and others close to me. Please, Master Luray?" he asked with steely determination, sincerity and a hint of grief. Luray looked into his eyes and saw, staring back, the fire of a true martial artist. Someone willing to do what he must to protect his friends.

Master Luray responded, "I could, but you must pass a test first and I must gauge your commitment."

Alexander looked at him and asked, "What's the test?"

Master Luray smiled. "You must land a clean hit on me to pass. Only your father was able to pass my test. You can start tomorrow since it's clear that you're still injured," said Luray.

"Very well," said Alexander "I will be back tomorrow."

"Do you have a place to stay?" asked the Master.

"Yes, I'm staying with my friend Samuel. I will return and begin my training tomorrow." Alexander was so excited at the thought of being trained by Master Luray. Everything though was still confusing, explaining the warriors and the content of the box was something he didn't want to talk about with anyone right then.

The next morning, Alexander walked into the clearing in the forest and saw Master Luray sitting in the lotus position. Sensing Alexander he arose at once, commanding, "Come at me!"

The Master took his stance.

Alexander, heart beating so hard he thought it may explode from his chest, got into his own stance, similar to that of a boxer but with personal alterations to allow more fluid movement.

Alexander, without warning, charged forward in attempt to catch the Master off guard, throwing a quick jab that was easily blocked. Trying to change tactics he went for a spinning kick, but the Master nonchalantly caught his effort, and he was thrown to the ground.

"That can't be all you got, boy," mocked the Master.

Alexander sprang back to his feet and went for a sweep, hoping to trip his opponent, but the Master easily jumped over it, returning with his own kick in the process, causing Alexander to fall down against the hard ground.

Sweat ran in rivulets down his face, while the Master remained relaxed. *The difference in our skill is too great*, thought Alexander. The Master smiled while Alexander found it difficult to breathe. Confusion was making Alexander feel light-headed, struggling to keep his balance he fell to one knee. *What is this? What is this feeling? Fear?* he thought. *Whatever Master Luray is doing is making me fearful.*

The old man took in Alexander's broken form.

"Having trouble with your balance, young man?" asked Luray. "Your father should have trained you to protect yourself from this attack."

Father did mention this attack! Alexander recalled, thinking back over the lessons his father had passed down to him.

Theodor was in front of his students in the dojo. Alexander stood in the front row of the class next to two other students. "Alright now we will learn how to defend against an attack known as 'Killer Intent' or as it's known in eastern countries 'Sakki'."

"First you must learn how to identify it; it will be a sense of dread or doom."

"How do you fight it, Master?" asked a student.

"You must counter with either pain or use your own will to fight it," said Theodor. "Sometimes you'll need to summon all of your will just to overcome it."

"Now we will begin our lesson with me unleashing only a small amount." *As his eyes narrowed the students instantly started to have difficulty breathing. Several fell down from the fear alone. Alexander found it hard to breathe also before collapsing.*

"Use what I have taught you."

Alexander started to move his foot as he fought the oppressive feeling being given off by his opponent. "Impressive, a few seconds under the *'Killer Intent'* and already able to move." Luray kept his attack going. He had no intention of allowing Alexander an easy way out.

Alexander overcame the feeling of fear by biting his own lip, inflicting pain on himself and effectively releasing the effects of the intent. Trying to gain the upper hand he immediately rushed the Master, but quickly the Master reacts, grabbing Alexander's shirt and throwing him effortlessly to the floor. "Here is a hint, child. It isn't always the strongest that wins, sometimes it's the craftiest."

Alexander steadied his breathing, relaxing before kicking his shoe across the loose ground, throwing dirt into the Master's eyes.

Alexander believing he had the advantage by temporarily blinding his opponent, charged the Master.

"Clever. That's more like it," the Master acknowledged as he closed his eyes. "It will though, however, take more than that to beat me."

Changing his style once more, the Master beckoned Alexander forward once more. "Let's see how you fair with this one, young man. The previous stance was Snake-style Kung Fu, useful if you mean to end any battle quickly. This, however, is the Crane-style Kung Fu, useful more for parrying blows and more defensive tactics."

Alexander, going for broke, went for a punch, but his fist was again easily grabbed, as he was tossed once more by his aged opponent. "You'll have to do better than that, boy. Your father didn't struggle this much with my test."

Alexander huffed, his determination never wavering but rather getting stronger due to the Master's latest jibe. Flipping himself up again he landed on his feet and went in for a flurry of punches, every punch was again dodged or parried. Every kick was deflected or jumped over. *How is he dodging my attacks?* Thought the teen as he was effortlessly being blocked and dodged.

The Master chuckled as he deflected another blow. "You've lasted longer than most prospects, but you've yet to land a hit," said Luray as he dodged a punch just as it passed over his face. Grabbing the teen's arm he once more sent him flying a few feet back with a throw that contradicted his elderly status. "Taking advantage of my distraction, better."

Alexander was getting frustrated. His attacks were all proving ineffective. *Blast it. How can I land a hit?* Alexander asked himself. *His skill is too great.* He breathed in and sent a powerful kick at the master, but it was blocked with both hands.

"Powerful. Not bad, but not enough," said Luray calmly. Alexander then twisted around and tried to kick with his other leg, but the Master blocked it with his own leg. "Nice try, boy," as he once again threw the boy back with a slight thrust.

"Want to come again, or have you had enough?" He seemed to have no issue goading the teen with his words.

Alexander was now breathing harder and replied. "I will fight until I land a hit,"

The Master smiled kindly and then sighed. "Sometimes you must cut your losses on the battlefield and retreat to fight another day."

"You are saying an enemy would let me flee?" Alexander received a clap from the Master with that response.

"Very good, they won't, but you passed my real test. I will train you," said Luray

Alexander looked confused. "But I never landed a hit on you, Master." Causing the old man to chuckle.

"The point of this test wasn't actually to hit me, but rather to see your determination against a stronger enemy, which you have passed with flying colors. Most of my other prospects gave up before thirty minutes of failure had passed, and therefore failed my test. You, however, proved to me your worth. Now I'll begin your training. Meet me here whenever you're out of school," said the Master.

"Thank you, Master." Alexander bowed his head, as the master bowed in return.

"Let me write up a training schedule for you to follow when you're not with me. Meet me here after your classes tomorrow and I will give it to you then."

"Yes, Master," confirmed Alexander.

"Be ready to travel for summer training," said Luray.

The two bowed once more. Alexander left the forest, his body raked with pain as Master Luray headed back to his cottage. He was excited about the chance to train another pupil. It had been a long time—a long time indeed.

Chapter 3: Training

Three weeks had flown by since Alexander had been rescued by Luray. Each day he went after school to resume his training with the Master. Alexander had never been more exhausted in his life.

Luray was a brutal taskmaster, pushing Alexander to his limit and sometimes beyond it.

"I don't get it, Master. Why are we doing this exercise again?" Alexander asked as he secured a blindfold.

"When I lost my sight during your test, how was I able to find you and keep you from landing a hit?" Said the Master.

Pebbles were hurled through the air at Alexander as a slight breeze swayed the grass. "What would have happened if it was you, who had lost your sight in that fight? The enemy would not give you time to recover."

Alexander nodded his head. "Understood, Master," replied Alexander with a sigh, attempting to dodge and block the pebbles thrown at him with very little success.

"Feel the wind and it will tell you the location of the thrown pebble. Very few Masters have used blind fighting to its fullest, and even fewer have mastered being one with the earth and the wind. It takes enormous concentration," advised the Master.

Alexander managed to eventually block a pebble, only for him to be then hit in the arm and the leg. "But you used blind fighting on instinct when I blinded you," Alexander said.

"True, but you have to realize I have many years of experience under my belt. It is like comparing a cub to a fully grown lion. If I had as much experience as you or close to it, you would have beaten me with your youth, energy and stamina," said Luray.

"I understand that experience is a great advantage," said Alexander. "However, you outclassed me in everything except youth. You are faster and much stronger despite being older."

"True, but I keep up my training," said Luray. "Many fighters let their skills diminish after reaching a plateau or they get complacent from their victories rather than keeping their skills sharp."

"Despite our short time training, you are progressing much faster than your father," the Master praised. "You've been practicing a lot even without me and that takes true dedication and focus."

"Thank you, Master," said Alexander. He dodged a pebble to the right before catching another with his left hand. He hissed audibly as a large pebble smacked him in the left hand, expelling the pebble he still held.

"Don't get distracted. It will cost you," said Luray. "All it takes is one second of losing your concentration to cost you your life in battle."

"That's enough for today, Alexander. You may go and rest up for tomorrow's lesson. Since it's the start of summer vacation, meet me here at six in the morning and come prepared for a summer-long survival trip," said Luray before he started to gather up the training equipment.

"Yes, Master," said Alexander rubbing the swollen red spot on his hand.

The next day, Alexander carried a large backpack with survival equipment as he headed to

Luray's cottage. He packed everything from the list the Master had provided and whatever else he felt he needed, he bought it with some of the money that was left to him. The Master walked out of his cottage, his own backpack across his shoulders.

"Good. You are here early. Now you're going to learn how to survive in the wilderness, I want you to be prepared for the worst. We will walk there, but it is a three-hundred-mile journey. We will have to survive along the way by hunting and foraging for food; you will learn how to make a shelter and find good sources of water," the Master instructed.

Alexander nodded. "Understood, Master."

The two turned and began their long trek north.

"I will be telling you about every poisonous fruit and plant that you will come across," Luray said as the two companions stopped near a bush, abundant with tiny red fruit hanging from its small branches. "This fruit is called the bittersweet nightshade, it's fatal if ingested." He warned. They continued walking alongside each other in almost complete silence, with Master Luray stopping from time to time to point out various plants. The tall trees blocked out most of the summer sun, but the heat was proving harsh. After an exhausting day of walking, they stopped for the night.

"To survive, you'll first need to find a source of water, preferably while looking for shelter nearby," he instructed Alexander as they began scouting around for a suitable place for the campsite.

Alexander saw a clear river running to the west, with a small cave in the hillside and thought, *This may work*. He rushed back, shouting to his master. "Master Luray! I think I found a perfect place to spend the night!"

"Show me where it is," the aged master replied, following Alexander to the river. Master Luray looked around. "You've picked a nice location, Alexander, with a water source and a cave that can be used to protect us from the elements." They searched the cave and were happy to find that it was not inhabited. "Well done. Let us set up camp and continue your practice."

Later that night Alexander went to his Master's tent. "You need something my student?" asked the Master as he put down a book.

"I saw a photo in your cottage of you and a young woman," said Alexander. "I was wondering if you can tell me who that was."

"That was my wife of twenty years. Her name was Elisa. She was beautiful and strong both mentally and physically."

He got a wistful look as he spoke of his wife. "We met at a local tournament as adversaries. We fought in the finals and I defeated her. I offered to treat her to some dinner and she accepted. We had a lot in common and a year later we married. We were happy for about fifteen years until she was diagnosed with brain cancer," the Master said as his emotions took over and a single tear ran down his face..

"I am sorry for asking, Master."

"It's alright," said Luray. "It will take the burden off my chest."

"By the time we discovered her condition, there was little we could do. She was told she only had five months to live, but being physically active helped her live another four years before she started to deteriorate. It was horrible watching her suffer and I did my best to provide for her. She died a year later after it became too much for her, and I never married again."

"Please forgive me for bringing up such bad memories," said Alexander.

"It's not a problem. Please, leave me to gather my thoughts, Alexander; I will wake you early tomorrow."

"Are you alright, Master?" asked Alexander the next morning as Master Luray got ready to head out.

"Yes, thank you for your concern and please remember showing sadness isn't shameful. Showing emotion, it is part of what makes us human."

"Yes, Master, I will cherish that advice," said Alexander.

"Now, we shall continue where we left off." The two began their intense spar which persisted into the night, Luray always dominating the fight and giving advice to his pupil. The next morning, they trekked up north into another part of the forest while Luray tested Alexander's endurance and survival skills. At night, they continued their martial arts lessons.

After two and a half days, they finally got to their destination. Trondheim. Master and student made their makeshift tent, protecting themselves from the elements with leaves and branches woven into a bivouac. They sat down to eat the food they had collected along the way, which consisted mostly of berries and nuts, but also some rabbit they had trapped on their trek. "We made it, Alexander, and you have learned much in such a short time," praised the master.

Alexander bowed. "Thank you, Master."

***

In the temple on the mountain, Kira was trembling, her shirt shredded. "You failed me, Kira and you lost three of my acolytes. Those scars will remind you not to fail me again," boomed the voice.

She remained on her hands and knees, feeling every one of the burns across her body and the cuts on her exposed back. "Forgive me, Master, but a Guardian intervened," she grunted in pain.

"I want results, Kira, not excuses! Get out of my sight!" bellowed the voice with anger as lightning struck the ground in front of her.

She got up, still quivering from the pain and fear. "Of course, my Lord," she said meekly as she limped away, blood dripping from the newest gash on her leg. The punishment for failure ever high.

"Nicolson! Come here now!" commanded the voice.

"Yes, my Lord?" answered a young man of roughly thirty years with wild black hair. Bedecked in black scale armor, a huge sword strung across his back. Walking out of the shadow of the temple wall with confidence and arrogance, he bowed to his Lord and master.

"Nicolson, as one of my personal generals, you have great skill. I have a mission for you," said the voice.

The young man bowed to the statue. "What is your command, my Lord?"

***

Deep in the forest, the master and his student were sparring hard, the bruises on both of their bodies proof of Alexander's rising skill. It had been a month since they had arrived in Trondheim. Sparring had for a while been accompanied by lessons in woodwork as they felled trees in preparation for a shelter. The end result was a well-formed log cabin, small but meeting their needs for shelter.

In a nearby town, Master Luray had arranged for his student to do odd jobs to learn work ethics. Whether it was delivering newspapers while running to increase speed and reaction time or construction work to increase his strength, Alexander never complained and did his work completely and without complaint.

Later that evening, Alexander watched from behind a tree as Luray put salve on his shoulder, tending to a sore area repeatedly struck during training. This proved to Alexander that he had come a long way in his training. Alexander could not begin to imagine how much he had improved. Still he knew, there was still much more learning to be done.

Master Luray also taught him to meditate so he could gain more focus. He taught him to strike a tree or boulder to increase his pain tolerance. By the end of each day, Alexander's fists were bloody and sore just in time for another sparring session with his Master.

As part of his education Alexander was also shown how to play Chess and Japanese pastime Shogi, utilizing how to use them in a fight with the aim of positioning his opponent in a more favorable position for him to attack. Alexander often got less than five hours of sleep, due to his rough training, but never complained.

One day Luray decided it was to be the day Alexander was made aware of what he held and its significance. "Alexander, it's time to tell you what you hold and how important it is," said Luray frowning, which was very rare on the usually kind and smiling Master. Alexander immediately stopped the stance he was practicing. Seeing he had his student's attention Master Luray continued. "The key you have in your possession holds the power to release a great evil."

"Who or what is it?" asked the student.

"We don't know his identity, but he is labeled as a demon with no morals. He is the one known as the Lord of Shadows, a violent and evil monster who has tossed away his humanity for dark power," said Luray.

"Why tell me?" asked Alexander. "Why was my family involved?"

"You are his target, Alexander, because of my mistake," said Luray.

"What do you mean, Master?" asked Alexander

"I gave your father the key to keep it hidden away from the Lord of Shadows," said Luray. "Don't worry, I will fight to the death to protect you, my student."

Alexander balled up his fist and spoke with a fire in his eyes. "Master, I hope it never comes to that, but if it does, we'll fight together."

"No! You will run when I tell you to, without question! The key should never fall to the Lord of Shadows. Your duty is to protect it at all cost," a stern solid tone in the Master's voice could be heard. "I failed your family already, you will not throw your life away for my mistake."

"But…" started Alexander until he saw his Master frown with a disapproving look. "Understood, Master."

***

Summer came and went, as Alexander turned seventeen. His birthday for ever held dear by his Master presenting him a medallion containing five crystals, colored brown, blue, red, green, and yellow. Each in turn symbolizing the elements, each element separated by thin lines of silver. Each shone brilliantly and Alexander had never seen anything like it before. All Luray said in presenting Alexander with his gift was a short, "Happy birthday."

***

That night Alexander was sleeping when he started to toss and turn, before screaming. Luray heard his student and rushed over. "Alexander what happened? Wake up!" shouted the Master.

Alexander woke up with a jolt. "Master? Why are you in here?"

"I rushed to see what was wrong," said Luray. "You had a nightmare?"

"It seems so," said Alexander, sweat running down his face.

"You want to talk about it?" asked Luray.

"I just saw my parents being murdered by a shadow then it went after my friend Samuel and killed him and his family as I watched. I was next to die."

"We should increase your training," said Luray

"Thank you, Master," said Alexander.

***

He returned home from Trondheim with his Master by foot in just two days. In the month since they had returned back, Alexander soaked up his lessons like a sponge, proving him to be a quick learner as he mastered the last tier of both fighting styles. As a gift for his accomplishments, Master Luray gave Alexander a scroll containing the last of the five animal fighting stances: Dragon, Tiger, and Leopard. Alexander was to master these styles with no tutelage.

Master Luray had never personally mastered the three contained within, but had located the scroll for it. Alexander looked at the scroll, and in doing so saw the different exercises for them and a method of training.

As he bowed to his Master, a black shadowy movement in the forest caught Master Luray's eye. Springing into a guard position, he motioned Alexander to move in behind him with a jerk of his head.

Moving swiftly to his left, Luray caught rocks thrown at him from the tree line with a deft movement of his hand. "You'd better come out!" He yelled out as he prepared himself for an attack.

A tall figure strode from the trees, a short sword strapped to his back. "I have come to kill you and take the key you possess, old man."

"Who are you?" asked Luray, biding time to further assess his opponent.

"You can call me Nicolson and I am your death," replied the stranger as he drew out his short sword and advanced.

Master Luray glared at his challenger, "I will not make it easy," he warned, as he drew out a jagged sword, which had remained sheathed so long that even Alexander was oblivious to its containment on Luray's person.

"Your toy won't help you now," said Nicolson. "I have killed stronger opponents than you."

"Alexander, leave now," Master Luray commanded as he charged towards his attacker, his jagged sword held firmly in his hand.

Alexander stood there frozen as his Master fought with the assassin. Watching as Master Luray went for a stab, his assailant narrowly avoiding being caught. Nicolson then slashed down but Luray blocked, quickly he disengaged and parried a diagonal slash that was thrown back by Luray.

Master Luray growled, "What are you doing here?" looking across to his student he again implored, "Alexander! Leave! You are no match for this opponent!" Focusing again, just in time to blocked another forceful strike.

"Master," whispered Alexander as he closed his eyes and ran into the forest.

Luray turned to his opponent, his blade turning purple as he spoke. "This blade is now poisoned, one cut will kill you within just a few short minutes."

The general smirked, no emotion portrayed across his face. "You are truly a master of the Snake Assassin style, old man. Using poison just like a cobra. I have heard of you from my master. They may refer to you as The Cobra of the Order, however, you're now well past your prime and have gotten weak in your old age," exclaimed the dark general as he attacked again.

Master Luray keen to again get the upper hand, started to attempt to push the general back with rapid thrusts of his blade.

The general simultaneously charged forward, disarming Luray by parrying his attack, and slamming the pommel of his sword onto the Master's hand. Nicolson keen to press home his advantage went in for another strike, but the shorter Master grabbed Nicolson's sword hand and threw him to the side with just a seemingly effortless flick of his wrist, forcing Nicolson to release the grip on his own sword. The general tried to rise only to be sent back down with a sweeping kick.

"You are getting annoying, old man," said the general, kicking out at the master while on the ground, making him also fall towards the ground. Luray recovered himself before he reached the ground, flipping himself back to get some distance, regaining his balance he got into a strong stance. "If you were younger and in your prime you might have stood a chance. Too bad for you."

Luray rolled up his pant legs, unveiling several ankle weights wrapped around his ankles. A smirk crossed his lips as he came back with, "You think I was trying my hardest?" As he released the weights from his hands, letting them drop and imprinting the soil below. "Now let's see you keep up with me, youngster." He launched himself forward, moving at much faster speeds, landing a strong punch on Nicolson's chest, sending him back against the trunk of a tree.

"So you're a little faster, old man, you will still die." Nicolson wiped the blood from his lip with his hand. "I'm still faster, stronger."

"That you may be, but I have more experience and that is what it will take, I will end you here and now," replied Luray.

The general smiled back. "Did you actually believe I would come alone?" the general asked as thirty more soldiers came out of the trees, each fully dressed in leather armor and armed with various weapons ranging from swords to bows and arrows to staffs. "The weak old man with his stupid sense of honor."

"You've got no honor. I have always known this day would come and I'm prepared, as all warriors should be, to live by the blade and die by the blade." The thirty soldiers charged at the lone master. He eyed each warrior with no fear and in turn met their attacks, striking the first soldier in the chest. One by one, he slashed and cut his opponents. Luray saw movement behind him but was unable to defend against the cowardly attack as a sword pierced his back. With the little strength that remained Luray managed to kick out, sending Nicolson into a tree, making the general cough up blood.

"You will die painfully, old man, from the slow-acting toxin on my blade. There is no antidote that can help you now," gloated the general as he got up from the last attack, still unsteady on his feet. The field was littered with the bodies of twenty-nine soldiers, the one remaining alive was struggling to breathe through his wounds, only to be silenced by the general after he regained his composure.

His work complete Nicholson hands gestured through the air, seemingly forming some kind of intricate message. A black portal appeared, and Nicolson walked through, leaving the carnage behind.

Alexander had stopped in a clearing a short way away to think about his next move. Hoping he was not too late he turned and ran back to the fight. Greeted with a scene of utter devastation he knelt down beside his master, carefully turning him over.

Luray's breathing was labored. "Why did you return? That was foolish!" Luray admonished in a raspy voice that betrayed the immense pain he felt.

"Master, let me get you to a hospital maybe they can still heal you?" said Alexander.

The old man reached up with his one good hand, his left hand lying limply at the side. A long cut ran from his wrist to his elbow where one of the soldiers had caught him, making it useless. "It won't matter, my student. He hit me with a powerful poison that has no antidote. I have five minutes or so of life in me." Master Luray flinched a little from speaking.

Alexander started to cry. "Stay with me, Master!" His master smiled back, sure that he had prepared Alexander as best he could for the battle ahead.

"I have nothing left to teach you, but I have one last request," the dying master coughed as he tried to get all of his message out.

"Yes, Master?" said Alexander as he tried to put on a brave front.

"Find the other Masters of the White Rose and learn all you can. Do it not for revenge but for peace. Honor my request, Alexander, please?" The Master implored his student.

"The medallion will point you in the right direction of the nearest Master, known to our kind as a Guardian. If a Master dies, one of the pieces in the artifact will turn black and crack. If they're mortally wounded, it will crack first. You were my greatest student and it was an honor to teach you all I know," he says with pride.

Alexander took out the medallion given to him by his master on his last birthday. Holding his Master close and sobbing from sorrow, Alexander implored his teacher, "Don't leave me, Master, please."

Luray coughed. "Promise me, should he regain his freedom, that you'll defeat the Lord of Shadows and bring peace to this world once again,"

His message passed on, he closed his eyes and passed away before his student could reply. A weak 'Yes, Master' stuck on his lips, never to be heard.

The cracked crystal piece in the medallion that signified Luray's life force turned black, signaling the Master's death.

Alexander held his masters' body as further tears ran freely down his face. The bodies of the soldiers killed by Luray dissolved in the clearing as though they had never been there. Strange magic was happening.

"I'll do as you have requested, Master," Alexander said, this time more clearly. With more conviction.

Gathering his items, he slung his bag over his shoulder, ready to begin his journey to find the other Masters. But first, he had to retrieve the box from Samuel's house. It was hidden in a safe place. He was no longer a minor in Norway at seventeen and he told the family he was going to find his way in the world.

***

In the temple on the mountain in northern Norway, Nicolson presented the Master's blade to the voice, one knee on the ground in a show of loyalty. "Forgive me, Lord. I couldn't catch the boy, but I killed his Guardian. I am ready for any punishment you deem fit for my failure," said the general.

"You did more than anyone else, so your failure will be forgiven this time," said the voice. "One less Guardian to deal with."

"What now, my Lord?" asked Nicolson.

"I think a change of tactics is necessary," said the voice. The general looks confused. "It's too risky to reveal ourselves further. There is time. We will search for the other keys, the boy isn't going anywhere. Have some men keep us aware of his whereabouts."

"As you wish, my Lord."

Chapter 4: Journey of a Hero

Several days had passed since the death of Master Luray. Alexander looked at the medallion, noting one of the spaces was glowing bright. He breathed in as he looked for another Master. It was hard to focus when he was still coming to terms with his Master's death, a man who was like a second father to him.

I must be heading in the right direction, he thought. Earlier, he had turned north, and the glow had become dim. He had turned to the west, and it glowed brightly again. Lacking any greater sign, Alexander took a train to the western town of Stavanger.

Reaching port the medallion continued to try to take him west. *It seems I must cross the Atlantic,* he mulled, but not wanting to leave a paper trail at the airports his only route seemed to be through the off chance someone was looking for workers.

Looking around the port he came across a 'Help Wanted' sign on the side of a United States cargo ship. Alexander walked up to one of the sailors and asked politely, "Do you need a worker?"

"The captain needs some muscle to help with our cargo of food to New York. You look like a strong young man. You need to earn some money then?" asked the crew member.

"I need to get to the States. Where do I sign up?" Alexander asked.

"We'll need your passport first," said the same crew member.

Hesitant to pass on his details it seemed Alexander's only option, so he went aboard the ship and filled out all the paperwork needed for the job. Where the form asked for family information, Alexander spelled out the dreaded word *deceased*.

"Everything seems to be in order, young man. Welcome aboard. Let me introduce to you our captain," the sailor said as he escorted Alexander to the ship's bridge.

The captain was wearing a white sailor suit with gold-colored stripes on his shoulders. He was a medium-sized man but had a very strong, muscular build. He was surprisingly clean-shaven, throwing any image Alexander held of a stereotypical sailor with a beard straight out the window.

"So you're the new hand." The Captain stated, shaking his hand, "you look very capable. I am Captain Hathaway. We leave port tomorrow in the morning. 4am to be precise. I need you to help with the rest of the loading tonight, then we will be ready as soon as we have passed through Norwegian customs."

Alexander worked hard over the following hours, eager to prove himself an asset as he helped with the loading. As promised the ship took out of port early the next morning.

They stopped in Iceland to refuel and stayed for a few days. Alexander was given some time off the ship, so he headed to the bazaar in the local town. He was relaxing and looking in shop fronts when he saw a stand with various weapons, manned by a man of oriental descent. "Sir, I'm looking for a weapon, so I can move my training up," said Alexander.

"What are you looking for?" asked the man. "My name's Cao Cue and I have been collecting weapons for twenty years."

"Well, I'm currently learning swordsmanship with a bokken and was hoping to begin working with a real sword," explained Alexander.

"What type of sword are you trying to master?" Cao asked holding his hand under his chin while listening intently to Alexander's answer to his question.

"A short blade so I can wield two," said the teen.

"Hmm, I'd recommend a Kodachi and a Tanto so you can get a feel for the two before moving up to two Kodachi, said the merchant. "Look around and see what strikes your fancy."

Alexander looked around and saw a beautiful, short curved blade around 40cm in length with a black hilt and several kanji. "What do the kanji stand for?" he asked.

"It is translated as 'the way of the sword,'" replied Cao. "Flip the blade and you'll see another set of kanji that can be translated as 'Bushido,' which is the samurai code," said Cao.

"How much is it?" Alexander asked as he stared at the swords.

"To you, my friend, five hundred dollars," said Cao.

Alexander bought both the Kodachi and a Tanto, which was around 18 cm in length and more of a dagger used for stabbing, and had them wrapped. A few days later, the ship left the port and headed on to New York City.

Weeks of hard work followed, interjected with Alexander learning to play poker with the sailors, where he won an impressive amount of money from his wins, and fishing. On occasion Alexander would catch enough fish, with a few sailors, to cook them for the crew.

Finally the ship docked in New York and together they unloaded the ship. The captain thanked the teen and handed him his check to cover his hard work aboard his vessel. Alexander was left knowing that a place for him always remained aboard the kind Captain's ship.

The captain and his crew wished Alexander the best and told him not to hesitate to ask for any help he may need. The teen walked into the busy city to continue his search, and the Captain furrowed his brow and turned back to the ship right before glancing in Alexander's supposed direction.

Alexander got a hotel room and slept for the rest of the day. While resting he turned on the TV flickering through the channels when a mixed martial art show called American Fighting Championship caught his interest. He watched as a master of Muay Thai defeated his larger opponent within thirty minutes of the fight beginning.

***

Alexander walked out onto the streets at a little after noon. With no destination in mind he managed to find himself in a dubious area of time. Looking for a way back to vague familiarity he came across several thugs pestering what appeared to be a young adult female with long black hair, wearing jeans and a white shirt, in an alley.

"Come on, babe. Just one night," the leader said as he advanced on the outnumbered woman.

"What part of no don't you understand?" growled the woman. "I've got a thing against trash."

"Don't be like that," said another thug.

"Sorry, I don't go out with the garbage. Now, beat it," the woman replied without a worry.

The man leered at her with a smile. "I like them feisty."

"How about I just humiliate you then call it a day?" she asked.

"All right, we'll do this the hard way." He cracked his knuckles and his men snickered at the woman, who looked bored.

"Today's spring cleaning. It seems it's time to take out and clean up this scum," replied the female.

"Is that right? Come on then, boys. Let's show her what happens when you don't accept my invite."

"You might as well save yourself the trouble of fighting and just fall down, because the ground is where you're going to be," she said getting into a defensive posture.

Alexander had seen enough and strode down the alley to stop the crime about to take place. "I think the young lady said no, gentlemen," he said, glaring at the thugs.

"This is none of your business, punk," said one of the thugs as he took a pistol out and pointed it at Alexander's head, the cold steel touching his forehead.

Before the man could voice another threat, he found himself dropping his gun and clutching his chest in pain as Alexander's right fist flashed out. Alexander followed with a spin kick, knocking the man to the ground, out cold.

As the other thugs advanced on Alexander, the leader was attacked by the young woman with a swift knee attack in a Muay Thai style. The leader losing consciousness as blood poured out of his nose. For good measure, she kicked him between his legs, felling him for good.

Seeing that the other thugs were knocked out, the young female visibly relaxed. Alexander joined her, "I guess you did not need help after all. Did you have to hit him there?" he winced.

The young lady glared at him. "I didn't need your help at all. Don't interfere next time," she replied before storming away with a scowl on her face.

"You're welcome," said Alexander to himself. He took out his medallion and turned south as one of the crystals glowed brightly. Leaving the thugs on the ground for the police, or whoever, he walked away.

Alexander continued to follow the direction of the medallion and found himself at a dojo for Muay Thai. He knocked on the dojo's door, and an older man in his thirties with black hair and bandages around his fists appeared. He had a scar over his right eye going from top to bottom.

"May I help you, young one?" asked the man.

Alexander bowed his head and said, "I would like to take lessons in Muay Thai. May I speak to the Master?"

The man looked at Alexander. "I am Master Paul Thompson of this school, I'm going to need to see where you are to be placed, said the master.

"No problem, Master," said Alexander as he bowed again. "I saw that you won the match this morning at the AFC. It was a great match."

Master Thompson walked into the dojo, motioning for Alexander to follow him. "I would like to see if you have any skills, and in which form." Alexander joined the Master in the middle of the mat as the ten students present in the dojo gathered around them both.

The Master addressed his students, "This young man would like to join the dojo. To help gauge his competence I will now allow him to face our star pupil."

A young woman, clearly agitated, appeared from behind the Master. "What are you doing here?" she asked rudely.

Master Thompson looked at the exchange with puzzlement. "Hey, fancy meeting you here," replied Alexander, a little embarrassed.

"So you're the one I am fighting," she said with a snort.

The Master looked at both with amusement. "You know each other?"

"Yeah, this loser intervened in a fight with some thugs that were trying to force themselves on me," she glared at Alexander.

The Master sighed. "You shouldn't be too proud to accept help when it is offered, Lenora. Being overconfident will lead to your defeat if you're not careful," said Master Thompson with a disapproving look. "You two can settle any differences in the ring."

Alexander faced his opponent and bowed to her. Lenora bowed as well. Alexander then positioned himself in his favored Crane style.

That stance he is using leaves very little opening to any attacker, thought the Master.

Lenora got into her stance, ready to show the upstart why she was Master Thompson's star pupil.

"Begin!" shouted the Master.

Alexander keen to be on the offensive, went for a backhand to Lenora's face, but throwing her forearm up she blocked it with ease. She then thrust back with her knee. Alexander grabbed with an open palm, hissing with pain as the knee connected with his hand. His strength though throwing her off balance as he pushed back against the blow.

Alexander kicked low, hoping to make the woman lose her balance for a moment, but she remained elusive, jumping forward and connecting a knee to Alexander's chest. Losing his stance, Alexander stumbled back. Before she could force home her advantage, he recovered and blocked a second attempted knee with his arm. Spinning on his standing foot he landed a forceful kick to his opponent's side, striking her midsection and making her growl in annoyance.

Lenora launched a return kick to his midsection, but the fluidity of movement possible by using the Crane Kung Fu's style easily allowed Alexander to dodge the powerful kick. Sensing the chance to go on the attack once more, he changed his style to that of the Snake and started to use fast jabs, his superior speed allowing him to land a combination of blows.

Alexander and Lenora were breathing hard, reaching a stalemate as they grew tired, more and more blows landing successfully on the two opponents. Master Thompson choose this point to step once more into the middle, raising his hand. "This match shall be called a draw as Alexander has proven to be a very capable fighter. I shall be honored to teach him our style in the dojo," said the Master. Gesturing for Alexander to follow he crossed the mat and headed to his office.

The Master sat down behind his dark brown, uncluttered desk. "What's your name?" he asked the young man standing before him.

"I am Alexander Theodorson, I have just arrived in New York from Oslo, Norway," said the teen.

"From what I saw today, you were trained by Master Luray. Am I correct?" asked the Master.

Alexander was shocked and tensed up, quickly ready for either fight or flight while asking his question. "Master Thompson, how did you know?"

The man chuckled. "No need to be paranoid, Alexander. The Masters of the White Rose keep in touch. He contacted me about his new student, but he never gave me a name. Though I can tell from your eyes that something is wrong. What happened?" The Master asked looking concerned.

Alexander took a breath. "Master Luray was recently killed by a general of the Lord of Shadows, trying to help buy time for me to escape their clutches."

The Master sighed at the news. "I didn't want to believe it when Luray told me about the murder of his old student. Now Master Luray is also dead." The Master ran his hand through his hair, before adding, "This complicates things greatly."

Master Thompson got up and looked at Alexander with a serious expression. "Your training will be difficult because it seems we've got to get you as strong, if not stronger, than each Master. Are you ready to push yourself beyond your limits? Your bones may be broken and battered from the training, but we have no choice, it is the only way to reach the levels that we need you to achieve."

"Whatever it takes," responded Alexander.

Master Thompson rose from his chair and the two left the office, he spent the next hour guiding Alexander on a tour of the dojo. "The students live at the school during their training." He informed the teen. He moved forward to show him the room that would become his temporary home. "The room may be small, but it's got a cot and the bathroom is down the hall to your left. We believe in simplicity and we show it in how we live our lives."

Alexander bowed his head. "Thank you, Master."

As he was leaving, The Master turned to Alexander, "After the training, I promise that you'll hate me. Training starts promptly at five every morning, so be punctual." With his message delivered, The Master left his newest student to get acquainted with his new surroundings.

Alexander settled into his room and placed the box with the key under the cot, hoping that no one would ask him questions about it.

Chapter 5: Death of a Master

In the temple on the mountain, three warriors stood in front of the statue that held the banished Lord of Shadows.

"Where did the boy go?" said the voice.

A small man stepped forward and said, "Our spies have again located him, my Lord."

"Where is he, Kyral?" asked the voice in irritation.

"He's in the city of New York," said Kyral. "He is learning Muay Thai with one of the Guardians in charge of a key."

"Did you find any of the other Masters?" asked the voice.

Kyral nodded his head. "We found another, Americo Estefan in Brazil, but he's well-guarded by his disciple, who is proficient in Brazilian Jujitsu and Capoeira. The others we have so far been unable to locate, my Lord."

"Very well. Kyral, take who you need and deal with Master Estefan. Bring me the key. Do not fail me," said the voice.

Kyral bowed and replied. "Of course, my Lord." Drawing his triangular-shaped throwing knife and his sharp ninja stars from his clothing his eyes glinted. "I'm not the best at Ninjutsu for nothing. He shall die quickly, my Lord." He held the two weapons between his fingers, a bloodthirsty smirk present on his face. His arms moved fluidly, in patterns that would seem random to any witness, but as he finished a black portal appeared before him. Walking forwards and disappearing, ten more shadows exited the temple and followed him through the portal.

"I'm getting tired of these constant failures, he had better succeed," growled the Voice as lightning shot down, striking the middle of the room.

***

In a temple well-hidden, deep in the Amazon jungle, a dark-skinned man with prayer beads around his neck was walking alongside a young man. The tanned, black-haired youngster appeared to be around fifteen years of age, and sported a pair of spiked black gloves. "Mason, I sense an ominous presence. You must leave at once. You've completed your training and are now the Master," said the man, the concern apparent in his voice.

"But, Master Estefan, why?" asked the young teen, confused as to why his Master would now choose to send him away.

The man put his hand on the boy's shoulder. "When I was mediating, I had a vision. It seems you have a great mission to accomplish. A blond-haired boy, not much older than yourself, will present you with a medallion like this one," said the master taking out a medallion and handing it to his student. "I want you to train him in our fighting style so he can protect the world from evil." said the Master.

"Master, let me help!" implored the student.

"I told you this day would come, my student. Now go," said the Master, a stern look across his face.

The tanned teen hugged his Master and fled with the medallion in hand through the back exit of the temple. Estefan's gaze softened as his watched his young student depart. Turning around he readied himself to face his enemy.

Exiting the front of the temple, a dagger immediately grazed Estefan's cheek, drawing blood. Estefan still remained calm. "I'll take you down, foolish assassin," said the Master as he blocked a series of throwing stars with his hands His gloves of tough leather successfully protecting his hands.

Estefan looked around, a smirk beginning to appear on his face. "I was picked as a Guardian because I'm in tune with nature," he informed his attacker. As he spoke three jaguars bounded from the jungle and stood, ready to attack, next to the Master. "They are aware of when I need assistance.

"I'm so scared of your kitties, old man. I'll make a coat for myself," Kyral said, as he crouched confidently unseen on a high branch. His confidence was short lived though, as he was forced to jump from his perch to narrowly avoid a tree branch swung in his direction by an angry monkey. Another of the Master's assistants it seemed.

Landing in the clearing below he was immediately charged by the Master. Kyral's skill set didn't involve physical combat but rather more hit-and-run tactics from a distance. "It seems you are truly worthy of fighting," said Kyral as he successfully blocked a kick, the surprising power of the Mater sending him backwards. *I have to get some distance between us.*

As Kyral retreated he loosed a trio of daggers. With gloved hands, Estefan blocked the projectiles and continued to advance on his attacker. A noise from behind caught the Master's attention. Turning around he saw he was also going to have to try and contend with ten warriors, garbed in black tunics. Blocking the first punch, he moved quickly to grab and throw his assailant into another warrior. The rest however continued to surround him.

Master Estefan tightly held the beads around his neck, bowing his head as the warriors again closed in.

After the fight, the assassin, Kyral, ransacked Estefan's temple. He had welts on his arms from the punches. Before locating the key he fell to the floor. "Damn that Master," said Kyral, his voice wavering in pain. After a minute to compose himself, he tore up the temple in search of the key. Finally in the darkest corner of the temple he came across floor boards that had their corner slightly raised. "He should have hide it better."

Kyral located the cube, gestured several intricate movements, and then disappeared again through a black portal.

***

Arriving back at the mountaintop temple, the assassin walked up to the statue, placing the cube onto the pedestal that matched the carvings on the cube. "The first of many, my Lord," confirmed the assassin.

The statue cracked a little further. "Now I have a full fifth of my power," the voice chuckled, before continuing. "Kevin, I want you to kill the Shaolin Master Shin. Once you are successful you can burn the temple."

A previously unnoticed man wearing a black cloak walked in from the shadows and replied, "Of course, my Lord."

***

Master Thompson looked at his medallion and saw a part of the crystal crack. *Oh no! Another one has fallen*, he thought. No sooner had it cracked though, the crystal's section mended and became bright again. *Good, a successor was picked*, thought the Master as he began meditating.

I think I might have to choose my successor soon, or all is lost, thought the Master.

Chapter 6: Out with the old and in with the new

Alexander was breathing heavily, as was his opponent Lenora as they sparred again. They had spent many hours together over the previous two months. They sparred daily, and had gradually grown to respect each other's skills.

The headstrong, young nineteen-year-old woman had finally apologized for the way she had acted on their first meeting, and eventually thanked Alexander for helping her out.

Alexander had now advanced in Muay Thai sufficiently to be equal to the level Lenora was at when they first met. Lenora has also progressed and was now able to fight her Master to a standstill.

In becoming closer the pair gradually began to confide in each other over more personal aspects of their lives.

In the two months that passed, Alexander taught Lenora and the other students the basics of the Snake stance. Those that excelled and who passed the first tier, he moved on to show them more advanced moves. He also finished the scroll of the Dragon and Tiger stances and was now working on the Leopard. Alexander was now sure that all the Masters were insane in their training. He was bruised and battered from both the exercises and the beatings he endured during the initial spars with Lenora. He had even had to strike a boulder with an exposed knee one hundred times with each leg. His Master watching as he increased his leg and knee strength. During spars, he was being limited to

Muay Thai only, causing him several painful defeats by Lenora before he was able to better defend himself against her attacks.

Part of his training also included the ankle weights that his first Master, Luray, had used. Building his speed up by rigorously training with the additional weight.

**

In the Shaolin Wu Shi temple, a bald-headed monk was meditating with a medallion on his lap. *So how many of us are left?* The monk considered, looking at the artifact. The Master that had recently passed had evidently picked a student to replace him, as the medallion was lit up where previously it had been dark.

A figure approached the monk at speed, as three others followed behind, nearing the monk he exclaimed, "Sifu Shin, an intruder is heading this way!"

Shin got up and grabbed a bo staff. "I'll deal with this. The rest of you stay here," he said, forcefully. "Tell Guan that he is in charge should I be killed."

Using his staff as a cane he slowly walked out of the temple and down the path to the grounds where the monks trained. A robed figure approached as he reached the bottom.

"Master Shin, it's a good day to die," said the intruder as he took off his hood, revealing the slicked-back brown hair beneath. Holstered on his back were two pikes.

"May I know the name of he who I'm facing?" asked Shin.

The man bowed and answered. "My name is Kevin of the Wind, one of the five generals of the Lord of Shadows' army."

The monk brought his staff to a ready position as Kevin pulled a pike from its holster. The two opponents charged forward.

Shin took the offensive as he went in low with a calculated swing, but Kevin was swift to block the attack as the two weapons locked together. Shin pulled away, managing to trip his opponent with his foot as he retreated with his staff. Kevin rolled off the ground, swinging his pike as he rose, Shin managing to redirect it to the side before it smashed into his midriff.

Kevin growled as he pulled out a second pike. Spinning them around, he went for a strike with one only for it to be parried. He slashed at the monk's staff with his second pike, cutting it in clean in half.

The Master, sensing defeat, backed up and went into his monkey stance ready to fight his assailant to the death. Alert to his advantage Kevin threw one pike at the elderly monk, but it was successfully blocked with the remaining section of staff he still held in his hand.

Kevin rushed forward trying to stab him with the blade of his remaining weapon, but he failed to land a hit as Shin evaded the blade. Shin followed this by disarming Kevin of his pike, hitting his palm hard against the hand of his attacker and simultaneously kicking him back.

Kevin went into a Kenpo stance as Shin stayed in his favored Monkey Kung Fu position. Both enemies stared each other down before rushing forward.

Kevin went for a punch to the chest, but his fist was parried and he was flipped to the right as Shin moved his bodyweight to the left. He rolled away as Shin jumped down with both feet, a move Shin aimed for his opponent's esophagus, trying to end the fight with one killer blow.

Kevin raised himself up onto one knee and grabbed his fallen pike from the ground beside him. He was backed up though as Shin attacked with the second pike, Kevin's other weapon grazing his chest as it was used against him. As he started to raise his own pike, the other pikes' blade was placed against his throat by Shin.

"Do it. I lost." Kevin dropped his pike, awaiting death as Master Shin raised his blade, ready to strike.

"You fought well and have some honor," Shin said before he gasped and started to stumble, droplets of blood appeared at the corner of his mouth.

Kevin looked up to see a dark warrior with a bloody sword, impaling the Master in front of him. The Master's body slid from the sword and fell down in a heap as his expired before Kevin's eyes.

Kevin stood and bowed to the fallen Master. "This was one-on-one. Why'd you attack him from behind?" growled Kevin as he turned to the soldier before him.

"I was ordered to help you win any way necessary," replied the solider.

Cleared unimpressed, Kevin bent down to retrieve his pikes. "Let's go. We've got a job to do. As much as I hate killing without honor, I realize we have orders to fulfill."

***

"Alexander, you want to get some lunch at the mess hall?" Lenora asked as they completed their latest bout of sparring.

Alexander messaged his sore neck, "Sure, I'm famished," he replied, moving on to rub his stomach. The two left the mat and headed to the dojo's mess hall. Collecting their food they sat at a table across from each other, away from the other students. "So how's your training to become a Master going?" Alexander asked through a mouthful of pasta.

The young woman chuckled at the painful memory of her training over the past few months. "Never have I been this tired in my whole life. Now I know how you felt when you started the training under Master Thompson," she responded.

"Didn't he train you just as hard?" asked Alexander.

, yes, but not as bad as you. I told him off at first for going easy on me. After that it was harder, but I persevered."

She turned serious, "I wanted to prove that women can be just as strong as men. There's no need to be handled with kid gloves."

Alexander grinned at her. "You want proof that women can be just as strong? Just look at the bruises that you gave me during our sparring sessions."

Lenora smiled at her friend's attempt to encourage her. "Thanks."

Alexander took another bite of pasta and swallowed. "Listen to me, Lenora. I'm glad you don't let others dictate what you can or can't do. Only you can decide how strong you are through hard work and resilience."

"A very wise statement, Alexander, and very true," said Master Thompson as he walked up to the table with his own tray.

He looked at his star pupil. "Heed his advice, Lenora, and you'll surpass me in skill," the Master said kindly as he put his hand on her shoulder.

"It's true that only you can determine your own worth, no one else, only you. That being said, we can certainly help you when you need it. We're a family not by blood, but by bond. A family that stands together." He smiled kindly as the two students got up and bowed to their master, who bowed in return. "I need you both in my study after you finish your meal. I need to discuss something with you," he said seriously. The two nodded their heads as Thompson walked away.

Later, the two students of the dojo walked to Master Thompson's study and saw him writing. "There's been an attack on several more Masters of the White Rose and we've lost a second key," he said with sorrow.

Lenora looked at her Master with confusion. "What're you talking about, Master?"

"I'll explain, Lenora, since only Alexander and I know what's going on." She glared at her friend, unimpressed that he hadn't chosen to share this with her.

The Master attempted to ease the tension between the friends, "I told him to not tell anyone except current Masters, so don't be upset with him, Lenora. I've been in contact with the other Masters and they're concerned. We might all be targeted, myself included."

Alexander nodded his head. "It looks like they are taking out each Master individually, but aren't killing all of the students, which is odd."

"Maybe they think you aren't a threat to their plans or worthy of killing? We can hopefully use that arrogance to get strong enough to fight them. To them you're nothing but children and can be dealt with at any time," surmised the Master.

"Why haven't the Masters come together?" asked Lenora.

"Lenora, let me ask you this: We are vulnerable to attack at any time, including in a crowded area. What would happen if the Master took a plane or train station? You think the Lord of Shadows army won't use leverage against us with a hostage?" asked Alexander.

"That makes sense," said Lenora.

"We can't endanger other people who have got nothing to do with this battle," Alexander told her.

"Plus," added the Master, "the Masters are around the world and we shouldn't come together. In doing so we would be making ourselves a bigger target. Let them expend themselves in finding us, that way they'll need more resources to try and take us out. Brute force isn't the only way to fight."

"Luray said subterfuge and cleverness is a greater weapon than brute force, and I agree with that completely," Alexander agreed.

Master Thompson stood. "Yes, Luray was the most tactically minded of the current Masters. Before retiring I have one last thing to do so I can sleep better. Please step forward, Lenora."

Lenora rose and approached the Master, unsure of what he was about to do.

"Lenora, as of now you're my successor in the Muay Thai style," said the Master as he handed her his own medallion. "Use this artifact to let you know how many of us are left. Alexander will teach you how to use it."

Lenora was visibly shaken. "Are you planning on dying, Master?" she asked quietly.

Master Thompson closed his eyes and sighed. "It's very possible. We have lost two just recently and Luray a few months ago."

Alexander walked forward. "Which ones have been murdered?" he asked.

"I just found out that Master Shin of the Wu Shi academy, Master of the Shaolin Fist and Monkey Kung Fu, was killed, and Master Estefan of Brazil, Master of Jijutsu, before him," said the Master.

"Did Master Shin manage to select his successor in time?" asked Alexander

"Yes. Before he passed, he chose a young monk named Guan Jiao, who's considered a prodigy in the style. He is both honorable and level-headed."

Lenora bowed her head. "Thank you, Master, for this honor; I shall do all I can to help protect this world from the Lord of Shadows' evil," she declared, her voice strong with determination.

Alexander turned to her and bowed. "I shall assist you, Master Lenora," he said, causing Master Thompson to smile.

***

In the temple on the mountain, five figures were standing in a circle clothed in black cloaks and hoods.

"Good, all my generals are here," the Voice noted. Two cubes now sat in their places on the pedestals. The crack in the Norse statue had grown further with the addition of the second cube. "I'm at two-fifths of my power thanks to the recent extermination of Master Shin and the burning of his precious academy. I can feel myself growing ever stronger."

Kyral walked up and smirked. "Too bad the only one who failed to get a key was Nicolson."

Luray's murderer growled. "Say that to my face, you little punk!" he shouted as he pulled out his sword.

Kyral pulled out his dagger and licked the blade. "Please, like you can even touch me, let alone beat me."

Kevin removed two pikes from his holster and addressed the pair, "Will you two show some respect to your Lord and stop your pathetic bickering?" his deep voice containing a threatening tone.

"He had an easy opponent," said Kyral with a sneer.

Kevin slammed his pike down on the ground, cracking a tile on the temple floor. "Fool! Each guardian must be approached with caution. You both fought like amateurs against your opponents."

Kyral snickered. "Like you did any better, Kevin of the Wind."

"I'll admit that I was caught off guard by Master Shin's skills. Truly a worthy and honorable enemy," said Kevin touching the scar he got from the fight with Shin. "Respecting one's enemy is the first step to defeating them."

Kyral growled. "You always had a silver tongue, Kevin, but each of us has a kill." He smirked, very satisfied with himself.

"Silence! I have let you three have your debate. Stop your pettiness and get me the third key!" screamed the Voice.

A figure walked out of the circle. "Allow me to retrieve it, Master," said a female voice.

"I've got someone more suitable for the task, Shun Xian," said the Voice.

The female bowed and retreated. "Of course, Master, but my claws haven't tasted blood since the murder of the Bolshevik family at their dojo in Siberia," she said grinning. She reminisced as she stroked her fingers, pulling out two metal claws that reached out a good eight inches. Specially made to fit only her fingers, Shun Xian took great pride in her lethal weapons.

"Vladimir!" shouted the Lord of Shadows from his prison. On hearing his name a huge man, a black tattoo of a viper on his bare arm and holding a massive hammer walked up from the circle. The lion skin he wore across his shoulders had belonged to a lion he had felled with his bare hands, before he had ripped the skin from its body.

"Yes, my Master?" His Russian accent thick and heavy.

"I want you to kill Master Thompson of the Muay Thai, the reigning champion of the North American division. Take as many of your hunters as necessary to kill the fool's students and find the Key," said the Voice of the imprisoned warlord. "Do NOT fail me!"

The man got down on one knee. "Of course, my Lord," he said, before walking out.

"Why start killing the students?" asked Nicolson.

"If any of the students survive, they will only grow stronger and oppose us," said the Voice.

"Bet you he fails," Kyral smirked.

"Say that to his face," Kevin replied.

***

The lastest American Fighting Championship was taking place. In the most recent match, the Master of Muay Thai stood over his beaten opponent. "The winner of this bout is Master Paul Thompson!" shouted the announcer as the Master raised his arm in victory.

"The next match will be Master Paul Thompson against an opponent whose size towers above all. Using Russian wrestling and some martial arts to overcome his adversaries, he is steamrollering all before him. -Vladimir!" shouted the announcer as the giant man, reaching an impressive seven and a half feet tall and all muscle, walked into the arena. "Begin!"

Master Thompson moved fluidly from his stance and thrust his knee at the giant man. His attack was easily caught, but the elbow he followed up with caught the giant Russian, making him release the Master. Vladimir growled, and struck back with his foot, his attempt intercepted by the Master's knee. "You shall be my next victim, White Rose Master," he threatened as he stalked the Master.

So I'm the next to be targeted, thought Thompson.

Vladimir threw another punch, but the Master moved his head to the side, letting the punch sail past. "I'm sure you can do better than that," goaded the Master as he hopped around in his stance.

In the stands, Lenora and Alexander were cheering their Master on. "There's something off about this Vladimir," Alexander whispered.

Lenora saw the worry on her friend's face. "What is it?" she asked.

He turned to her. "We've got to stop this match. Master Thompson is in trouble. Look at the way this Vladimir is attacking."

Lenora looked at him like he had lost his mind. "What are you talking about? I don't see any..." she says before realization strikes her. "Those attacks."

Alexander left his seat. "He's using kill shots with his attacks." His franticness making Lenora's eyes widen. "Throw in the towel, now!"

It can't be. They wouldn't reveal themselves to the public, would they? She thought, as she grabbed a towel from the bench and ran to the stage.

"He forfeits the match!" shouted Lenora as she threw in the towel for her Master.

The giant of a man glared at her. "This is my mission, girl." Raising his arms, a series of movements caused an eerie blue glow to appear around the fighters. "This is a barrier that'll only drop when one of the fighters is dead."

***

Back at Master Thompson's dojo, thirty men heavily armed with hammers approached. "The dojo's closed," stated one of the students as met the group at the door. Seeing the weapons they carried, the young man dropped into his stance and kneed the first attacker.

The armed men charged the lone student, overpowering him as they rushed over his body and into the dojo. The rest of the students stood, scared and outnumbered, ready to risk it all to defend their home.

After ten minutes of fighting, only three students were left to battle the twenty assailants still standing. Two students charged and engaged the overwhelming odds as one fled to sound the alarm.

He managed to evade the enemy long enough to press the switch, before he was killed by a dagger to the back.

The leader looked around. "Find the key now!" His men divided up, tearing up the dojo looking for the key. Failure to find what the Lord of Shadows needed was not an option.

"Sir, I found it!" shouted one of the men as he took it from a safe the man busted.

"Excellent, man. Leave the bodies here and follow me." The group of attackers left with the wind, leaving the bodies of ten students, all teenagers, and eleven of their own men.

***

The battle taking place in the tournament was becoming one-sided. Master Thompson, his energy failing him, was starting to slow down The hits from the Russian giant were stronger than any he had ever faced.

Lenora was still trying to get into the fight, past the blue force field, but was forced to watch as her Master fought vainly for his life. "Master, don't give up!" she shouted, hoping now for a miracle.

His opponent relocated several of his joints as Thomson's throws found some success, but he seemed unstoppable. He had multiple bruises on his body and blood on his face and chest.

"Well, this is the end for you, fool!" Screamed the giant as he punched the Master in the chest, throwing his weight behind the strike and sending him crashing to the floor. Coughing out blood, the Master tried to rise. Vladimir grabbed the Master's throat, lifting him from the mat, and began to crush his esophagus.

"That monster's won already due to forfeit, and by the rules he needs to stop his attack. I need security!" the announcer called with panic.

Several men in uniforms rushed to the stage guns in hand but were stopped by the invisible barrier. One slammed his stick into the barrier only to find it bounced back. "We can't get in," said one of the security guards as they looked for any weakness in the field.

"I won't go down this easily." Rasped the Master, using his remaining strength to head butt his opponent in the temple.

Vladimir stumbled back, letting go of the Master just as a knee was sent into his chest. "Pathetic!" growled the man mountain. "I'll kill you slowly." He continued to circle his target as a predator does its prey.

The Master jumped up hitting the assassin in the air with a strong knee to the ribs. "Time to end this." The Master's strength though had gone. A bone protruded from his knee where he had struck the Russian. "That attack and he's still alive and fighting," said the Master as he fought to mask the pain.

Vladimir walked to the injured Master who was trying to get up and stepped on the Master's one good leg, snapping it and making the Master scream in agony. Grabbing him by the throat he again lifted him from the mat, his broken legs dangling beneath him. Crushing his windpipe he threw the brave fighter, dead, to the floor.

Lenora screamed as the barrier finally dropped. The security officers near the barrier tried to apprehend the killer only to be thrown toy-like from the ring.

Lenora charged the giant man but was easily backhanded back out of the ring by Vladimir. Alexander also charged, hitting the giant Russian in the throat, making him stumble, but he recovered and punched Alexander back out the ring and into the crowd.

He opened his hands, moved his arms in a figure-eight motion and a black portal appeared before him. Turning to Lenora he goaded, "Your Master was easy to kill, girl. Pray I don't come for you next."

Lenora fell down and cried, holding her bleeding Master's head in her lap. "Master!" she vainly cried as Alexander limped to her side. He knelt down and hugged her, as tears ran down her face.

***

In the temple, Vladimir approached the statue and saw there were now three cubes on the pedestal; he smirked. The crack had extended still further on the statue, the flesh of the Lord of Shadows peeking through.

"Well done, Vladimir," said the Voice. "However, you shouldn't have made such a spectacle of the attack."

"I'm sorry, my Lord. It was the only way to fight him," said the Russian.

The Voice responded, "Since you have successfully completed your mission, I shall forgive this transgression."

"Thank you, my Lord," Vladimir said, getting down on one knee and crossing one arm over his chest.

The Lord chuckled deeply. "Soon I'll be free of this accursed prison."

***

Back at the dojo, the two newly-minted Masters were horrified at what they saw. "Who'd do this to such innocent children? This is horrible," a tear-stricken Lenora said. All of the students' bodies still littered the floor, along with numerous dark-clothed assailants.'

Alexander balled up his fists. "Damn!"

The two sorrowfully gathered the dead bodies of their fellow students and buried them at the rear of the dojo. Granting the orphans the little honor they could provide in death. The assailants' bodies burned with the dojo as the pair destroyed the building. Laden with supplies for their journey, the Masters left the scene and went in search of the remaining Masters.

***

One week later, traveling by train and guided by their medallions, the pair arrived in Brazil. Using funds Alexander has drawn on before leaving The States they rented a car, taking them across country to the edge of the largest rainforest on earth.

"It's huge. How're we going find the master in this place?" asked Lenora as they arrived at their latest destination. "Can the medallions still guide us through here?"

Alexander held her close. "We'll do it together," he said reassuringly. Lenora smiled back at the young Norwegian and returned his hug.

Chapter 7: The Three Pupils

Alexander and Lenora had been in the rainforest for a little over two days, walking as much as possible and resting only when they could walk no more. No sign of any habitation could be found, only mile after mile of wet flora.

"We've been searching for days. Where is he?" asked Lenora.

As another day drew to a close, Alexander had his medallion out and was using it to guide them to the Master. Lenora heard a small roar ahead. "What's that?" she whispered.

Alexander looked around. "Sounds like a wild cat. We'd better find shelter for the night," he replied. Making their way to a small cave nearby, they lit a fire outside the entrance big enough to illuminate the immediate area, got out their sleeping bags and lay down. Time passed and the roaring grew more distant but the pair found themselves still unable to sleep.

Alexander looked at his partner with worry evident in his eyes. "What's wrong?" he asked.

The young woman had her arms around her knees shaking. "I wish my Master was still here," she said, fighting back the tears.

Alexander put his head down in a slight bow. "I know, I felt the same way when Master Luray was killed," he admitted, a tear threatening to run freely down his face.

The two continued to sit in silence as darkness fell on the rainforest.

***

At the temple, Nicolson was kneeling in front of the statue as Kevin stood alongside.

"I need you to go to the Amazon with Kira and deal with the two successors of the Masters. We must prevent them from finding the other Masters before we do," the voice commanded.

Nicholson bowed his head. "Yes, my Lord." A black portal opened, and he walked through, followed closely by Kira.

Kyral walked out of the shadows. "I hope you sent some men with them. Otherwise, they'll fail you," he said with a smirk.

"Don't question what I do, Kyral," the voice was irritated.

"My Lord," said Kevin. "Why go after the small fry now?"

"They are away from civilization and we can kill them with no attention drawn to us," said the voice. "We can retrieve the key the boy has on him. How's my army coming along?"

"The men are almost ready. They are now ten thousand strong with access to modern weaponry and there are still more to come."

"Excellent. I want them ready by next year," said the voice.

Kyral bowed. "Of course, my Lord."

***

In the rain forest, Alexander and Lenora continued their trek. A nearby roar bringing them to a sudden stop.

Alexander turned his head. "Did you hear something?"

"You mean the roar?" asked Lenora.

Alexander shook his head. "Well, yes, but not just that. I can hear human voices as well."

Following the sound, the two young Masters snuck towards the edge of a small clearing. Three men armed with rifles stood over the bodies of several jaguars, some being so small they could only be cubs. The forlorn roar was emitted by a lone, injured jaguar in a nearby trap. They listened to the men converse as they circled the wounded cat.

"Man, these jaguars sure are a pain to kill," said the largest of the three men, as he looked down at the injured female jaguar lying on the ground. Toying with the scope on his rifle he prepared to finish the job.

The two Masters saw the jaguar vainly struggling to get free of the trap. "Poachers," said Alexander as he turned to his companion. But the girl was gone.

"Lenora, where are you?" he whispered. Turning back to the clearing he saw his friend stealthily approach from behind one of the three poachers, knocking him out with a punch to the back of his head. "She's going to get killed if she is not careful," Alexander stressed as he followed after her.

The two remaining poachers heard the sound of their friend hitting the ground and turned around.

"What're you doing here, girl?" accused one of the men, fully decked-out in camouflage gear, his finger firmly on the trigger of his rifle.

"These animals are protected from hunting and smuggling," she replied. "But then I suspect you already knew that!"

The two men laughed.

"We were going to sell the babies but they got a little rowdy so we put them down," said the camouflaged poacher's associate from under his safari hat. Lenora saw red and attacked the first of the two men, knocking him out with a quick knee thrust to the chest followed by a swift kick to the head. In her rage she lost focus, the second poacher hitting her in the temple with the butt of his rifle, and knocking her to the ground.

The man stood over her, rifle pointed between her eyes. "So long, girl," he grinned, his finger on the trigger.

Lenora, still dazed, closed her eyes and readied herself for the end. But it never came. Before her attacker could fire the fatal shot he collapsed across her. Behind him was Alexander, hands raised in a karate chop stance. "You know I really hate those who tear apart a family. They're lower than dirt," he said, reaching down to help his friend up.

Getting the rope from his bag the pair tied the three poachers together. Lenora tried unsuccessfully to get close to the injured jaguar, but it snapped at her, warning her to stay away.

Alexander walked up to her. "You're approaching her too fast." Slowly he crept up to the giant cat, careful not to make any sudden movements. The jaguar continued to growl at the two but was no longer snapping. Alexander approached the trap and released the injured cat.

He saw the animal's leg was bleeding and maybe broken, so he took a clean cloth from his bag and once again approached the cat, gingerly tying the cloth over the wound. Snapping a branch from a nearby tree and cutting down some vines he fashioned a makeshift splint onto the cat's injured leg. The jaguar looked at her rescuer's eyes and walked toward him as he walked away.

Alexander turned around and smiled. "You want to come with us?" The jaguar nudged his hand in confirmation.

"You've got a way with animals," said Lenora. Unable to believe what she was witnessing.

"They aren't mindless creatures like many people think. Show them respect and they won't harm you," lectured Alexander. "Show them kindness and they'll remember it for their whole life."

"I'll have to remember that." Responded Lenora. "We'd better get to work burying the deceased Jaguars."

***

The two fighters and their feline companion, having completed the shallow burial of the dead jaguars, walked further into the rainforest, leaving the men in the clearing tied up. Taking out his medallion Alexander saw that it was glowing brightly. "This way," he confirmed.

The three continued to walk deeper into the jungle for hour after hour until Alexander suddenly pushed Lenora to the ground as an arrow flew by where she had been stood only a moment before. "You know you shouldn't attack people you don't know." Shouted Alexander to their unseen attacker.

A young, black-haired boy wearing spiked gloves appeared from the trees. Holding a bow in his hand, a quiver of arrows were slung across his back. "What're you doing here?" he questioned, keeping an arrow notched on his bow string and his eyes on the two humans and their companion as he waited for their answer.

Alexander took a brief glance down at the medallion he held and saw it glowing. "Are you a master of the White Rose?"

The boy tensed up. "Who are you?" he asked cautiously.

Alexander smiled, the boy's response all the confirmation he needed. They had found another Master.

"Why don't you take a look at your medallion?" He gestured at the medallion the boy had around his neck. The young boy raised an eyebrow, took the medallion and pointed it at the two newcomers, seeing it glow brightly. "Very well. This is all the proof I need that you mean me no harm. Come. Follow me and I'll take you to my campsite," he said as he headed off through the trees.

They were led by the boy to a clearing less than a mile away. A log cabin stood near the center, land left free on all sides to no one to sneak up catching the boy unawares. "Welcome to my humble abode. My name is Mason, and I'm the former student of Master Estefan. Since his was killed I'm the current Master."

"I'm Alexander, former student of Master Luray," Alexander replied.

"And I'm the former student of Master Thompson. The name's Lenora."

Alexander turned to the jaguar. "And this is a jaguar we saved from some poachers after her babies and mate were killed."

Mason nodded. "What'd you do with the cubs and their father?"

"We gave them a burial, it seemed the right thing to do."

"Glad to see there's still compassion in this world. May I ask why you're walking in the rainforest to begin with?" asked Mason.

Alexander sat down on a log near the entrance to the cabin. "We're looking for allies, either Masters or their recent successors, to help prevent the rise of the Lord of Shadows."

"I thought that may be the case. My Master was killed a few months ago, and I have been trying my hardest to keep the poachers out. I've also seen the medallion crack twice since my master was killed."

"All of the Masters but one have been killed. Can you help us?" asked Alexander.

Mason sat down beside Alexander. "I will assist you since it was my master's last wish to help you. But first, we need to get stronger. Otherwise, we stand no chance." Alexander and Lenora nodded in agreement.

The next morning, the three arrived at a nearby river with a clearing and the three stood facing one another. "We need to have an idea of what we've got to work with."

"I'll start," began Mason. "I know the Brazilian style of jujitsu, and I'm a master at using my spiked gloves that can extend with a hidden button. I've studied, but have yet to master, another form known as capoeira, which is a dance style of fighting."

Alexander went next. "I know the five animal kung fu styles plus Muay Thai. I can use a tanto pretty well, but have yet to master it. I have mastered a short sword and am working on dual wielding."

Lenora looked at them. "I have mastered Muay Thai, as well as Snake and Crane. The only weapon I can use with any proficiency is the staff, but I prefer to use my knees."

"I'll teach you Jujitsu to give you both more styles to use and maybe confuse your enemy." Mason got into his stance with the other two doing likewise.

Xxx

In the middle of the Amazon, Nicolson and Kira appeared from within a black portal. "Let's find these weaklings and call it a day," said Nicolson as Kira stayed silent. "I thought you'd be excited to fight this boy, since your last mission was interrupted." He smirked.

The red-haired woman growled in response, "Don't mention that failed mission, Nicolson," she said with venom.

The man chuckled. "Or what? You aren't near my strength or any of the generals. You're kept around purely as a meat shield and for eye candy."

Kira growled while fingering her sword. *Just a little slash and he won't be bothering me*, she thought, anger etched across her face.

The two walked up to a clearing and saw the tied-up poachers that the Masters had left. "What do we have here?" he asked, as Kira gave them a disgusted look.

The poachers looked at the two. "Those two little brats jumped us and prevented us from catching our prize," said the one with the hat.

Nicolson bent down and untied them. "What did the brats look like?" He gave them a creepy smile.

"A young woman with black hair but no weapon," said a poacher. "I did not see the one who knocked me out.

"Do you want revenge against them?"

The three looked at each other and nodded their heads. "Yes," the leader said.

The general laughed. "Good. 'Cause those two are our targets. Help us kill them, and you'll have your satisfaction," he told them cutting them lose.

The five left the area in search of their quarry and headed deeper into the forest.

***

The three were resting in the log cabin when Mason woke up, startled. "Someone triggered an alarm!" he whispered waking up the other two. Looking at the clock it was five o'clock in the morning.

"We're about to have company." As they got their equipment, the jaguar woke up and joined the three, curious. The four walked out and saw five figures approaching from the East.

Alexander's eyes widened with shock, but turned into pure rage and anger as he shouted, "You murderer!" He pulled his short sword from its sheath.

Nicolson smirked. "It's been awhile, boy, since I killed your master."

Alexander tried to calm his emotions and steady his breathing. Kira fleetingly looked at the two with sorrow in her eyes before she steeled her features. Mason caught her expression. *Why would she be sad? Isn't she on their side?* He thought.

"I will take the woman. I need to see something," Mason told Lenora who nodded.

"I will deal with the three idiots with guns," Lenora replied.

Nicolson smirked and charged forward, attacking Alexander with his sword. Alexander blocked the initial strike and then span and kicked in response. "I will avenge my master." He put his sword diagonally over his chest in a defensive posture.

Nicolson chuckled as a maniacal grin was formed on his face. "We'll see." He in turn pulled out the jagged blade that he took from Master Luray's corpse, further fueling Alexander's rage.

Alexander was engaged in a sword duel with Nicolson, and neither was backing down. "You won't win, boy. I've got more experience in swordsmanship than you do." Nicolson blocked a blow with his sword and hit Alexander with the end of the handle, knocking him back. Alexander pulled out a long knife from a hidden sheath in his pants and started to fight his enemy with both weapons.

Noting the skills of his young combatant, Nicholson spoke, "You fought well, boy, but you'll die like your pathetic Master."

At this latest jibe, Alexander put his sword away and instead got into his Muay Thai stance. The general laughed. "You were foolish to put your sword away, hoping I'd do the same. I have no honor and don't care about any of my opponent's handicaps!" He rushed Alexander with his sword raised, ready to deliver the killing blow.

He thrust down, only for Alexander to turn his body at the last second, the attack flashing past him without contact. Alexander twisted something in his hand, and struck Nicolson's chest. Blood poured from the wound.

"So… careless…" gasped Nicolson as he fell down, a small dagger protruding from his heart.

Nicolson was dead and Master Luray was finally avenged. Alexander exhaled. He put his back on the tree he was next to. He covered a wound he'd received in the fight with the remains of his shirt, and waited for his friends to show up.

Xxx

Mason was currently using capoeira against his opponent, who was using the same style in reponse. "You really don't want to fight, do you?" he asked. "Your attacks they are too predictable for a trained assassin."

"I've got to. My feelings don't matter." She spun on her hand and tried to kick Mason.

"Moron! Your feelings do matter, not what other people think," Mason countered as he tripped Kira with a kick, pinning her to the ground.

Kira growled. "Do you know what suffering is? I was kidnapped by Nicolson when I was two years old," she told him as she tried to get out of his grasp.

"So? I never knew my parents either. I was raised by monks and nuns at the monastery, but it was burned by the acolytes of the Lord of Shadows!"

He continued, "I would've died that day, if it weren't for my master, who rescued me. For the first time, I knew what having a father was like, but I never felt complete, as I still wondered if my parents abandoned me," Mason told her as tears fell down his face. "You're not the only one who hassuffered."

"You might've had it rough, but at least you had people who cared about you! I was trained only to be a killer and a fighter—no childhood and no friends!" shouted Kira.

"My master discovered and found out that I was found by the monks on a street corner." His opponent was bleeding from a knife wound in her side. "I begged my master to train me. He refused for the first month, but I was persistent, and he finally agreed. I could've gone down your path if I still wanted revenge for my first family's death." He got up freeing his opponent.

"I pity you," said Mason as he got up and lowered his arms. "Now's your chance to prove that you've got no feelings. Kill me in cold blood and we'll see how you feel."

Kira drew a knife. She brought it up, but then couldn't bring it down. "Why do you care?" she cried.

"Because we're the same. We have both lost something early in our lives, but the difference is, I found something to protect." Mason looked into her eyes and only sorrow. "What's wrong? This fight won't end until you strike me down."

Kira growled and raised her dagger higher but threw it on the ground in frustration and stormed away from her fight.

Mason had a sad look on his face, and he shook his head. "She would make a decent ally if she conquered her superficial demons." He turned around and picked up her dagger and rushed to the other fight.

Xxx

Lenora walked away from her battle with two of the poachers dead, and a third on the ground unconscious. One dead after being mauled by the feline; the other one hit with the blow to the head.

The third poacher began to stir. Coming around he pulled out a pistol and got up suddenly and smirked. "Take this, you bitch," he said as he pulled the trigger.

Lenora screamed as the jaguar fell to the ground in front of her with a bullet wound on her side. "No!" she yelled as she rushed up to the last poacher and killed him with a knee to the temple. She rushed up to the giant cat and checked for any sign of life. She put her head down after finding no pulse or heartbeat and started to cry.

With the adrenalin wearing off, it hit her she had killed three people. She started to shake from shock. Mason ran up from the edge of the clearing. "Lenora, you okay?" he asked.

"I killed them," whispered the female master in shock.

Mason grabbed her shoulder. "Look at me. It was them or you," he said. "Did you like the feeling of killing them?"

"It sickens me," said Lenora as she stared at her hand.

"That is all that matters," said Mason. "Let's see if Alexander needs help."

Alexander breathed in as Lenora and Mason walked into the clearing, carrying the dead jaguar between them. Lenora spoke first, "My opponents are dead after one of them killed our feline friend."

"My opponent fled, so our battle was indecisive," said Mason as Alexander breathed in.

"I killed my opponent and avenged my master's death," Alexander responded. "We've got to give the jaguar a funeral. It fought bravely and it's the least we can do." Alexander clutched his wound and grimaced as he spoke.

Alexander's wound was cleaned by Lenora, before Lenora and Mason dug a grave, laid the dead jaguar in and prayed for its soul.

Following the funeral, Alexander was helped back to the cottage where Lenora was able to better clean his wound. As night fell, the three slept, their opponents reduced to ashes in a bonfire.

***

In the temple, the Lord of Shadows was furious after getting a report back on the fight. "Nicolson is dead, and Kira left her fight unfinished!"

Kyral smirked. "I knew we should have killed her."

"This is not a laughing matter, Kyral. You need to know when it's appropriate to crack jokes," said Kevin. "We lost a great asset, and another might've betrayed us."

Enough!" shouted the Lord of Shadows. "Shun Xian, I want you to exterminate the final master in Korea."

The only blond-haired, female general, with a slim body made for speed, giggled. "Yeah, it's my turn." She got excited as she vanished in a black portal.

Chapter 8: The Fall of the Last Master

In a temple on the outskirts of Seoul, South Korea, a black-haired woman of roughly forty years, walked down a stone walkway to a farm that she owned, in a long, red dress with a sword at her side.

"Where is that lazy student of mine?" she wondered as she looked around. She rounded the corner to see an older teenager laying on a pile of hay, sleeping peacefully, his green vest exposing his chest. The woman sighed and kicked the hay. The boy tumbled to the ground, hay falling on top of him.

"Mistress Wu, I was sleeping," he complained as he got up.

The female sighed. "Yuan Sang, have you finished your chores?"

The teen groaned. "Most of them, Mistress," he yawned.

The woman glared at him hands on her hips. "You're a genius in fighting, but in your work ethic, you're lazy," she said with exasperation.

"Not my fault that the hay looked comfortable," he said shrugging his shoulders to get the cramps out.

"The point of chores is to finish them, not to make a lounging area," said Mistress Wu with her hand on her head. "You cause a lot of headaches for me. Lunch is ready. Come inside. When you're finished, you can stack the hay and feed the chickens."

The boy finally jumped up. "Yes, Mistress, let's eat!"

Xxx

A portal opened in southern Kumi, South Korea, and the blond-haired female general walked out. On her hands eight inches claws that were curved down at the end. She headed north on foot talking to herself as she went, "The joys of the kill, the flesh being cut by the blade - I am so excited!" She licked a claw of her blade and smiled.

She had only been traveling a short while when she came across a crossroad. Five armed men appeared from behind a building.

"Look at what we have here, gentlemen. What about it, sweetie? Give us what you own, and nothing will happen to you," said one of the group. By the way he spoke first, she assumed him to be the leader.

The general shook slightly. "I am scared. How am I going to fight five big, strong men?" she said, faking a frightened voice.

The men leered at her, and the leader spoke again, "Just the way I like my victims, scared of the situation." The five advanced on the solitary female, determined to have some fun..

A few short minutes later, the female general skipped away from a scene of utter carnage, her claws red with blood. *Fools*, she thought as she started to giggle, "Now, that was fun."

Xxx

Mistress Wu was sipping her tea when the cup cracked. *Could it be?* She thought. Placing the damaged cup down on the table before her, she stood and walked out of her small house.

Across the yard she saw her student working on his chores. "Yuan Sang, I need to talk to you," she said. Her student looked at his teacher and saw concern on her face.

"What is it?" asked Yuan.

"I need you to take this and flee," she said as she handed him a medallion.

"Why? What is going on?" he asked.

"Assassin of the shadows," said Wu.

"But according to your stories, they were defeated," Yuan replied, the worry evident on his face.

The woman sighed. "They could always return, and I am the last of the older masters. I want you to find the other pupils, who have now been elevated to masters, and help them any way you can," she said.

"I will, mistress," he replied as he left the grounds and fled into the forest.

The master sat in a lotus position with her sword sitting on her lap. "This will be my last fight," she said.

Shun Xian approached the temple with a carefree expression on her face. Seeing the female master sitting, she smiled. *So, she has been waiting for her death,* she thought as she walked up to the master.

"I have been waiting for you, assassin." Mistress Wu got up, her right hand holding the curved Chinese sword of plain design.

"Today you will die, dear," the general mocked Wu. "Just like the other masters before you."

Wu got set into her stance, ready for the battle. "Your master will not take from me what he seeks!" she declared charging against the female assassin.

Shun ran at the master, claws raised, only to be blocked and kicked back.

Shun spun in the air and landed on her feet. "I guess it won't be easy," said the crazy female as she held her arms apart, claws extended. "That's good. I need some extended fun!"

Wu held her sword to her side, pointing the blade down. The Shadow assassin ran forward, scraping the dirt with her claws as she approached. She brought them up as she reached Wu, and flicked dirt into the master's eyes, temporarily blinding her. She thrust forward to take advantage, but missed the master and was kicked in return to the right side as Wu held her position. *So, she can fight blind*, thought Shun as she smirked. *Finally, a challenge.*

Xxx

Yuan ran through the forest, trying to get as far away from danger as he could. A sudden feeling made him stop and look at his medallion. It went dark, and then cracked a few minutes later. Knowing what this meant, tears fell down his face as he silently wept for his mistress's death.

Xxx

Back at the Wu's temple, the blond-haired assassin strolled off the grounds, holding in her hands the cube. Noticing the blood on her claws, she stopped and licked the blood from the blades. "The stronger opponent always has the better blood," she said out loud. A bloodlust look in her eyes as she opened a black portal and walked through it, leaving the body of Mistress Wu on the ground, several deep holes covered her chest.

***

At the edge of the Amazon, the three fighters looked down at their medallions and saw them all crack simultaneously. "Things are happening too fast," said Alexander, voicing what they were all thinking.

Heading back to the rental car they drove to the airport.

***

In the temple in northern Norway, a black portal opened and Shun stepped through. "I got the key, Master," she said, placing the fourth key on the pedestal.

"Well done," said the voice. "Soon I shall be free."

The remaining four generals each dropped to one knee as the Lord of Shadows laughed darkly.

Chapter 9: The Gang and the shopkeeper

On the west coast of South America the three young masters were looking out at the Pacific Ocean. Alexander had his medallion out as it glowed brightly, indicating the location of the latest successor. "The last master has fallen." Alexander looked at the ocean. He turned and faced his comrades. "We have to head to Asia and locate that master's pupil before the assassins do."

***

In the temple, the four generals stood in a circle around the statue. "We need the last key, but for now, lay low," said the disembodied voice.

Kyral was snickering. "Why? We could take the last key right now, my Lord."

Kevin growled in annoyance. "Watch your tongue, Kyral. The Lord of Shadows' word is law."

"Enough, fools! The reason we don't want to move against him is because we can't have the governments of the world alerted to our presence. We already caused a stir with our attack on Thompson, so, for now, we lay low, said the Lord of Shadows.

"Understood," said Kyral as the rest of the generals bowed in agreeance.

***

On a boat, the three young masters headed across the Pacific Ocean towards China. When they landed onshore, they headed into the city and looked around. "So where is this guy?" asked Lenora.

Alexander looked at his medallion as it glowed. "It looks like it is heading out of the city to the south." The three duly headed south, trekking for a few miles before they reached the edge of a forest.

Entering it they saw the serene and peaceful beauty of Sakura trees. Lenora looked around. "This seems so different to the Amazon, it's nice here – somehow calming," she said.

As they continued to explore, they failed to see a figure studying them in a nearby. Before they noticed him, he moved from tree to tree away from the group and deeper into the forest.

"This forest is bigger than it looks," noted Alexander as they continued in.

Mason looked down at the crumpled map he held in his hands. "There should be a small village on the other side of the forest. We should be able to get supplies there, and maybe some answers?"

The other two nodded as Alexander spoke up. "What is the name of the town?"

"He Fei," replied Mason. "It was a fort during the Three Kingdoms era, following this it was converted to a town. The walls are still there now," Mason explained.

"How do you know so much about this country?" inquired Lenora.

Mason smiled. "Master Estefan had me study the history of different countries and their fighting styles. I have always found Asian history fascinating."

A couple of hours of walking later, the three came out of the forest and saw the walled-off city of He Fei. The gate to the town was wide open and they entered without questions. Heading into the town, they concealed their weapons. "I will go and find a grocery store, while you two try to find a place to sleep," Alexander said.

His two comrades nodded in agreement and walked away.

As Alexander looked around, he saw a stall that may just have some things they could use. Walking in he came across three men with automatic rifles, talking to a clerk with a balding head and a gray shirt and jeans. "We own this town, so give us your payment, and you can stay in business," said one of the thugs.

The clerk backed up. "I gave you the fee for this month already. Why do you keep harassing me?" he asked.

The leader snapped his fingers, and one of his thugs threw down a shelf. "You know the deal: no money, no business."

Alexander walked up to the counter. "I need these items," Alexander said as he placed some provisions on the counter.

The leader growled. "Leave now. You cannot buy anything from this store!"

Alexander's eyes narrowed and he spoke Chinese in a growl that his master had taught him. "You might think you're strong with your friends behind you, picking on a defenseless clerk. However, we both know you're weak against a real fighter."

The leader chuckled and walked up with the other two, cracking his knuckles as he approached. "Let's teach this stupid boy a lesson."

The door opened behind Alexander, and Lenora and Mason walked in. "Need help?" Lenora asked, smiling.

Alexander grinned in return. "I got this."

Mason smiled. "Don't do too much damage," he said as he and Lenora left the store.

Outside, the two masters waited until the three thugs were kicked out of the stall, one after another, sporting bruises and broken bones. In the doorway, they could see Alexander brushing his hands.

"There goes the trash." Alexander turned back toward the clerk and walked up. "So as I was saying, I would like to purchase these items, please."

The clerk nodded his head. "Sure thing, sir. Anything else?" he asked.

"Is there a place in town that sells exotic weapons?"

Alexander's question caused the old man's eyes to narrow and he asked, "May I ask why?" At that moment Alexander's medallion glowed in his pocket. Noting this the old man added, "You have a White Rose Medallion I see." He went to the front door and put the 'Closed' sign on it. "Follow me." He indicated and the trio followed the old man towards the back of the stall.

The shopkeeper led the masters through the back and down to the basement, where they saw a forging shop complete with pit and steel-making equipment. "Tell me the real reason you want a weapon!" demanded the old man as he pulled out a smaller version of the medallion. "Each member of the White Rose, regardless of rank, gets a medallion. However, they get smaller with each lower rank.

"There are four levels: One is the lowest and four is the highest, save the fifth level, who is the grand master."

"Wait, why didn't you fight those thugs?" asked Mason.

"They would have taken it out on the town, so I couldn't," the man explained.

Alexander sighed. "I see. We are looking for allies to fight the Lord of Shadows, and I need a weapon made for Lenora."

The clerk sighed. "Do you have an idea of the kind of weapon you need?" he asked.

Lenora took some notes out of her bag and handed them to the shopkeeper, who said, "I can make it, but it will take me a week to forge it.

Lenora got up. "Thank you. By the way, we have never been introduced."

"You are correct. My name is Bain Yu, and I am the weapons maker of the Order of the White Rose."

"Mason," said the jujitsu master, extending his hand.

"I am Lenora," said the female master of Muay Thai.

"I am Alexander."

Bain nodded his head. "Very well, I will have your weapon ready in a week."

The three warriors bowed and left, leaving the man to his work. From the stall Lenora and Mason led Alexander to a hotel they had found.

Once in the hotel, the three sat in a room in a circle to discuss the situation with the local enforcement gang. "We have got to do something," said Mason.

Alexander thought for a bit. "If we can capture a member, maybe we can interrogate him?"

The three set to work on a plan to capture a member of the gang. Several hours, and many efforts, later the trio retired to bed, the formation of a plan complete.

The next morning, the three returned to the stall. Bain Yu turned around as they entered. "Good morning, Masters. Is there something you need?"

"We need your help, Bain Yu" said Alexander.

"Let's hear it," said Bain.

Alexander told him the plan, and Bain agreed, though some doubt remained. "This had better work."

Later that same afternoon, three thugs came into the shop. Approaching the desk, the larger of the men demanded, "Give us the tax for the week!"

Bain handed the thug some money and they left, not noticing the three figures following them.

After leading the Masters across town, the three thugs entered what appeared to be a Buddhist temple. Walking in, the thugs were greeted by a man, dressed in orange monk robes, and sat behind a desk. "You got the fee?" asked the apparent monk.

One of the men stepped forward. "Yes, sir, we have the whole amount."

The monk's eyes flicked to the corner of the entrance behind the men. "You have been followed," he said to the thugs, "Leave. I will deal with this." The three bowed and walked away.

Once the thugs had departed, the monk spoke again, "You three can come out. I know you are there, Order of the White Rose." He threw a medallion on the table.

The three revealed themselves as the figure dressed in the monks' robes dropped his hood, revealing a young male of teenage years with six dots across his bald head. "Welcome, Masters. My name is Guan Jiao, and I am the student of former Guardian Master Shin."

Chapter 10: The Final pupil

"Why are you in charge of a gang, and why are you forcing the townsfolk to give you money?" Alexander demanded.

The teen bowed his head. "It's just a farce to keep the suspicion off us. We have been hunted by the Lord of Shadows' minions, and from the two hundred students that were at the temple, only seventy are still with me now, and the number is getting smaller."

"I see. By acting like a bandit, you are basically trying to fool the Lord of Shadows into thinking you were all wiped out, because monks are usually peaceful and try to avoid conflict," surmised Mason.

The monk nodded his head. "That is the gist of it," he confirmed.

"So what now?" asked Alexander.

"Simple. I must join you and leave someone else in charge of this group," Guan said.

"Jun!" he shouted, and a young woman of Asian descent with black hair walked out and knelt before him.

"What is it, Sifu?" asked the young woman.

"I have to leave now to help the order. You are in charge of this group. Try to lay low, and hopefully remain safe."

The young woman continued to kneel. "Yes, Sifu."

"When the time comes, I might call on you and the others to fight. For now, try to gather more soldiers, as discreetly as possible," said Guan.

The young woman bowed her head. "Of course."

***

In the temple in Norway, the four generals were decked out in full armor. Kevin's armor was green with spikes on his wrist, symbolizing the wind's sharpness.

Kyral had black armor that blended into the shadows. The armor, symbolizing the cunning of a ninja, had holsters for his kunai and shuriken. On his back he carried a short blade.

Vladimir wore a dark brown armor with many layers to symbolize the strength and the protection of the hard earth.

Finally, Shun Xian wore a dark-blue leather armor to symbolize water. Highlighting the way she moved fluidly like a stream or river.

Behind the generals stood two thousand soldiers, equipped with old, yet functional, weapons: staffs, swords, pikes, arrows, and daggers.

The Lord of Shadows spoke, "It is time to begin. I have contacted my proxies in several countries and have told them to begin their mobilization. Kevin, you are going to take five hundred soldiers and head to Laos and attack Vietnam and Indochina."

"Shun Xian, you will take another five hundred and head to Uzbekistan to help with the mobilization. Take out the weak countries that broke away from Russia."

"Vladimir, I want you to head to Zambia and conquer the smaller countries in Africa. And finally, Kyral, you must go to the Congo. Take control of your surrounding areas. Dismissed!" the Voice commanded.

***

The rest of the week went by without incident, and Lenora returned to the stall and collected the weapon from Bain Yu. It was a bo staff constructed of lightweight but hard metal. In the middle of the shaft was a small button, used to extend a sharp blade from one end of the staff.

Fully-armed, the four headed south in search of the final pupil. Resting at a small inn, they planned how to stop the Lord of Shadows.

"So, you have the last key in your possession, but the evil one has the rest," Guan said grimly, getting clarification.

Alexander nodded his head. "I have kept it on me all this time."

"It's strange that the Lord of Shadows only attempted to have it retrieved once," Lenora said.

"I can only think of two reasons why this would be so," said Mason, as he leant back against the wall.

Guan, who was sitting in a lotus position, nodded. "I have a theory as well, but first let us hear yours. Mason."

Mason cleared his throat. "I think that they want us all together in one place so they can get rid of us in one movement, or The Lord of Shadows is laying low so he doesn't alert the world's powers to their plans."

Guan closed his eyes. "Those were my theories as well, but they could also be biding their time because they don't have the manpower for a world search or conquest yet," he said, adding to the list of possible reasons.

"Now, what should we do?" asked Alexander.

"We need to continue to gather allies for this battle," Guan said. "The Lord's army will not be small."

Consulting his medallion, Alexander confirmed that the journey ahead was to the south, and the four headed out. They took the train to South Korea, and after a few days on the train they disembarked in Seoul and headed to a nearby hotel.

The next morning, Alexander's medallion led the group to a forest, and in turn to the site of a temple. Approaching the entrance the group discovered a mound of dirt with what appeared to be a tombstone on it. "This must be it," stated Mason, seeing his own medallion glow brighter.

Guan looked at the makeshift tombstone. "It is unmarked."

The four entered the temple and looked around. "Who are you?" questioned a voice.

The group all looked around, trying to find where the voice was projecting from. "I will ask again: who are you?"

The medallions, in unison, glowed behind them. "Are you a disciple of a Guardian?" asked Alexander.

"How do you know about that?" replied the voice.

"We are disciples of the Guardians as well," said Guan as the four took out their medallions to prove their claim.

A red-haired teen, with hardened eyes walked out. "What are you doing here?" he scowled.

Alexander stepped forward to speak for the group. "We need your help to fight the Lord of Shadows."

"You wasted your time. Leave," he said, before turning his back on the four masters.

Lenora stepped forward. "At least hear us out," she pleaded.

"I have no interest in this war. Let me be at peace," he said.

"If you don't help, there won't be peace only darkness," Mason responded.

"Leave. I will not ask again," said the teen as he drew his sword and pointed it at the four warriors.

Guan walked toward the teen. "Tell me, did your master die also?"

"Yes. Now leave," growled the teen.

"We have all lost someone precious. It is how we cope with this loss that determines our path," the monk sympathized.

"If you don't leave, I will force you out," the teen repeated as he got in a guard position with his curved sword held out before him.

The four turned and left the grieving boy alone in the temple. After they had exited the boy dropped to his knees and tears started to flow down his cheeks. *I am a coward and I can't help them*, thought Yuan.

"So what now?" asked Alexander, as they came back out into the sunlight.

"Let's head to the next town and think of a plan," said Mason. "Whoever he is, we need him."

The masters headed to a small town nearby and found a couple of rooms at an inn where they could clean up and work on how they were going to persuade this strong-willed teen to join them.

Back at the temple, the teen still sat on the ground. *I can't involve myself in this battle,* he thought.

"Why not?" replied a familiar female voice.

"Mistress Wu?" he asked, getting up and looking around. Unable to believe what he had heard.

"You need to help them, and you need to stop blaming yourself for my death. Yuan, it is not your fault."

"I should not have left you!" he shouted out, trying to convince himself.

"Foolish student; it was my choice to fight and to make sure you lived."

He looked down at his medallion. "What magic is this?" Yuan asked, angry at this perceived trickery.

"This is no trick, my student."

"What do you mean?" asked Yuan.

"As you know, I am the only master to have used chi energy to its fullest. I have imparted some of my own into this medallion to give you one last message."

"Help the others fight the darkness," implored Wu's voice.

"I can't. I don't want to lose anyone else," said Yuan.

"Then you have failed already by giving up."

Yuan put his head down in shame.

"Help them. I knew the risks of ordering you away from the battle and have accepted it. You have not. Help them as my last wish, my student," said the spirit of Yuan's former master.

"Yes, Mistress," He got up and went to his master's headstone to pray one last time before heading into town.

Chapter 11: Order of the White rose

The four disciples sat in a room where they watched the television. The local newscaster informed the group, "Breaking news: War. Several third world countries have formed an alliance and have taken over neighboring countries. No one knows why these countries have suddenly declared war, but the world's powers refuse to step in, calling it a regional conflict," said the reporter.

Guan closed his eyes. "That is mistake number one for the world powers. It will haunt them later."

"I did not think they would move so fast or so soon," said Alexander.

"What was that?" Alexander said when they heard screaming in the street. He rushed to the window and saw cloaked figures killing the townsfolk below.

Guan joined him. "We will have to fight our way out and get what is left of the town to safety."

They rushed out of the hotel and saw around fifty men, one of them about ready to kill a child.

"No!" shouted Mason as he ran at the attacker, knocking the man to the ground.

"The targets are here," stated one of the cloaked figures as they surrounded the masters and charged.

Lenora kicked one back with her knee, as Alexander dodged one attacker before he drove through another with his sword. Guan moved between enemies hitting pressure points as Mason dodged and landed his own blows.

The sheer number of attackers meant they started to back up to the entrance of the town, protecting what was left of the citizens as they tried to flee. Lenora took out her staff and knocked a few attackers out as Mason used his spiked gloves with some degree of success.

No sooner than they had overpowered the first fifty, more attackers started to come in. "They are using waves of attackers to wear us down!" the monk said as he struck one of them between the eyes, killing him, before roundhouse-kicking another coming in from behind.

The warriors began to tire under wave after wave of attacks. As the soldiers of darkness advanced on the group, an arrow flew into one of soldiers, before a hailstorm of arrows followed. The dark-cloaked leader looked up as a man wearing a cloak with the symbol of the White Rose on the chest appeared on the hillside above, followed by another until the hill was filled with members.

"You will not stop the shadow!" the dark-cloaked leader shouted as he and his army charged the hilltop, hoping to kill some of the White Rose reinforcements in a futile gesture.

"Attack!" was shouted by one of the White Rose members as the order attacked the army of darkness.

In the ten minutes that followed, the shadow army was wiped out, staining the town and hillside with their blood.

One of the members walked up and bowed. "I'm glad we made in time." The man lowered his hood, revealing himself to be Bain.

"Thanks for the help," said Guan as the rest bowed to their savior.

"We have to get back to the hideout. We can't talk here," urged another member, keen for their conversation not to be overheard.

Alexander remembered the voice, "You're Captain Hathaway of the ship that took me across the Atlantic." The man lowered his hood, confirming Alexander's suspicions.

"It has been a while, Alexander," the captain said as further members revealed themselves to be the crew of Hathaway while others were townspeople of Hefei.

"We must leave now before more show up," urged Bain.

"That will be for the best," Mason agreed.

Alexander looked around, suddenly panicked. "No! My bag with the key is gone. They must have gotten it during the fight!" cried Alexander.

"The Lord of Shadows can now be resurrected," said Mason, worry etched on his face.

***

At the temple, a cloaked figure walked to the pedestal and placed the final key in its slot. "It is time for your resurrection, my Lord."

The eyes of the statue glowed, and it broke apart, revealing a black-armored, demonic-looking being with a metal mask. On his back was a massive jagged sword. He looked at his minion. "Your usefulness is over. I thank you for your services. I will take your life force to get the rest of my strength back. Know that you have served me well." He stabbed the solider through the chest with his sword. The dark lord's eyes glowed red. "Now for my final conquest," he said as an orb of black energy was shot from his hand to the sky, spreading darkness around the world.

***

Kira looked up and closed her eyes. *So he has done it. I have got find a way to stop my former master*, she thought with bitter hatred.

***

On the road from the temple, Yuan's medallion exploded into shards. "No! It is too late!" he cried as he rushed to the Order of the White Rose's camp.

The four newest Guardians watched as their medallions simultaneously cracked into shards, as the members of the order looked on in horror. "He has risen," confirmed one of the members as the sky became completely covered with dark energy.

Chapter 12: Elimination

In the Temple on the bleak mountain, the Lord of Shadows was sitting on his throne with his generals at his side. "It is time. Find any fighters with tournament rankings and eliminate them, all of them. Leave no one standing."

"Yes, Lord of Shadows." The four generals disappeared in a black vortex.

I shall not make the same mistake again; those who can oppose me will die, the evil one thought.

***

In a small dojo with swords decorating the walls, a man in a blue haori and black pants was sitting down meditating. A sword lay on his lap in its sheath when a black portal opened in the room.

"What in the world…?"

Kevin strolled out with two pikes pointing sideways out of the holster on his back. "Oroki Yu, you are due for extermination," said the general drawing a pike from the holster and spinning it before him.

Oroki grabbed his Katana off his lap. He took it out of its sheath. "I don't know who hired you to take me out, but I will beat you here and now," said Oroki.

The two charged. Kevin barely had time to block as the Katana got close enough to draw blood from his cheek. Kevin growled, clashing with Oroki as the swordsman parried the pike, forcing Kevin off balance. Kevin eyed his opponent and pulling out his second pike, he attacked from a distance, throwing a gust of wind of Oroki.

Oroki was picked up by the wind and slammed against the wall as Kevin charged forward.

Oroki seeing Kevin charge pushed himself off the wall and tried to strike his opponent with his blade. Kevin blocked it with one of his pikes and tried to stab Oroki in the chest, but this move resulted in having his shoulder grazed slightly.

"You are skilled," Kevin said with respect as he spun the pike forcing Oroki to be on the defensive as one of the pikes got past Oroki's guard and severed his left arm.

Oroki looked at the general with defiance as he tried to slash with his good arm, still holding his sword, but it was kicked away as he was stabbed in the chest. Kevin sighed and bowed to his fallen opponent. Turning away, he headed back through the portal.

Xxx

In a small forest in France, a man was chopping trees with his ax when he felt the energy of a Shadow and threw his ax into the forest. A black blur rushed out. "So the rumors of your skills in hatchet throwing are not exaggerated," said a voice. Pulling out another hatchet, the man blocked knives being thrown at him with his ax. Kyral appeared before the man with his tanto posed to strike.

"Who are you? Why are you attacking me?" asked the man.

"I have been ordered by my master to eliminate you."

"I, Léon, will not lose!" the Frenchman defiantly declared as he swung his ax, nearly taking off Kyral's head but Kyral managed to block the ax with his Tanto.

Kyral was forced onto one knee as the Frenchman's strength started to overwhelm him. Smirking, he disappeared in a black mist surprising Léon for an instant, before, again, he was quickly on his guard. *I see he will be a difficult opponent*, thought Léon as he looked around. Suddenly, he heard a noise and blocked a kunai but he was run through by Kyral's tanto. Kyral pulled out his weapon as the body of Leon fell lifeless to the ground.

***

After a short wrestling championship, the winner was in the locker room when a portal opened up revealing Vladimir who said, "Brother, it has been a long time."

The other man eyed the giant. "You have a lot of guts coming back to Siberia after the stunt you pulled."

The general walked up to the champ. "You're not happy to see me, Sergei?"

"After murdering our parents, I am not overly thrilled to see you," said the wrestler Sergei, with a clear dislike of Vladimir.

Vladimir charged his brother, starting a grappling contest. Vladimir proved to be stronger, tossing his brother over his shoulder and into a locker. "Is that all you got, Sergei?"

Sergei got up and sent a right hook into Vladimir knocking him back. Vladimir smiled and said, "That is the only attack you will land on me." He then rushed his brother and grabbed his neck, slamming him into the ground. "This was fun, brother, but I have other people to murder." He punched Sergei in the temple, killing him.

***

Meanwhile, in Manhattan, a champion boxer by the name of Clay was taken out before he knew what hit him. Shun Xian hid in the shadows of a building and, with her lethal claws, grabbed Clay out as he walked from the boxing arena. His body would be found sliced to ribbons. "Well, I was hoping for more of a challenge," she said with a bit of disappointment.

And so, one by one, the generals dispensed of well-known fighters around the world, showing no mercy.

***

In the Lord of Shadows' temple, the evil one opened a portal and went through it. *I guess I should take care of him, the one with the item,* he thought.

At Mt. Everest, close to the base of the high mountain in Nepal, a man with a white beard and white robes, his body adorned with circular bladed objects, was climbing down the slope when he sensed a presence before him.

So it is time, thought the man as he grabbed his bracelets which doubled as circular daggers, one in each hand. "To what do I owe the pleasure of this visit, evil one?"

A dark-armored figure appeared. "You have something I want," the Lord of Shadows said, pulling out his jagged sword.

The Ancient spun his bracelets from his wrists and swung them towards the Lord of Shadows. "Chakrams," said the Lord of Shadow as he blocked them effortlessly with his sword.

The old man jumped back, took small blades from several hiding places in his robe, and threw them at his attacker. The Lord of Shadows effortlessly blocked the first with his sword and grabbed the second with his armored hands.

Sensing a counter attack, the old man blocked the sword that was swung at him with the chakrams he pulled out from his robes and the two warriors stayed locked for a few seconds. The old man broke the deadlock with an effective sweep kick, forcing the evil one to back away.

"Impressive," the Dark Lord responded. He fired a dark orb out of his hand, hitting the sage in the chest sending him to the ground.

The old man struggled to his feet, and ran forward throwing his Chakrams, forcing the Lord of Shadows to avoid them by lowering himself into the ground. As the old man frantically searched for the evil one, he reappeared behind the Ancient and ran him through with his sword, killing him instantly.

"Now, to find what I am searching for." He stepped through the open doorway, into a hut that belonged to the Ancient and with no effort saw a red orb out in plain sight. "I have the first elemental Orb of fire!" He exclaimed. Retrieving the object, the Orb sank into his body and his eyes glowed a dark, ruby red.

***

The Lord of Shadows reappeared in the temple. Sitting on his throne he looked around. His three generals appeared before he needed to summon them. "Have you done what I asked?" he demanded.

Kyral smirked. "Léon is dead, my Lord."

"Oroki Yu has been killed," said Kevin.

"I am the only one left of my family." No remorse could be found in his Vladimir's voice.

Shun walked in and said, "That boxer had no skills. His blood was wonderful for my blades."

The generals continued to tell of the extermination of renowned fighters around the world.

The armed warlord gave out a deep chuckle. "It is time to show the world my might. Are the troops ready for total conquest?"

"We have twenty thousand troops and thirty naval ships, my Lord," said Kyral.

"We shall start our conquest in Norway followed by northern Europe. Kyral, you are in charge of this operation. Don't fail me.

"Of course, my Lord," Kyral said, disappearing in a plume of black smoke.

The Lord of Shadows sat on his throne, looking out from the bleak mountain his temple was situated on. "Let us see how this plays out," the Lord of Shadows chuckled darkly. "Now to tie up that one loose end."

***

Kira had been in the forest since her battle with Mason. After their fight has come to a premature conclusion she had escaped via plane. Keen to get herself far away from the Amazon, she soon found herself in Norway again several days later. Unbeknown to Kira, she was being tracked through the seal on her wrist.

Kira found herself walking through a dense part of the forest when her musings were cut short. She heard voices echoing in the brush.

"Why did our Lord send us to kill the traitor and not send his generals?" asked one voice.

"The Lord of Shadows chose us to take care of this traitor, and his word is law to us as it will soon be to the world," another voice responded.

Kira tried vainly to get out of sight as the figures came into view, but they saw her and prepared to attack.

"Kira, you are to be terminated by orders of the Lord of Shadows," the leader said as around fifty more black-garbed warriors surrounded her. She rushed forward, trying to attack with the element of surprise. The tactic seemed to work as she killed two of them with a knife she had hidden in her sleeve.

Once the surprise was gone, she quickly lost ground due to the relentless numbers assailing her. She found herself backed up against a line of trees, when an arrow lodged itself in one of the soldier's arms.

The leader of the Dark Lord's men turned his head to find out where the assailant's shot came from, just in time to catch an arrow with his bare hand. Momentarily distracted he was struck down from behind by a figure carrying a mace. One by one, the soldiers were taken out by the black-robed newcomers. Kira took a good look at one of the men and noticed him wearing black robes with a white rose. More warriors dressed the same appeared and after a short battle defeated the soldiers. "

Come with us to camp," said the one of robed men.

Kira looked at the man with confusion, "Who are you?" Not ready to trust her saviors just yet.

The man sighed impatiently and took off his hood, revealing a bald head with a tattoo of a rose. "My name is Rashid, second in command of the Sharp Thorns of the Order of the White Rose."

Kira looked at him with curiosity. "The Order of the White Rose?"

The man nodded his head. "More will be explained when we get to camp, Kira, former Captain of the Lord of Shadows. Our commander would like to see you," Rashid said as he was joined by another member. "Report!"

"We have discovered the order for the termination for Kira by the Lord of Shadows. It seems he is also looking for the elemental Orbs."

Rashid closed his eyes. "This will complicate things greatly. Come with us and you will be protected until we get to camp." Rashid motioned Kira to go with him.

Kira sighed and thought, *I've got no other choice*. She walked with Rashid.

At a small camp, a half hour's walk from the scene of the battle, Rashid headed straight to a tent decorated with flags, beckoning Kira to follow him. "Commander, I have brought Kira as requested," said Rashid as he entered the tent.

"She may enter," replied a female voice.

Rashid nodded his head and motioned for Kira to enter the tent. Inside, she was greeted by a red-haired woman, dressed in a similar black robe with a white rose. "Hello, Kira," said the woman.

"Who are you?" Kira asked nervously.

"My name is Kin, and I'm your twin sister." The red-haired woman stated with her eyes closed.

"My twin sister?" Kira said with shock.

"You were kidnapped by one of the Lord of Shadow's generals after he killed our mother. Our father was a member of the Order. He spent years trying to find you and even lost his life to an acolyte of the Lord of Shadows in his pursuit of you." Kin responded. "You must have many questions for me, sister."

"Yes. But first, I was told this is the Sharp Thorn of the Order of the White Rose. What is that?" asked Kira.

"There are four branches of the Order. First is the root that consists of the Artisans who make the weapons and the farmers who provide food and supplies, like a root who gathers nutrients from the soil.

Next is the Stem or the soldiers who fight on the front lines. The stem is the strongest part of the rose.

"The next one is the Sharp Thorn, we who work behind the scenes, including spies and assassins. Like a thorn on the rose, you won't know you have been pierced until after you have put your hand on the stem."

"Finally the Masters branch, known as the Commanding Petals, which is situated at the very top of the flower, from where it commands the rest," explained Kin.

"So why did you want to meet with me?" asked Kira. "Surely it's more than me being your sister?"

Kin looked at Kira. "Simple. We need your help in stopping the Lord of Shadows. This monster must be defeated."

"I don't know how I can help. I can give you information but he and his generals are much stronger than I am," said Kira.

"True they are now, but we will train you to fight like us so you can help on the battlefield," said Kin.

Kira looked up and nodded.

"Rashid, can you take Kira to her tent?" asked Kin.

"Yes. Right this way, Kira." He escorted her out of the commander's tent.

A moment later Rashid walked back into Kin's tent. "We have a problem," he said.

"What is it?" asked the commander.

"The evil one is searching for the elemental orbs."

"Send an alert to all of the members including the Masters. If he gets all of the Orbs then it will truly be Armageddon."

"I shall do so. A question if I may?" asked Rashid.

"Go ahead," said Kin.

"How should we train your sister?" asked Rashid.

"You will train her in strength and I will train her in speed. Marduke will train her in tactics. After that we will teach her how we engage the enemy without engaging."

Kira woke the next morning and saw a white tee shirt and a black robe with a white rose draped across a chair. She put them on and marched out of her tent. Rashid strolled up to her and said, "Kira, come with me. I will be training you first. You will call me Master while I am your instructor."

"Yes, Master."

Kira followed Rashid to a circle in the dirt. He held up two wristbands and ankle weights. "Put these weights on your arms and legs." Kira did as she was told. "We will start with forty pounds on your body and increase them gradually so you can get your strength and speed up."

"Now, I want you to do fifty push-ups and thirty squats. Get to it."

Kira started her pushups as Rashid watched, and then squats. Kin came to observe Kira.

After an hour of doing exercise, Kin approached a panting Kira. "You did well. Now to build your speed up."

"Follow me," said Kin as Kira followed her sister.

They came upon a field with a dirt track. "I want you to run two laps with your weights on and I will time you," said Kin.

Kira walked to the starting line and Kin took out a timer "Go!"

Kira ran around the track twice and got back to the finish line as Kin stopped the timer. "A mile in four minutes and thirty seconds. Not bad for a rookie. It is not fast enough to match even our slowest runner, however."

Kira was wheezing and her muscles were sore with extreme fatigue. She dragged herself back to her tent and fell onto the cot.

In the main tent, Kin was talking to Rashid. "She has the potential to be stronger than any one of us. Have the leadership of the rose replied back?"

"Yes, the elders who are in charge until the new Masters are prepared have sent this letter; they have requested that we try to locate the Orbs with our spies," said Rashid.

"Send out the spies immediately. We have got to secure at least one or the alternative will be catastrophic."

"Yes, Commander." Rashid bowed and left.

Kin walked to Kira's tent the next morning. "It's four A.M, time to continue your training," Kin said, waking her sister. "Get dressed and meet your instructor at the training ground."

Kira got dressed and went to the training field. She got there and saw Rashid standing in the middle. "Master Rashid, how are you this morning?"

"I am fine this morning, Kira, and you?"

"Tired." Kira rubbed her eyes. She let out a yawn.

"Waking up this early is part of your training, I woke up two hours before you and I went to bed at eleven last night."

"What does that accomplish?" asked Kira.

"Excellent question, Kira," he praised. "We need your body adjust to getting very little sleep. We must be ready at a moment's notice for any mission."

"So what's on today's agenda?"

"First we are going to warm up with some basic exercise, and I will do them with you. Ten sit ups, ten pushups, and ten squats," he said as he sat with her.

After doing the warm up, they stood. Rashid turned to face Kira. "Now we are going to have a sparring session."

"I want you to come at me with everything you have." He got into a stance putting one leg in front of the other and his palms out in front of his chest.

"Tai Chi, interesting choice," Kira said as she started to dance like a break dancer. She went for a kick as Rashid blocked and slammed a palm on her shoulder sending Kira to the ground.

"Is that all?" said Rashid as Kira got back up and went for a low sweep. Her kick was grabbed and she was thrown. "You can't beat me with your limited knowledge," said Rashid, his posture relaxed. "I will teach you my style while others teach you their styles. We have much more training to do."

Kira got up and nodded her head.

***

The Lord of Shadows was sitting on his throne. "Kyral, what have our spies found about the location of the Orbs?"

The small ninja jumped down from the rafters, landing softly at his master's feet, and said, "We have found two of them. One is in China in the Forbidden Palace, guarded by the president's elite guards. The other one is in a tribal area in Uganda. The one in China is the wind element and the one in Uganda is the earth element."

"I shall claim the one in China." The Lord of Shadows, rose from his throne and summoned a black portal before him. Without looking back to his Generals, the Dark Lord strode through the portal.

In the Forbidden Palace, the Lord of Shadows walked out of the portal, and straight into a soldier. "Halt," said the solider, a Chinese Flag on the shoulder of his uniform. Hearing the commotion, five more soldiers ran out from the palace, semi-automatic guns pointed at the Lord of Shadows.

Looking unperturbed by his predicament, the Lord of Shadows confidently addressed the soldiers before him, "It looks like I am outnumbered. But you will do well to remember what they say about a trapped rat, -we bare our fangs."

"Shoot him down," ordered the commander. The Lord of Shadows raised his hands, a few elaborate movements and he had formed a black barrier between himself and the soldiers. The bullets sank into the barrier and disappeared.

The Evil Lord pulled his jagged sword from its sheath and charged the soldiers, cutting them down with his sword as the commander fired his machine gun in response. Nothing could touch the Lord of Shadows as he effortlessly weaved between the men.

"I was hoping for some kind of challenge," the Lord of Shadows said as the last soldier's body dropped to the ground and he walked into the Palace.

***

In the Order of the White Rose Camp, the Masters were now sitting in a tent with the more experienced members of the order. "What are the elemental Orbs?" enquired Guan.

Bain replied, "They were said to contain the power of the elements. There are five in all, each carefully guarded by either a sage or heavily guarded by members of the order. If the Lord of Shadows collects all five, it will complicate things greatly, and his power will be limitless."

"Do we know the location of any of them? If we can secure one it will even out the odds a bit," suggested Lenora.

"One is in the United States guarded by the president of the country," said Bain.

"Can we retrieve it?" asked Alexander.

Hathaway, who was sitting on Bain's right side, looked at the newest-minted Guardians. "I will contact the president."

***

In the Forbidden Palace, the Lord of Shadows tore through the Chinese Special Forces as their bullets continued to be absorbed by his magical barrier. Seeing that their bullets had no effect on the intruder, they changed tactics and began to attack with their combat knives.

The evil dictator chuckled darkly as a frightened soldier got close with his combat knife, only to have a sword flash past and pierce his chest. "I am once again disappointed. Now you will all die," he said rushing forward, taking apart the soldiers at will.

A lone soldier glared at the murderer. "I have called for backup," the soldier defiantly said, before his assailant drove his sword through his chest.

The Lord of Shadows got into the throne room and came upon the case holding the green Orb. "At last, the second Elemental Orb," he cried, then his maniacal laughter echoed from the walls as he strode out of the palace and into a platoon of infantry and five tanks.

"Only *five* tanks? I am insulted," said the evil one. The soldiers had their guns pointed at him, obviously unaware of their futility.

A man appeared out of the centre-most tank. "Surrender yourself, by order of General Tang."

The Lord of Shadows absorbed the Orb like the one before it and his eyes glowed a dark green. Clapping his hands, he sent a gust of wind at the platoon of infantry, sending them crashing back into the walls of the palace. "Let's see what the almighty Chinese military can do," said the evil one as he charged the tanks, slashing his sword through them like a knife through butter.

"Shoot him!" Cried the officer as his men all fired their guns, but the soldiers bullets never found their target and bullets and soldiers alike were shredded by a high-powered wind blast.

The Dark Lord, surrounded by death and destruction was not impressed. "Weak." He uttered, before opening a portal. As he went to leave he turned around to see the injured officer and said, "Tell your president this was just a taste of things to come." He then turned and disappeared through the portal leaving the massacred soldiers behind.

Chapter 13: The Beginning of the Norwegian Invasion

Kyral stood in front of the temple facing his fifty thousand soldiers. "Men! The time has come! Let us conquer Norway!" The soldiers held up their guns and eagerly shouted in praise of their general.

The attack progressed quickly, Kyral and his force overcame the northern half of Norway in short time, killing all those who stood in their way.

In Oslo, the Norwegian Prime Minister was in a meeting with his cabinet when a soldier burst in, paused to catch his breath, and then spoke, "Sorry to interrupt, Prime Minister."

"What is going on?" The Prime Minister demanded.

"The northern cities have been attacked, sir. We don't know by who," said the panicked soldier. Everyone looked around in shock at the events unfolding before them.

"Do we still have our airfields?" asked the Prime Minster.

"No, Mr. Prime Minister, they have all been taken," the soldier replied.

"What do our attackers look like?" asked the Prime Minister. "Any identifying insignia, do we know who is butchering our people?"

The solider regained his breath and said, "From what I have been told, they have black leather armor and they carry the Symbol of Darkness on their chest plates."

The Prime Minister closed his eyes and sighed. "I know who attacked our cities."

"How would you know?" a member of the cabinet asked in disbelief.

"They have attacked us before. As Prime Minister, I have access to a carefully guarded historical account of a battle that occurred two hundred years ago that they kept from the history books," said the Prime Minster.

"So who is the aggressor?" asked another member.

"The Lord of Shadows," grimly said the Prime Minister.

"What are we going to do?" asked the Minister of Defense.

"We are going to do all that we can do. We are going to fight. Mobilize all military personnel for full combat status, war has arrived!"

***

At the Sharp Thorn camp, Kira was sparring with Rashid. She sent a palm thrust at Rashid, who blocked it and motioned her to end the spar. "You have improved by leaps and bound in the last month, Kira."

"Thank you, Master Rashid," she replied, as she grabbed a towel from a post.

The conversation was broken as a man ran towards the pair, "Commander Kin wants all warriors in a meeting. It's an emergency!"

The two headed to the command tent. Crowded inside the tent were all warriors from the camp.

"Scouting report!" said Kin.

A man knelt before the commander. "Commander Kin, I have heard from my informant in Norway. The Lord of Shadows, through one of his Generals, has launched an attack."

"He is moving too fast, as well as recklessly, unless he is confident of his successes," said Rashid.

Kin sighed. "Nevertheless, we must send some help. I need some volunteers for a mission that will be undoubtedly be very dangerous."

Kira stepped forward and said, "I will be honored to take this mission, Commander."

Seeing this, ten more volunteers stepped forward.

"Kira, I am placing you in charge," said Kin.

Kira was shocked. "Why me? I only just joined you and renounced my ties to the Lord of Shadows. Yet you trust me to lead your soldiers?"

"I think it is time to give you a field test, Kira, to see what you can do," said Kin.

Kira looked down at her feet unsure of herself and said. "What is the mission?"

Kin explained. "We need you to lead a mercy mission to evacuate the southern towns in Norway."

"Did the Prime Minister request it?" asked Kira.

"He did. He requested we try to save as many civilians as we can," said Kin.

"I accept the mission," said Kira with pure determination.

"One more thing, Kira. Only engage if there is no escape. The evacuation of the people is our main priority."

***

Near Oslo, the Norwegian military had taken a great number of casualties from the Army of Darkness's advance. Their modern weapons had little to no effect against armor full of mystic energy. The Army of Darkness advanced up to the Capital city's limits then stopped. "Lord Kyral, why are we stopping?" asked a soldier.

"Simple," replied Kyral. "The Lord of Shadows is sending reinforcements to our location."

***

In the residence of the Prime Minister, the leader was listening to his commander. "They have stopped at the city limit, sir."

"General, I need you to help with the evacuation of the citizens. Then I want you and my cabinet to leave the country," the Prime Minister ordered.

"What about you, sir?" asked the general. "You should leave as well."

"I will stay here and hold the commander of the aggressors off."

"Sir, we must make sure you escape."

"No, I will do what I can for the citizens that elected me. You have your duties and I have mine," said the Prime Minister resolutely. "One more thing, commander. Several people wearing black robes with a white rose emblem on the chest will be arriving before you. Have them assist with the evacuation."

The general walked out of the palace heading to the battlefield. The Prime Minister sighed, *I will do what I must to make a stand,* he thought.

The general got to his soldiers and ordered them to cover the civilian retreat south. A private ran up. "General, we have people wishing to talk to the commanding officer."

After briefly confirming that these were the Order of the White Rose sent to assist, he responded, "Send them to my tent, Private. The Prime Minister was expecting them to show up."

"Yes, sir," said the soldier.

Kira was escorted to the tent by a soldier. Her comrades were held back to make sure they were not a threat. "Thank you for this audience, General Howard." Kira said showing respect.

"I was told you were on your way here," said the General, "The Prime Minister wants you to help with the evacuation of the citizens."

***

Kyral was sitting in his tent as a scout appeared from the flaps. "General Kyral, I bring news."

"Yes, report. And for your sake it better be worthwhile," Kyral said. The scout gulped. "Well, what is the report?"

"I did a reconnaissance of the capital outskirts and have seen soldiers getting ready for an evacuation of the capital and all surrounding areas."

"Well done. You have just bought yourself more time in my fold." said Kyral.

"What are your orders, General Kyral?" said the nervous soldier.

"We will wait and attack when we get our reinforcements and not before," said Kyral. "They will appear in no more than two days from now. Then we shall eliminate all opposition. Dismissed, soldier." The solider saluted and walked out. When outside, the scout breathed in a sigh of relief, glad to be out of sight of his commander's oppressive presence.

***

The panic of the people was evident as cars and buses left the city in droves. The soldiers made sure, as best they could, that there was not widespread hysteria.

Kira looked around the empty street. "Status report," she ordered through a headset.

"Most of the civilians have evacuated the city. Just a few stragglers left."

"Are you with the Prime Minister?" she asked.

"Yes Ma'am, we are in position."

"I will join you shortly," said Kira.

She was heading to the Prime Minister's residence when a soldier ran up from a side street. "The enemy has begun their attack!" cried the solider.

"Get the order from the commander. I will assist in holding them off!" She yelled in response.

Suddenly Kira heard a muffled cry. She rounded a corner of a building, following the sound. On the front porch of a house sat a small boy of about five years old with tears staining his face. "Where are your parents?"

"I don't know," cried the boy.

"Don't worry. You can come with me. My name is Kira and I will get you to safety. Just stick with me, okay?"

"Okay," replied the child and she scooped him up onto her back. "I am Jon."

Kira watched as the sound of fighting began. *I thought we had more time,* she wondered, worried.

"Ma'am, the Prime Minister has ordered every soldier to retreat at once, including us," said a man in her headpiece. "He had some men place some surprises in the city for our attackers.

"We were told by our commander not to engage unless we are attacked. We will pull back with the military. What about the Prime Minister?"

"He is staying until everyone is out," said the general through the headset.

"Everybody fall back to the south," General Howard ordered what was left of the military and withdrew out of the city.

"General Kyral, the enemy has left the city."

"Advance and kill anyone that was left behind," Kyral said. *"This is too easy,"* he thought.

The soldiers stormed the city and headed to the residence of the Prime Minister. They saw the Prime Minister sitting calmly behind his desk.

He rose from his chair and addressed the soldiers before him, "You are not welcome here; You may think that today you have won a great victory…" His arm dropped out of sight under the desk as he reached for a hidden button. "… but I feel I may have the last say on this most momentous of days." The Prime Minister pushed the button. Across the city, a series of bombs went off, killing large section of the attacking army. Finally, the Prime Minister's office exploded killing both the soldiers and the Prime Minister himself.

In the distance, the surviving army watched somberly as their capital went up in a huge blaze. "Everyone head to Denmark; the world is to be at war soon," said General Howard. The army turned and followed there General away from the devastation, looking to find safety and hopefully a chance to regroup.

***

Kyral was standing in front of his master. "Norway has been taken, my Lord."

"Too bad the Prime Minister destroyed his capital as well as himself," replied the Lord of Shadows.

"What do you mean, my Lord?" asked Kyral.

"His death will inspire other countries to fight harder against us." The Lord of Shadows smiled wryly. "It makes little difference whether it is one or a million soldiers who oppose us."

"What shall we do?" asked Kyral.

"We will strike Sweden quickly; we have tripled the size of our armies with alchemy and the weaponry we have attained," said the Lord of Shadows.

"Let me finish Scandinavia, my Lord." Kyral said.

The Dark Lord chuckled. "My, aren't you eager, Kyral. Very well, take over Sweden and any other nations you like," encouraged the Dark Lord.

Kyral bowed. "Yes, my Lord."

***

Kira was running to the refugee camp in Denmark, Jon was gripping tightly to her back. "We are almost there, Jon." Her comrades were ordered to report back to Kin while Kira escorted and found protection for the little boy she had rescued. She arrived at the edge of the North Sea. "We will rest at the hotel up ahead and then get a ferry to the camp."

They got to the hotel and found it deserted. Kira took keys from behind the desk, found a room, and placed the boy on the bed. "Get some rest, little one; we will find your mother."

"Miss, I am scared." He replied, pulling the sheet up to cover his face.

"Call me Kira," she told him gently.

She sighed and started to hum a lullaby until the boy fell asleep.

After walking down to the first floor, she sat in the foyer and closed her eyes.

During the night Kira heard footsteps coming down. "Miss Kira, I can't sleep."

Kira sighed and asked, "What's wrong, little one?"

"Mommy used to tell me a story before I could fall asleep."

"Alright I will tell you a story of a young girl who lost her way." Kira sat the boy sat on her lap and began to tell a story:

"Once upon a time, there was a young girl named Jane who did not know who her parents were. She was raised by a man known in his village for being a bad guy. Teaching his way to Jane, she lost the right path and did many bad things, like stealing things that did not belong to her. One day, she met a kind monk while out in a market thinking about stealing some fruit. The monk was meditating on a rug and he grabbed her hand just as she was about to steal an apple. The monk held on to her tightly and he stopped her from doing a bad thing and do you know what he said?" asked Kira.

Jon shook his head. "The monk told Jane this: 'Despite your past, you must look to the future and make a better one for you and everyone.' After that Jane gained a new purpose in life. She ran away from the bad man and from then on, she did only good things in the world. She never forgot the monk who gave some advice which she would always carry with her," Kira said with a smile.

Kira looked down and saw Jon sleeping on her lap. *Is this what it is like to have a child and someone to protect?* She thought. Kira head up the stairs and placed Jon back in the bed. She knew tomorrow would be a long day.

The next day, Kira got to port and paid the ferry to get herself and Jon across to Denmark. After a three day voyage, they arrived at the refugee camp and there Kira was able to reunite the boy with his mother who had been frantically searching for her son after they got separated in the evacuation of the city.

After squeezing the boy to her chest, the mother said to Kira, "Thank you so much for finding my boy. We were separated and one of the soldiers told me they would look for him. I almost gave up hope."

"I was happy to." Kira smiled as she watched the mother and son have their reunion.

The young boy escaped from the crush of his mother's arms and ran up to Kira. He hugged her and said, "Thank you, Miss Kira."

"It was my honor to keep you safe."

Chapter 14 The Lightning Orb

Alexander was sitting in the hidden camp in France with the other masters and the elder. "It is time," said Bain as the newly-minted Masters looked up.

"What do you mean, Bain?" asked Alexander.

Bain replied, "You are not real masters, yet."

"I am not following. I thought we were masters?" Lenora said uncertainly.

"You have the title but you don't have the experience. Every guardian before you had to go to the Temple of the Rose and pass their respective tests, three in all."

Guan had his eyes closed. "Where is the temple?"

"It is in the rural village of Quedlineburg, Germany. It was carefully hidden from view to keep tomb robbers out," said Bain.

"Why there?" asked Yuan.

"The founder of the Order of the White Rose was Qadir the Goth and the first Grand Master during the Dark Ages. He lived in that area and bought land to build the temple. He then recruited other members around Europe into the Order of the White Rose," explained Bain.

"What do these trials entail?" asked Guan.

"That is for you to find out," said Bain. "You must travel on foot to remain inconspicuous; it will take a day for you to travel that distance."

Hathaway ran up. "President Newman of the United States wants to meets with a guardian."

"I will meet with him," said Alexander.

"I will take you on my ship, just like the first time we met," said Hathaway.

Lenora looked at Alexander and said, "Be careful, Alexander. I don't want to lose you like I lost Master Thompson."

Alexander walked up to her and hugged her. "I will join with you and the others after I talk to President Newman."

Lenora said, "Just please don't be reckless."

Alexander smiled and said playfully, "No promises."

Lenora chuckled. "You big dummy, I want to do one thing before you leave," she then kissed him on the lips. "That is for being there for me."

Alexander reached into his pocket and pulled out leather string necklace with a silver charm of a four leaf clover. "This is a necklace I had Bain craft for me. I want you to have it so you know I will come back," said the young master as he broke off the hug. "Wait for me."

***

The Lord of Shadows was sitting on his throne in the Parliament building as the self-declared Prime Minister of Norway. A soldier approached. "My Lord, our spies have found another Orb."

"Oh?" said the "dictator." "Which one?"

"The Lightning Orb sir, protected by the President of the United States," said the soldier.

"I will retrieve it. Gather up ten thousand soldiers for an attack on the United States of America," said the Lord of Shadows. Getting up from his throne he turned, crafted a portal, and then walked through.

***

President Newman was a well-built man with brown hair and eyes in his late thirties. Some considered him too young to be a president but the voters put him in office and he was determined to defeat this growing threat.

He was wearing a suit but he loosened it as he was sitting in his office with his Chief of Staff and the Secretary of Defense. "Are the troops ready?" asked the Commander in Chief. The president was a former soldier who had served in the military and fought in the first Gulf War.

"Yes, Mr. President, sir," General Howe replied. "We have the Lightning Orb surrounded by thirty Special Forces."

***

On the outskirts of the capital, Washington D.C., a black portal opened and the Lord of Shadows walked out. Soldiers from his temple appeared from another portal alongside him. "Attack the White House!" Screamed the Lord of Shadows' as his soldiers started to attack the civilians.

The President had foreseen such an attack and had an army stationed in the streets. Realizing the immediate threat they fired at the oncoming Shadow Army.

The Lord of Shadows saw a bullet hit one of his soldiers. "I see they were expecting me." He snapped his fingers and a black barrier appeared absorbing the bullets.

The US Army pulled out their knives, seeing as their bullets were not doing anything, and charged the Shadow Army. The Dark Lord's army has no such trouble with their own guns, armed with semi-automatic guns they began to fire at the American military, causing massive casualties.

Three US tanks appeared and provided cover fire enabling those soldiers who remained standing to get close and fight in hand-to-hand combat with their army issue knives. A US soldier saw the Lord of Shadows and motioned his platoon towards the evil dictator.

"They are brave, but foolish," the Lord of Shadows said as he ran at the charging platoon, hacking through the twenty men with no mercy shown. He saw one solider rush him, killing several of the Shadow warriors as he attacked. "Go to hell!" the brave private screamed as he grabbed the Lord of Shadows and pulled the pin out of a grenade in his hand. The blast engulfed both in a final effort to kill the dictator.

When the smoke cleared, the Dark Lord was still standing, brushing all manner of debris from his armor. "That actually singed my armor," the Lord of Shadows commented. The US army backed away, pure fear etched across their faces

The Commander of the battalion saw the losses before him. With no other option, he ordered what remained of his unit to withdraw.

The General phoned the President. "The defense has crumbled. Out of the 3000 soldiers we sent less than 500 have survived. We won't last more than a few hours at this rate," said Howe gravely.

The president sighed. "Have all citizens evacuate the area?"

"What about you, sir?" asked Howe.

"You have your orders, General, I will stay back." said the Commander in Chief. "Dismissed."

***

Alexander and Hathaway landed in the Potomac River in DC. "They have begun their assault," Hathaway said as he went below deck. He came back with a five-foot-long great sword resting on his shoulder. "Let's head to the White House and rescue the president," said Hathaway.

"It's a Zweihänder. I hear it is hard to use due to the weight," said Alexander.

Hathaway nodded his head "My blade is nine pounds of metal in the blade and two pounds in the handle. However, it comes with a major disadvantage; I need two hands to lift it."

When the pair arrived in the city, they found it overrun by soldiers decked in black armor. Alexander removed his twin swords and rushed the soldiers. Hathaway came after him swinging his giant great sword with ease and killing many of the soldiers opposing them.

***

The Lord of Shadows blasted the door of the oval office down with pure, evil energy only to see the President calmly sat at his desk drinking wine. "I have come to talk about the terms of your surrender," said the villain darkly.

The president smiled as a battalion of Special Forces appeared holding pistols. "I think not," the Commander in Chief declared with confidence.

"Your secret service will do you no good," said the Lord of Shadows. He rushed the guards as they started to shoot with more pouring in.

"Get the President out of here!" shouted one of the men, and as the Special Forces attempted to subdue the Dark Lord, The president was escorted out of the White House.

"Your guns are useless against me," the Lord of Shadows said, shooting fireballs at the agents. The Lord of Shadows raised his other hand and a gust of wind blew at those agents still standing, shredding the ones who got too close.

The President was successfully escorted to his motorcade, but the Lord of Shadows appeared, blood dripping from his sword. The president took off his jacket and pulled a gun from the back of his belt.

The five guards along with the president fired their guns, but the barrier's ability to absorb the bullets prevented them hitting their target.

The Lord of Shadows rushed forward and brought his sword up ready to end the American leader's life.

It came down, but was stopped as Alexander appeared on his knees blocking the blade with his twin Kodachis.

"Guardian of the White Rose," said the Lord of Shadows with distain as Alexander kicked him with a knee thrust forcing him backwards

Alexander helped President Newman too his feet and the two fled before the Lord of Shadows regained his composure.

The Lord of Shadow growled, "Perfect. I can kill two birds with one stone." He stalked up to the guardian and the president but found his way blocked by Hathaway.

Hathaway threw the orb to Alexander and stood in front of the Lord of Shadows, his great sword in hand. "Go, Alexander. Take the orb and escape with the President. I will hold him off, as long as I am able."

Alexander looked on. "Get the hell out of here, Alexander. If you fall, we will have lost a guardian. You must do what is necessary to attain victory!" Hathaway continued.

Alexander nodded his head to show he understood, closed his eyes briefly and ran out with the President.

Keen to buy as much time as possible for the retreating pair, Hathaway ran at the Lord of Shadows slashing his sword. "I will end you, Lord of Shadows!" Hathaway screamed as he forced the villain onto his knee from the sheer power of his blows.

"Impressive strength; however, I killed stronger enemies two hundred years ago," the Lord of Shadows returned, before he disappeared in a cloud of smoke. "I have yet to use all of my skills," the evil one said, his voice echoing around Hathaway.

Hathaway, unable to tell where the attack would come from, brought his sword closer to his body. Still though, when the attack eventually materialized, he was unable to block in time as the sword pierced his body and he slumped over.

The Lord of Shadows bent over the fallen warrior. Reaching down he took the warrior's sword from his weak grasp. "I will add this to my wall," he said as he stepped over Hathaway, leaving him to bleed out on the floor.

Alexander was hidden in a building as several soldiers passed his hideout. "Let's go," Alexander whispered. The President met his savior's gaze and nodded his approval.

"Did you get my wife out the building?" asked the President.

"I had some of my comrades sneak her and your son out," Alexander confirmed.

Keen to keep increasing the distance between themselves and the Lord of Shadows, the pair made their way towards the ship, but were stopped as they encountered a small group of ten shadow soldiers.

The shadows soldiers advanced on the two, but as they closed in shots rang out from all sides as five men in suits appeared holding pistols. The shadow soldiers not killed in the initial burst of fire soon fled as the reinforcements arrived.

"Is everyone out?" asked President Newman.

"We have evacuated most of the citizens, Mr. President," said one of the men.

"Now we are escaping as well," said the young leader. "There is nothing more we can do for anyone else."

The group got to the ship with no further attacks.

"Dad!" A black-haired boy of about eight years ran up to greet his father. Right behind him followed a blond-haired woman in her thirties.

"You escaped," said the woman as she hugged her husband. The relief evident across her face.

"If it weren't for this young man and his comrade, I would have perished," the President said, motioning to Alexander.

Alexander left the group in the meeting room to pass on the news of Hathaway's passing to the crew. His voice was solemn as he explained, "Hathaway died a hero, and he will be honored and missed by us all."

The crew, as one, put their heads down in respect.

Xxx

In the captain's quarters, the President was talking to Alexander and his staff. "I have to try and warn the United Nations of this threat. We might be able to stop the Lord of Shadows with a preemptive strike."

"With all due respect, sir," responded the leader of the President's secret service, "modern weapons did not do a damn thing against that madman."

"I see your point, Smith, but I noticed that as long as the Lord of Shadows was far from his troops, they, at least, were susceptible to bullets," said President Newman.

Alexander thought about it for a moment, before adding, "But it was not significant enough to give us any type of edge in a shootout, Mr. President, sir."

"Our think our best course of action is going to be to meet with the rest of the guardians and get more input," decided President Newman.

"Agreed," the others concurred.

Xxx

The ship docked in a cove where the Order's camp was hidden. Bain greeted the party as they disembarked. "Alexander, did you succeed?" he asked.

Alexander nodded and replied, "Yes, however, we lost a great ally and friend."

"Who fell?" asked Bain.

"Hathaway."

"I see." Bain bowed his head.

"We must meet with the other guardians without delay. We need to get our trials started," said Alexander.

Bain nodded in agreement. "They are waiting for you."

Alexander walked into the room with the President.

"Alexander!" exclaimed Lenora, as she hugged him tightly to her chest. "Thank goodness you are safe."

Alexander smiled at his friend before the seriousness of their situation came back to him.

"Mr. President, please have a seat. We first need to get in touch with the United Nations and warn them of this threat," Alexander said grimly.

"All those lives have been lost due to this madman," the President said with his head lowered.

"We need to get ready for the trials. If we don't we won't acquire the skills nor the knowledge to win," interjected Guan, keeping a level head.

"According to Bain, we can't enter the temple until the Winter Solstice in December," countered Mason.

Lenora got up. "We can't afford to wait. The longer we wait, more countries will fall."

"We all know that, but we have really no option. The temple has been designed to only open at that time to keep robbers out," Mason replied.

"Somehow we will need to keep the Lord of Shadow's forces from gaining more ground. We won't be able to beat him, or his army, without discovering some kind of weakness," Alexander said.

"For now, we don't have any information on even a single weakness," brought up Lenora.

Guan was thinking. "Wait. Sifu Shin told me about these orbs. Whoever absorbs them will become reliant on them like an addiction and like all addictions, it has a downside."

"What is the downside?" asked Alexander.

"From what I understand the orb is poisonous to anyone using it for an extended amount of time. The problem is he has to use it continually with no break,"

"So the power will corrupt the body but we don't know how," said Alexander.

"Then we should come up with a plan to utilize this information," said Mason, as Yuan stayed silent.

"What about the other orbs? Have we located any of them?" asked Lenora.

"We know one is in Uganda, and it is the Earth Orb. The last one we don't know yet, but our spies are looking," confirmed Guan.

"We will need to send two guardians to collect the Earth Orb. I think the best choice in this instance would be Mason and Guan," added Alexander.

"May I ask why you choose Mason and me?" asked Guan.

"Simple; you and Mason have the greater skills in diplomacy, which is what we need right now," Alexander said.

"There is one problem. How are they going to get there? Our fastest mode of transport is a boat," Yuan pointed out.

"I have a jet you can use, if that helps. It's located not too far from here, actually. Consider this a thank you for saving me, my wife and my son," said President Newman.

Chapter 15: Battle for the Earth Orb

In the White House the Lord of Shadows sat listening to his spies. "So the one in Uganda is protected by a tribe of warrior nomads, maybe I should pay them a visit."

An intricate dance of his hands and a portal appeared. Stepping through, the evil Lord headed to his next target.

***

In a small village in northeast Uganda a dark skinned man with beads around his neck was sitting, a staff lay across his lap. "I see there will be a great conflict in the not so distant future. I weep for the future of the Earth."

Getting up, he headed up the hill to his small cottage. Walking into the cottage his gaze moved to the left and to a brown spherical object that lay on the kitchen table. "I have to keep it away from evil at all cost," the old man though out loud. "Bash!"

A man entered, carrying a staff. He was well built and stood about six feet tall, "Yes, Elder Puck?" he said with a deep voice.

The elder took the orb from the table and moved to hand it to his assistant. "Take this and flee at once. We must keep it away from the Lord of Shadows," he urged.

"What about you, Elder?" Bash asked as he took the orb from his master hands.

"I will do what I must to keep this village safe, even if it costs me my life. I shall show this evil lord what true sorcery can do," Puck stated.

"What is this orb you are trying to protect?" asked the younger man.

Elder Puck replied, "That is not important at the moment. You have only one task: You must keep it safe."

Bash bowed his head. "I'll keep this safe at all cost. You have my word."

In the village, a dark portal opened and the Lord of Shadows walked out. Several more portals opened behind him as ten black-garbed figures appeared, their faces obscured by cloth, and each one carried a sword. "Find the orb and burn this village," commanded the evil Lord.

The ten figures rushed into the village as the Lord of Shadows looked on. A gravelly voice asked from behind the Lord asked, "Why have you come?"

The Lord of Shadows turned his head. "I assume you, old man, are the protector of the village. I am here looking for an artifact. Rest assured, I won't leave here without it."

Elder Puck brought his staff up. "That power should never have seen the light of day!" The old man shouted as he pointed his staff at his enemy. A stream of fire shot out of the tip of the staff hitting the Lord of Shadows, making him stumble back, with a look of shock on his face.

"So, I see you are a shaman. Your magic means little to me. Here, let me show true magic, old man" said the Lord of Shadows as he launched a wind blade from his hands right at the mystic before him. The old man slammed his staff onto the ground and as he did so a wall of earth rose in front of him, blocking the attack. "Not bad, mystic," acknowledged the evil Lord.

The old man twirled his staff above his head in defiance. "The torrent of the ocean," he said and a huge wave of turbulent water formed above his head. As the Elder lowered his staff, the wave came crashing down on the Lord of Shadows, sweeping him away. Keen to press home his advantage the Elder added, "I call upon thunder of heavens," and several bolts of lightning were shot toward the wet Lord of Shadows.

Slowly The Lord of Shadows rose to his feet, his armor cracked significantly in places. "I thought it impossible to damage my armor this badly," the evil Lord said with disbelief. "I shall repay you completely."

The old man slammed his staff down, his defiance growing in the face of danger, causing a minor earthquake and making the Lord of Shadows momentarily lose his footing.

Suddenly, pain coursed through the Elder's body. The old man grabbed his chest. *I thought I had more time,* thought the mystic.

The Lord of Shadows smirked underneath his damaged helmet. "You're skilled in the mystic arts, old man. However, your body can't withstand the power of the elements, anymore. It's a battle of attrition, old man. All I have to do is survive all of your attacks and you'll fall to your knees before me."

The old man let go of his chest. "You might have found my weakness. However, you will not survive this day. I shall put all my will into this attack. Even my life!" the mystic exclaimed as he slammed his staff into the ground. Five elements formed a circle around the man. "I shall end you now!" he cried.

The five elements caused an explosion of fire, wind, water, lightning, and earth as the elements mixed together.

The Lord of Shadows growled in defiance. "No, I will not end. I will NEVER end!" he screamed as the full force of the Elder's attack hit him.

As the cloud cleared away, two bodies could be seen on the ground: the old man, his bruised and battered body completely devoid of life, and the Lord of Shadows, whose armor had been completely vaporized.

Slowly, a movement, a flicker, as the Lord of Shadows firstly bends just a finger, and then his hand slowly clenches into a fist, as he slowly gets to his knees. Disbelief again evident in his tone, "I have never been so badly injured." Dark, black hair had fallen forward, the strands getting caught in the bloody cut that crossed from above his left temple down to his right cheek. Screaming in agony, he rose to his feet. Seeing the old man on the ground, lifeless, he approached the fallen Elder. Spitting at the old man's corpse he leant over the broken body before slamming his fist down in pure rage between the defeated Elder's glazed eyes.

The battle over, the evil Lord stumbled into the village, finding it deserted.

One of his men appeared and knelt before him. "The orb is not here, My Lord."

"Look for anyone in the vicinity. Someone must know the location of the Orb," replied the Lord of Shadows, his patience already wearing thin.

In the forest, Bash was running through the trees, in his haste, time and again, he narrowly avoided tripping and falling. Turning his head at a sound behind him, he saw ten soldiers closing in on him. Stopping, he drew his metal staff, slamming it on the ground before him.

The figures continued to run toward Bash who swung his staff to deflect their attack, sending the first one into a tree. Blocking a sword strike from his left, he then slammed the pommel of his staff into a second attacker, killing him instantly.

Bash, one by one, finished his pursuers before he continued running, determind to put distance between himself and the threat. Whatever it was that was chasing him.

***

"So do we have any clue as to where the Orb would be located?" asked Guan, as the small Jet flew over Uganda.

"Unfortunately, we only know the general area; when we get to a city we can search for information," said Mason.

"How about the leadership of the country; can we trust them?" asked Guan.

"We should land in the northeast area and go by foot to the nearest village. I think it best it do not get the government involved."

"Got that, pilot?" said Mason, tapping the plane's navigator on the shoulder. "I don't want to involve the government."

"Yes, sir. Understood. There is an abandoned airfield left over from the civil war a decade ago near our location," said the pilot.

"Take us down," confirmed Guan.

Landing in an unmarked airfield, the tires screeched to a halt. The two guardians walked down the ramp and were met by a crumbled air tower and several cracks on the runway. The passage of time, and obvious neglect of the airfield, were immediately apparent.

Guan turned to the pilot and said, "Conceal the plane as best you can; we will be back." With the pilot under no confusion as to what he needed to do, Guan and Mason headed deep into the forest.

While the two guardians searched the forests of Uganda, In the Order's camp, President Newman was addressing those that remained, "With our options decreasing, I believe the best way forward will be for me to head to Geneva where the United Nations will be convening."

"I will join you," said Lenora. Nodding toward Alexander, she added, "The two of us will escort you there."

Not looking to draw attention to themselves, the three got into an old red car stored inside the Order's headquarters. The peeling paint and the car's propensity to veer slightly to left a clear sign of the fact it had certainly seen better days. "Not luxurious, but something nicer will paint a nice big target on us," said Alexander. "Is this fine with you, Mr. President?"

"This car will certainly do for now. Does it run?" asked Newman.

"It will get us to where we need to go," confirmed Alexander.

***

Back at the forest, Guan and Mason made their way through dense forest. "We should set up camp for the night," Mason stated as they came out into a rare clearing.

"Very well. I'll gather firewood if you can pitch the tent we brought from the plane?" Guan asked, walking away as he received confirmation from his companion.

A short time later, Guan returned to find both tents up, and Mason arranging rocks to form the outer circle of the site chosen for their fire. "I will take first watch," said Mason, as Guan dropped the firewood down beside him.

Guan nodded in agreement and opened the flap of the tent to the left of Mason. "Wake me up in three hours," he stated to Mason, as his companion sat arranging the kindling into the base of the fire.

Roughly an hour later, Mason heard some rustling coming from the trees, "Guan, wake up," he said, scooting back toward the tent to make sure his companion awoke.

"What's wrong, Mason; an animal?" asked Guan as he saw slight movement in the treeline.

"I'm not really sure, Guan. But, there is more than one, whatever it is," said Mason, as several warriors holding spears and rifles stepped out of the trees.

"Well, we've found the locals," replied Guan putting his hands in the air. Mason followed his example. Keen to remain calm and gain the trust of their would-be attackers, the pair allowed their hands to be tied before they were escorted away.

Guan and Mason were taken to a small village, where the guards escorting them hurried them toward a ramshackle building at the eastern end of the village. "Elder, we found these two in the forest near the village," said one of the guards, as they entered the building.

A man with dark skin, wearing a traditional, vibrant-colored kanzu looked up as they entered. "Thank you. You can head back to the gates."

The six guards walked back towards the edge of the village, as the young leader pulled out a knife and slashed the bindings on prisoners. "Take off your blindfolds," he ordered. "I am curious as to why two guardians are wondering in the forest. It seems it is time you both started talking."

Mason and Guan tried to hide their surprise at the man's knowledge of who they were and were instantly on guard. "How do you know of the Order?" asked Guan.

"The leader before me was a member of the Root of the Rose," said the elder. "He told me many things. He told me of a threat that he knew was coming to break our peace."

"Before we tell all, why not start with the introductions? I am Mason and this is Guan."

"My name is Kiwi -like the bird. I am the leader of this village."

"It is a pleasure to meet you, Elder Kiwi," said Guan with a bow.

"Now on to business. Why have you come into this area?" asked the Elder.

"We are looking for an artifact we must retrieve before the evil one finds it," replied Mason.

"This village does not contain the earth orb," said Elder Kiwi, surprising them with his knowledge of the orb. "Though I do know where it is. Or at least where it was…"

"Can you tell us, Elder?" urged Guan.

"You are too late; it has been taken already. I sent soldiers to assist, but they were ambushed and killed before they even made it to the village."

"Can you at least tell us the location of the village? We might find some clues," said Mason.

Kiwi sighed. "The village is thirty miles to the south of here. I will have some of my men go with you. You are going to need all the help and support possible."

***

In Geneva, President Newman was in front of the Security Council. "We can't let this madman take any more countries. If he continues his conquests, who will be left to fight?" he explained to the Council. The fear was evident in his address as he struggled to contain his emotions.

The French ambassador rose and looked sorrowfully at the President. "We heard of the attack on your country and we are sorry to hear about it."

The ambassador to United Kingdom then also stood, "I agree with the President; we must do something. I have received concrete reports of Norway being taken, and the Prime Minster having to sacrifice himself in blowing up his office to take out some of the enemy's army."

"We shall take a vote. All who want to fight, please raise your hand," said the Russian President. As one, all of the leaders and diplomats present raised their hand. "Then it is decided. We shall fight."

***

Almost a day after meeting with Elder Kiwi, Mason and Guan were looking around the ruins of the village where the Brown Orb had been stored.

"This is very depressing," said Mason. The scenes of destruction left him feeling full of despair.

A warrior ran up to Guan. "Sir, we found something." The warrior lead them to a nearby hill top. On the ground the pair took in the body of the old man, covered by wounds of battle and spent of all his power.

"Who is this man?" demanded Mason.

"He was the chief of this tribe. He was a mystic of great skill," said the warrior with great respect.

"It looks like he put up quite a fight. There must be some clue as to the orb's location," Mason said.

The two looked around, still deeply saddened by the destruction of the village. Spying a small cottage, they crossed the village and entered.

"This must be the leader's home." Mason realized. The two looked around and saw a shrine with incense in the corner of the main living quarters.

"A shrine?" asked Guan.

After searching the cottage thoroughly, the Guardians walked outside only to see a man approaching them. As he walked he was flanked by three warriors.

"What are you doing here?" asked the newcomer.

Guan noticed a brown orb in the man's hand. "I see you have the earth orb," said Guan.

The man eyed Mason and Guan, his look showing clear proof he had yet to trust the pair. "Who are you?" he asked again.

"We are members of the Order of the White Rose. Who are you?" asked Guan.

"My name is Bash, protector of the chief of this village."

"We have need of the orb so it does not fall into the wrong hands," said Mason.

"How do I know you are telling the truth? As far as I know, you could be a general for the Lord of Shadows," said Bash.

"If we were, would we not just have attacked you?" retaliated Guan.

"I still need proof. There is a ritual duel that determines the pureness of your heart," said Bash.

"What are the terms of this duel?" asked Mason.

"We each place our weapons in a triangle and two of the fighters must enter the middle and do battle without stepping out of the triangle. It must be around a four foot area."

The two guardians and Bash put their weapons on the ground, creating a small triangle just enough for two people. "Which one of you will take up this challenge?" asked Bash.

Guan walked up, taking off his robe he revealed a white gi beneath. "I shall," he confirmed as he walked to the middle of the ring.

"Let us start," said Bash, going into wrestling stance with Guan going into Shaolin fist. Bash went straight for a punch, keen to make initial headway, but was blocked by Guan who pushed back, there was no way he was going to concede any ground.

This might be more difficult than I thought Guan said to himself. *The limited amount of room to evade attacks will make it harder for the nimble to not get hit.*

Guan threw a kick, but it was easily blocked by Bash who slammed a fist right into his shoulder. The crack of bone could be heard to all those surrounding them. Guan winced from the pain. "Is that all you have?" taunted Bash.

Guan, ignoring the pain, sent a kick into Bash's midriff, causing him to grunt in pain. Bash tried to respond and punch Guan, before he could retreat, but his attempt was easily dodged. Guan dropped low and sent his foot straight into Bash's face, hitting him to the edge of the ring.

"I see you could have won when I was still trying to recover," said Bash as he slowly regained his bearings.

"It would not have proven a thing to win with such underhanded tactics," said Guan.

"I see you were telling the truth. This was purely for me to judge your character. I think you can protect this better than I can," Bash said as he handed Guan the earth Orb.

Guan bowed. "Thank you, noble warrior. We have need of your skills to fight the Lord of Shadows. Will you join us."

Bash shook his head. "Alas, I cannot. But, send a message when you need an army. I will prepare my tribe for battle."

"Your tribe? Responded Mason, clearly confused. "I did not see anyone around."

"The tribe is in hiding, at the moment. When the time comes, we shall join in the war."

The two guardians bowed to Bash and retreated back toward the plane.

***

"Did you find the Orb?" asked the Elder when the boys returned to the first village.

"We have it. We had better take it to the White Rose Camp," reconfirmed Mason.

"My scouts reported soldiers from the Ugandan military are approaching," said Kiwi. "I don't know what they want, so be on guard. I have reason to believe they are in league with the Lord of Shadows. You must leave now with the Orb if you are to leave this area safely."

"Thank you, Elder, for your assistance." Guan bowed and they head out of the village toward the landing strip and their plane.

The soldiers entered the village an hour after the Guardians had left.

"What can I do for you, Captain?" asked the Elder.

"We are looking for two foreign fugitives; have your warriors seen them?" responded the Captain.

"Yes, one of my warriors saw them in the southern part of the forest. They were not a threat so we did not pursue them," said Elder Kiwi.

The captain chuckled. "I see," he said, turning away from the Elder. "However, I was not born yesterday." The captain turned back around and shot the Elder in the chest twice with his semi-automatic.

"I want this whole village arrested and the buildings burned to the ground," ordered the Captain.

The soldiers surrounded the stunned warriors and restrained them. As the farmers and families were herded out of their village, the Captain warned, "If no one tells us where the fugitives are, everyone will be executed."

One of the warriors spat in the Captain's face, "You will get nothing out of us."

"Perfect! You will be an example for the rest of the rabble," the Captain said and motioned forward a soldier. Pointing at the disobedient warrior he ordered, "Kill him."

The soldier pointed his gun and without no hesitation fired.

A woman nearby dropped to her knees. "You monsters!" she screamed, only to be backhanded by the soldier next to her.

"Firing squad, prepare to fire," said the Captain as the ten soldiers pointed their guns at the remaining villagers who were refusing to cooperate. "Fire!"

***

After hours of fighting their way through the dense forest, Guan and Mason eventually arrived back at the airfield. Being careful to approach cautiously incase their transport had been found by enemy troops, the Guardians boarded the plane and were relieved to find their pilot alive and well in the cockpit.

"Pilot, let's go," said Guan as he and Mason settled into their seats. A couple of minutes later and the plane was back in the air and heading to the Order's Headquarters, the Orb safely in their possession.

***

The Captain was in front of the leader of the Lord of Shadow's forces in Uganda. "We did not find the fugitives," reported the Captain.

"Do we at least know who was helping them?" questioned the leader.

"Yes, sir, but we executed all of the traitors," said the captain.

The leader growled his disapproval. "The Lord of Shadows will be very disappointed in your foolish choice." He pulled out a pistol and shot the Captain in the leg. "I now have to explain why we don't have a prisoner with the knowledge we seek."

Turning, the leader walked away as the Captain writhed on the floor in agony. A moment passed, before the leader seemingly changed his mind. Approaching the fallen Captain once again he raised his pistol. "Good bye, Captain." Two shots thudded into the Captain's chest, and the writhing stopped.

***

Mason and Guan took the time on their return journey to discuss their next move.

"We just need to gather the Water Orb," said Mason.

Guan looked ready to respond, but before he could the Pilot interjected. "There is a storm up ahead. Should we go around it?"

"What do your instruments say?" Guan replied.

"It says the eye of the storm is a little over two miles wide. It's a good sized storm," reported the Pilot.

"What about the wind speed; how fast is it?" asked Mason.

"It is roughly seventy miles per hour, but rising. I suggest we land at the nearest airfield."

"What is the closest country?"

"Currently we are flying over Egypt. Cairo is about fifty miles away. If we head directly there we can get there and land before we're hit by the full extent of the storm," said the pilot.

"Right. Contact air control. See if we can get permission to land," Guan ordered.

"Let me get in touch with them right now, sir" said the pilot, before pulling his radio to his mouth. "Cairo Airport. This is flight AF2019 from Uganda. Requesting permission to land."

"This is Cairo Airport, why do you request to land? Please notify us of your state of emergency," responded the control tower.

"We need to land before the approaching storm hits us," said the pilot. "We would like permission to land and, if possible, refuel."

"This is Cairo Air control, permission granted, flight AF2019. Please have your necessary paperwork prepared for arrival," said the tower.

"We appreciate it. 45 miles and closing," the pilot said with gratitude.

***

Karim Mushawi, the President of Egypt, was looking up the most recent reports of the international alliance.

A gentle cough caught his attention, and he looked up from the report to find a beige-suited soldier before him.

"Mr. President, sir."

"Go ahead, Colonel," said Mushawi

The Colonel saluted. "Sir, air control has authorized the landing of a Jet out of Uganda heading towards a storm in Cairo."

"I see. I have a feeling I know who they are," said the President. "I will need to meet with them."

"Then, I will be more than happy to escort you there, sir," said the Colonel.

The President closed down the report and stood. "Have men in position just in case, I don't foresee a fight, but we can't be too careful in these most dangerous of times."

The Colonel nodded his head in agreement before leading the President from the room.

Once the plane had landed and finally taxied to a stop, the two masters walked out to be greeted by President Mushawi. "Mr. President, it's an honor to meet you," said Guan as he and Mason both bowed.

Mushawi gave them an appraising eye. "So you are two more of the masters. I have been fortunate enough to meet a couple of your group previously."

"What other masters did you meet, Mr. President?" inquired Guan.

Mushawi explained, "Master Lenora and Master Alexander were at the UN Geneva conference I attended recently, so I am fully aware of the precarious situation our world finds itself in. We can get your plane refueled and you can wait out the storm here."

"Thank you, Mr. President," said Guan.

"I have arranged for a hotel to put you up while you wait out the storm," said Mushawi. "Captain, please give the two masters a brief tour of the city, before dropping them off at The Bakhoum."

"As you can see, we currently have a fair in remembrance of our country's previous leaders," the Captain explained to the masters as they walked through the business district filled with stalls.

Guan saw a child in rags on the street with a cup, dredging dirty water from a puddle to drink.

"President Mushawi has been trying to make new jobs to reduce our unemployment but it is hard. This is the homeless section of our city, despite the President's best efforts it continues to grow," the Captain explained.

The boy looked up from the puddle in time to the group as they passed.

"Captain!" He exclaimed, as he ran up to the soldier.

"I am sorry, I did not bring anything today," the soldier says with a sigh. The child put his head down.

Guan walked up to the boy and reached into his pocket for some money and handed the boy a collection of coins. "Please, get something to eat."

The boy hugged Guan's leg in thanks, before disappearing into the stalls that lined the street.

The captain smiled at Guan's actions, and said, "I am glad there is still kindness in this world. I will come by tomorrow with some food for these unfortunate children. I have been visiting these slums as often as time allows, and have been helping the homeless with medical supplies and food, even blankets when they are needed."

The tour ended in the rich section, here the masters arrived at the hotel known as The Bakhoum. The hotel had a large wooden door, gold-trimmed, with an expensive looking ornate, golden knocker. Even the roof had gold edges, a pair of giant, golden Eagles perched at either end.

***

The soldier took up a discreet guard position in the foyer of the hotel as the two sat and discussed their situation.

"We need to report back to the others; I'm sure they want to know that we have the orb," Guan began.

"As soon as this storm passes we will head out," confirmed Mason.

***

The storm raged for hours and night fell before it had passed. After a disturbed sleep, where one of the masters remained awake at all times, the morning was clearer and the pair headed back to the airfield.

Guan and Mason were in front of the jet, once again in the company of the President of Egypt.

"Thank you for your hospitality, Mr. President," said Guan as he and Mason bowed their heads.

"I was more than happy, too. Until we meet on the battlefield next to each other as allies."

The two masters boarded the plane. Their destination once again: The Order's Headquarters.

Chapter 16: The Water Orb

The Jet landed in a secret hanger at the Order of the White Rose's base. Mason and Guan disembarked, Orb in hand.

Alexander nodded, glad to see his comrades safely back, and the Orb in their possession. "The temple will be visible in one month. We will take our trials then, my friends."

"Have we located the last Orb?" asked Guan.

Alexander sighed, the disappointment etched on his face. "No, we have not."

"We landed in Egypt on our return journey and the leader said something about a coalition?" asked Guan.

"The United Nations has agreed to a unified front against the Lord of Shadows. They are sending their troops to be trained by the order," said Alexander.

"Good. The governments from around the world are joining forces for the first time," said Mason. "I just hope they are in time."

***

In the camp of the Sharp Thorn, Kin was stepping into her robes as she addressed her sister.

"Kira, you and Rashid will accompany me to the meeting with the masters."

"Is that wise?" Kira questioned her sister. "I have some history with several of the masters and I don't think they would be thrilled to see me."

"I think I know what I am doing. Just do what I say when we get there," said Kin, as she walked past Kira and out of the tent.

Kira nodded her head in resignation and followed. Once outside she beckoned Rashid to join them and they headed to the base.

Once inside the base, the trio entered the appointed meeting room. Kira upon seeing Alexander lowered her head in shame.

Kin nudged her sister. "You know what you must do, sister."

Kira walked up to Alexander and knelt before him. "Master Theodorson of the Order of the White Rose. I, Kira, have done you a great injustice that I cannot hope to atone for." Alexander eyed the woman as she continued, "I have come before you today for either forgiveness or death," she said placing her head down as if she were waiting for hand or blade.

Alexander unsheathed his blade and walked up to Kira. "I, Alexander, Master of the Order have made my decision. Kira, I forgive you for your transgressions," he said as he touched Kira's shoulder with his blade. "Rise. You are one of us now as we welcome you into our order."

Kira stood and, with a smile, acknowledged the man before her, "Thank you, Master."

***

In the temple in Norway, the Lord of Shadows was being fitted with new armor; midnight black with silver shin guards. As several slaves flitted around him a soldier entered.

"My Lord, I have found the location of the Water Orb." the soldier confirmed.

"Do tell," said the evil Lord, pleased. Finally some good news.

"We don't know if it is guarded as yet, but we have traced it to Australia," said the soldier,

"I will go and retrieve it." The Lord of Shadows stood and pushed away the slaves. Adding the last piece of his new armor he summoned his magic and created a portal. Striding through, three shadows ran to follow him.

***

The meeting was in full swing at the Order of the White Rose Base when a soldier knocked, before being summoned in.

"Forgive me for the interruption, Masters," he said. Acknowledging each of the attendees in turn.

"Report," Alexander said as he looked up at the soldier.

"We have found the location of the Water Orb, it is in Australia in a temple of the Aborigines," said the soldier.

"Yuan and Lenora shall retrieve the Orb," said Alexander, motioning for the two masters to rise.

The two masters stood as requested. "We will head out immediately," said Yuan.

Alexander gave them one warning. "If you two encounter the Lord of Shadows, do not engage; I would rather lose an orb, than the life of one of our remaining masters. At least, while we still have the Brown Orb in our possession."

The two left the meeting to head to Australia. The challenge was a daunting one. Undoubtedly the Lord of Shadows would be on to the remaining Orb. Could they retrieve it successfully from under his nose?

***

The Lord of Shadows struck another native down as he marched to the location of the Orb. Slaughtering his way to the temple, he showed no mercy. "The Orb is near, I can feel it!" he screamed. Grabbing an Aborigine by the throat. He pushed his face inches away from the man's, "Tell where the water orb is."

The man coughed blood in the Lord of Shadows' face. "You'll get nothing out of me."

The Lord of Shadows brought the man closer. "Too bad," he said, crushing the man's skull, before tossing his liefless body away.

Seeing a stone building ahead, the Lord of Shadows entered to find the Orb on a pedestal before him. "There it is. Not even hidden," the Lord of Shadows said. Reaching for it, it disappeared into his hand. His eyes glowed blue as he absorbed the new energy.

***

When two masters arrived at the aboriginal village they were horrified at the death and destruction they found.

"We are too late," said Yuan. His head dropping in despair.

Lenora rushed over to a man who lay face down, writhing in agony. "Who did this?" she shouted as she turned him over.

"It was a monster in black armor with a demonic helmet," said the villager as he coughed blood. "You must stop him!" His final words forced out before he closed his eyes and went limp.

Yuan glanced around in sorrow. "Looks like the Lord of Shadows managed to grab the Orb before we could secure it. The amount of life lost is tragic."

The two, unable to leave the bodies without the honor of a proper burial, prepared a mass grave at the southern end of the village.

"I can't believe he would even kill the women," said Lenora.

"He is a heartless monster," said Yuan clenching his fist. "We must stop him."

***

In the Norwegian temple, the Lord of Shadows was sitting on his throne as his four generals knelt in front of him. In each of their hands was a pendant of a pyramid.

"You have your orders. These pendants should get you in the temple without going through the trials. Go!" the Dark Lord commanded.

The four generals nodded their heads and disappeared to do their Lord's bidding.

"Your move, guardians," he chuckled darkly. "Soon all shall belong to me."

***

The five guardians, having realized that they must get to temple before the Lord's minions could do so had left for Berlon. Upon landing, they headed straight to the Quedlineburg temple. A huge building, it had a stone entry with five towers on the corners of the main building.

Alexander immediately noticed the main entranceway doors were ajar. "Looks like someone is here already. Be ready for an ambush," he warned.

At the door they were greeted by five different passages. "Which one?" asked Yuan. Unsure of how to proceed.

Alexander turned to the one on the far right. "Open up your senses, masters. If I concentrate I can feel that this path is calling to me," he said, walking down the path before him.

The other guardians in turn closed their eyes and each walked down a separate passage.

Chapter 17: Alexander

Alexander continued down the passage in the temple, after a short time he came across a small lake. Stood to the side of the lake, he found a man decked out in Samurai armor, holding a katana firmly in his right hand.

"So the prospect has arrived." The samurai stood as he addressed Alexander. "And, one taught by my student."

"Your student?" questioned Alexander.

"Yes, Luray earned my title after he beat me in a sword duel. Now, before the test, you must train under me."

"I don't have time. The Lord of Shadows is taking over countries as we speak, slaughtering innocents without regard," said Alexander.

"Let me finish," the Samurai lightly admonished Alexander. "Time is slower in perception. One day in your world is a least a month here in the temple so do try not to rush so."

"May I ask your name, Master?" asked Alexander.

"Certainly. I am Jin Misabusta. Now let's begin. To begin, I will teach you the first style that I mastered." The warrior raised his sword, with Alexander in a mirrored stance. "Remember, the sword is an extension of yourself; until you realize that, you will lose against superior enemies."

"Of course, Master," said Alexander as he went through the katas of his blade. The samurai master nodded as he observed Alexander's form.

For three hours Alexander followed Master Jin's teachings. Improving his style, attacking and defending against imaginary opponents and approaching various 2-on-1 and 3-on-1 scenarios was tiring. After the three hours were up Jin motioned to Alexander to take a short break.

***

After a month inside of the temple, or one day in Alexander's world, the young warrior stood in front of the former master. "Now for your test. You must crack my sword by any means necessary," said Jin.

The two stared each other down, daring the other to make the first move. Alexander grabbed his sword and rushed forward, but it was easily blocked by Jin's katana. Flipping the blade, Jin forced Alexander off balance, and he stumbled back. "Is that it?" asked Jin mockingly as he jumped over a sweep kick.

"I am not done, yet, Master Jin." Alexander slammed the handle of his sword into Jin's chest, catching him unprepared and making him stumble back.

Alexander, seeing an opportunity, rushed forward hoping to disarm his opponent. Jin intercepted the attack with his sword as both fighters attempted to overpower the other. Alexander's sword was forced down by his more skilled adversary.

"Not bad, Alexander, but my experience is greater than yours." Jin backhanded Alexander, knocking him down. Then, charging down the teen, he went for the final blow but missed as Alexander rolled away, grabbing his sword as he went. "Remember, Alexander, experience trumps all other advantages."

Jin held his sword to the side as Alexander ran forward, going for a strike which was locked by Jin's sword as he brought it before himself at the last moment. Seeing an opening, Alexander revealed a hidden blade in his sleeve and thrust it forward, forcing Jin to disengage.

Alexander rushed forward once more, avoiding Jin he jumped on a small ledge that ran along the length of the wall. Coming at Jin from a new angle, Alexander jumped off and slammed his sword down with all his might, forcing Jin's sword to crack.

Jin smiled and praised Alexander. "Well done, Alexander. Your next test is of the mind. Head through the door to your right and proceed."

Looking to his right, a door appeared where there was just a solid stone wall before. *Magic?* Alexander wondered. Bowing to the master, he walked through the door and on to his next challenge. His attention taken on going forward Alexander never noticed Jin disappear behind him into a light, grey mist.

***

The room that Alexander now found himself in appeared to be a library. In the middle of the room was a weathered, wooden table with a map of the world spread across the top. A man marched into the room through a door that Alexander was sure wasn't there when he first entered. The newcomer wore a German Stahlhelm helmet and a gray military uniform with the designation of a General.

Looking across the table, he addressed Alexander, "So you are the new master. I am General Alois, a soldier of Germany and a commander during the Franco-Prussian war," said the general. "I was Strategist of the Order during my time. I rarely fought unless it was needed."

"Alexander Theodorsen, Master of the Order of the White Rose." The young man confirmed as he bowed in greeting.

The general's gaze seem to bore into Alexander's soul as he appraised the young warrior, before his eyes drifted to the sword Alexander wore at his waist. "You will not need your weapon in this test. Not all battles are won with brute strength or superior numbers, some are won with tactics and strategy."

He pointed to the shelves of books that ran along all four walls of the room. "The books on shelf 1-250 are military tactics and related subjects. I want you to read the Art of War by Sun Tsu. The book is perceived by some to be outdated, but I strongly believe it contains many strategies you can still use in modern times."

Alexander nodded confirmation and crossed the room to where the General had motioned the relevant shelf to be. Shelf I-250 contained about fifty books on the subject of tactics as well as strategic games. Selecting the Art of War, Alexander took a seat and read it, cover to cover, before moving on to the next book suggested by the General, The Way of War. This latest book had been written by a French commander, one who was renowned for turning around losing battles.

Days passed in the library, Alexander trusting that what he had been told about the altered time was true. After reading many more war manuals, he closed the latest book and sat at the table waiting for the General to return.

Alexander thought he heard to soft click of a door close behind him, and turning round he found the General before him once again.

"You have learned what you can, young warrior?" asked the Prussian commander.

"Yes; I am ready," said Alexander with the determination clear in his response.

"I will be the judge of that." Alois motioned Alexander to sit at the table. "Let us play a game. What you see before you is a map of the area in which we will deploy our troops. The objective is simple, and that is to take the enemy base while keeping yours safe. You will have several bases, one supply base and a forward base to recruit more troops.

Alexander looked at the map on the table. "The dark brown terrains are mountains which will give your troop the best line of sight. The field, or the light green colored area, will be of less benefit to the troops, while the forest will be the least beneficial. Got it?" asked Alois as he explained the different terrains.

"There are two types of troops: artillery, which requires two or more soldiers - It will say on each card how you need to operate the canons, and then the riflemen are your infantry. You also have one medic which can in certain circumstances bring a soldier back to life. All right, let us start."

The two sat at opposite ends of the table and put their troops into position for the battle to begin. Alexander made the first move, putting two soldiers into the artillery and starting to pound Alois' line causing initial casualties. Alois went straight to the mountains, hoping to gain the advantage its height provided.

The battle continued as both combatants employed their individual strategies. After three hours, Alexander finally pulled a daring raid, killing the General's medic and taking occupation of the supply camp. An hour later, Alexander started his siege of the main camp.

Alois, seeing no other option, focused on hit and run tactics, which were doing heavy damage to Alexander's front line until Alexander successfully took out the raiding units. Several hours later, Alexander took the main camp, claiming victory.

Alois smiled as he saw his defeat. "You are a skilled commander to use such unorthodox methods. You succeeded in weakening my moral and throttling my troop recruitment to achieve victory. You have passed the second test," Alois confirmed.

Alexander bowed in acceptance. "Thank you."

"The next test will be on diplomacy. I wish you the best of luck," stated the General, indicating that Alexander should exit through a door that, moments before, the young Master was sure had not been present.

***

Alexander, on passing through the door, took a set of stairs to a floor above. He entered a room resplendent with the decor of a throne room. On the throne before him, sat a white-bearded man with an aura of nobility and wisdom.

"Welcome to the third test, young Master. I am Advisor Peter of Russia and a member of the Order of the White Rose before General Alois. Like Alois, my role was not as a fighter but rather a negotiator.

"Master Alexander of Norway," responded Alexander, bowing his head.

"My purpose was to prevent any conflict with a peaceful resolution," said Peter. "You will learn how to negotiate and debate with others to achieve the desired outcome."

"When do we begin?" questioned Alexander, keen to be finished.

Ignoring the question, Peter led Alexander to an ornate, golden table set at the side of the room.

Here he showed the young student various proven methods for solving problems. "This will be a written test," he confirmed. "The test is of different scenarios. You will need to write out how you would resolve each dispute."

Taking a seat at the table, Alexander carefully considered each scenario in turn. When he had finished, he returned to Peter, who looked over the test and before confirming that Alexander had successfully passed.

"Nicely done. Head up to the last trial."

Alexander climbed a further set of stairs. As he reached the top, he found a room set up as a dojo, complete with fighting mats and a ring. In the middle stood a man dressed in yellow pants and a blue coat, indicating the rank of Colonel.

"Greetings, I am Colonel Han of Prussia, 12th generation Grand Master of the Order of the White Rose 1805."

"Why would a Grand Master himself be testing me?" asked Alexander, confused by this latest development.

"You're the catalyst of victory in this conflict, Alexander. The temple is a living entity that has searched the heart of each master to decide who attains the rank of Grand Master. I, the last Grand Master, will administer this final test."

"Did the temple not give this test to my companions, or did they all fail it?"

"All masters since my time have failed this part. If you also fail, the temple will choose another from this generation. If none suitable are found, I will wait for the next generation. I will not teach you now, but rather I will go straight to the test," said Grand Master Han.

"What is the objective of the test?" asked Alexander, though he had a fair idea he would need to fight the man stood before him.

"You must defeat me. You can use any form of fighting but no weapons will be allowed," confirmed his opponent.

Alexander walked to the ring, followed by Han. The two stood at opposite ends of the ring and got into position. This was the moment of truth. A moment where Alexander could achieve something no other Master had done in generations, or should he fail, a moment where the Dark Lord's victory could be all but complete.

Alexander ran forward, hoping his youthful speed would catch his opponent unprepared. Going for a jab with two fingers at the Grand Master's eyes, he missed as Han redirected the attack with a dismissive swipe of his hand. With speed far superior to his years, Han grabbed Alexander and threw him across the ring, rushing at the young man as he lay on the floor.

Alexander, seeing his first style had no effect, sprang to his feet and immediately brought his knee up, thrusting forward and connecting with Han's chest. Seeing another opening, Alexander tried to follow with an elbow into Han's head but his older adversary was not to be caught twice and he easily evaded the attack. Dropping low, Han swept Alexander's feet from under him, knocking him again to the floor.

Alexander knew he had no time to catch his breath and flipped back to his feet. The two combatants nodded respectfully to each other, before charging with a flurry of punches and kicks.

Hours passed as the warriors fought, no man able to press an advantage home to completion. Both men were visibly tiring as Alexander attempted to slam a knee into Han's chest again, but Han blocked it and returned with a combination of swift punches at Alexander, before shoving him backwards across the floor. Han, evidently keen to keep on the offensive, charged forward at the young Master. Alexander, however, stayed motionless, waiting for Han to get closer. As Han got within range, Alexander dropped his left shoulder, avoiding Han's grasp, before spinning and using the Grand Master's momentum to throw him out of the ring, ending the fight and successfully passing the final test.

Han returned back to the ring and bowed to the victor. "That was your final test, Grand Master Alexander Theodorson of Norway."

"Thank you, Master Han," said Alexander as he bowed to the former Grand Master stood before him.

Han smiled and snapped his fingers. Alexander's robes turned blue as an emblem of the medallion appeared on the back. A passageway opened at a wall revealing a further flight of stairs.

"Take that passageway to the top of the tower," instructed the beaten Grand Master.

Alexander nodded in confirmation and exited the room.

"Finally, I can move on!" said Han. Tears ran down his face, the joy and relief evident as he disappeared in a gray mist, safe in the knowledge that the newest Grand Master was deserving of the title.

Chapter 18: Lenora and Mason's trials

Lenora entered her passageway and soon found herself in a dense, humid forest. *Why is there a forest in the temple?* she wondered.

Turning her head, she saw a dark-skinned man, war paint on his face and holding a spear, approaching through the trees. "Who are you?" she questioned.

"My name is Smoking Bill, Chief of the Sioux nation, Master of the Order of the White Rose, and teacher of Master Thompson," replied the man.

"I am Master Lenora of The Order of the White Rose, and former student of the late Master Thompson."

"Well, Master Lenora, I am here to take you through your first test. The test is one of tracking and stealth. You must find me without alerting me of your approach. If I hear you, I will move to another part of the forest. I am understood?" asked Smoking Bill.

Lenora nodded in confirmation.

"But before the test begins, I will teach you different tracking methods.

For a week in the temple, Lenora was taught the appropriate ways to track using all of her senses. It felt to the young Master as thought the training would never end, so it came as a relief when her teacher finally announced that the training was complete.

Lenora nodded her head confirming she was ready to start the test, and then Bill slipped away through the trees. Heading in a random direction, she looked for Smoking Bill. After about an hour of searching, she sighed in exasperation. *Where is he?* she thought. She could find no sign that he had even been this way. Heading back into the starting point, she analyzed the ground and discovered some snapped twigs in the opposite direction to her original choice.

Frustrated that she had overlooked the clue the first time, Lenora headed in the direction of the snapped twig. To avoid becoming disorientated she marked every third tree she passed with a knife. She found Bill within two hours, but he was alerted to her approach and disappeared to another part of the forest. Lenora started the search once again.

Bill had covered his tracks well and was hidden under some brush in the northeast corner of the forest. *She is using tracking skills, but her stealth needs work*, he thought. Feeling a tap on his shoulder, Bill turned.

"Found you, Master Bill," said Lenora in a sing-song tone.

The Native American grunted. "Well done on passing the first test, Master Lenora. The next test is through the door. I wish you luck."

The forest before Lenora gradually faded from sight and once again she found herself in the stone passageway. Lenora headed to a door that had materialized in the wall in front of her and went through.

Lenora found herself in a dojo with mat. On the mat she saw a man of Asian ancestry standing in the middle wearing a white gi.

He looked up at Lenora and spoke, "Greetings, prospect. My name is Lei and this test is a test of your skills, but first I will run you through my form. You hopefully will be aware of The Mantis."

"Of course, Master," said Lenora.

The master explained the form as one of counter and low attacks, making it hard to defend against. "There are two forms of Mantis," he explained, "the Northern Mantis Style and the Southern. I will be teaching you both." Adopting his stance, Master Lei stood with his right leg in an arch still on the ground, and his left leg behind slightly bent to provide support. His arms were bent downward, one in front of the other for quick strikes.

Lenora mirrored him, and fluidly copied the movements of the teacher before her.

Once Lei had shown and repeated all he could to the young master, he believed her to be more than capable with the new style. "You must land a clean hit on me to pass," he explained as he stood before her.

Lenora bowed and got into her usual Muay Tai style. Lei adopted his mantis style.

Lei motioned to Lenora that the time was upon them. "Let's begin!"

There was no time for the tension to build as Lei charged first going for a downward jab, but Lenora was ready, easily blocking the attack with her knee. Retaliating with a roundhouse, Lei sidestepped the attack before grabbing her leg and throwing her across the room.

Lenora managed to land softly on her feet. Immediately going back on the offensive, she ran forward sending a knee thrust toward Lei, who managed to once again evade. He then blocked an attempted elbow headed toward his face. Going low, he caught her unprepared as he tripped her with a disguised sweeping kick.

Lenora got to her feet just in time to block a kick from Lei. Gripping his leg, she threw him, trying to take the fight down to the mat. However, using the momentum of her throw, he flipped midair and landed on his hands before flipping once more back to his feet.

Lenora let out a growl in frustration, *His defense and recovery are superb,* she thought. *This was not going to be a short victory.*

Lei rushed her once more, sending out a short jab which was caught by Lenora inches from her face. Sensing an opening, she went for a knee thrust which was blocked by Lei's left leg.

Lenora smirked, and sent a strong punch with her free hand hitting him squarely in the chest and sending him crashing to the mat. Giving Lei no time to recover Lenora completed her victory.

"Well done. You have passed the second test," he said, rising to his feet and bowing to the victor.

"Thank you, Master Lei." Lenora bowed in return.

"Now head to your final trial," said Lei, and he disappeared before her eyes.

***

Lenora headed through the latest door to appear and found herself in what appeared to be a deserted western town. Looking around, she saw a tall, handsome man with a cowboy hat sitting atop his head and a Sheriff's badge on his dark brown waistcoat. At his waist were two pistols in holsters, his hands appeared ready to draw at any moment.

"Greetings, pretty lady. You must be here for your trials," said the man in a thick accent.

"Yes, I am," Lenora replied, a slight blush had come to her cheeks.

"My name is Sheriff Bob Jones, and I'm the weapons specialist of the Order of the White Rose," he introduced himself.

"Lenora," she said trying to regain her focus and lose the blush from her face.

You will choose your weapon of choice. Your goal is to disarm me, but in doing so you must not lose your own. Firstly, we need to get you trained with a variety of weapons," said Bob.

Following the Sheriff through a set of saloon doors, Lenora looked around and found walls covered with different hand weapons.

"Pick three weapons you would like to learn and I will teach you," said the Sheriff.

Lenora picked two daggers, a scimitar, and a short, straight sword.

Content that Lenora had chosen well, the Sheriff motioned for the young master to follow him through a further door and into a huge, barrel-vaulted training hall. "Let us begin." A construct of one of the weapons appeared in his hand and he approached his student.

The training lasted for a week, the Sheriff allowing only very small breaks through each day's practice, keen to make using the weapons almost second nature for his young student.

Dropping his short sword to the ground, he finally announced, "You have done well, Lenora. Now it is time for your test. You know the objective, correct?"

"Yes, Master." She confirmed, taking out her bo staff as another one appeared in the Sheriff's hands. The two faced each other.

After a short bow to confirm they should start, Lenora ran forward wildly swinging her staff, trying to unsettle the Sheriff with a unique approach. Striking down with one end of her staff she forced the Sheriff to block the attack with his own staff.

The Sheriff broke away with a strong twirl of his staff and brought it over his head to strike in response. Lenora blocked the blow but the force of the hit brought her to her knees.

"I am disappointed, little lady," the Sheriff taunted, "maybe you are not fit to be a master?"

"Don't count me out yet," she growled as she pushed back. "I have not yet begun to fight."

The Sheriff grinned as Lenora flipped her bo staff sideways and pushed down on his weapon. Bringing the other end of the bo staff up, she tried to hit him with repeated blows of her staff, forcing him to dance from side to side to avoid the attacks.

While spinning away from her, he failed to see the staff heading to his hands, slamming into them with such force to make him drop the weapon. The Sheriff let out a yell.

"Yaahoo! Very good little lady. You pass the final test. Head to the passage behind me, and go to the top of your tower."

Lenora nodded, then headed to the passageway. Climbing to the top of the stairs she found a black shroud present, hiding the other towers from view.

Her disappointment at being unable to make out the other towers suddenly turned to fury as a figure appeared out of the shroud before her. "You!" she growled.

A giant of a man stood before her chuckling. "Congratulations, weakling. Now I will end you like I ended your master," the giant taunted as he set his feet apart, spread his arms and readied himself to wrestle.

"Vladimir, I am not the same little girl you swatted away last time, you piece of filth," Lenora growled as she got into her Muay Tai stance.

Vladimir roared and charged, his fists flying as he sort to crush his opponent. Lenora dodged the flurry of blows and sent back a kick into his chest, making him momentarily stumble back. Vladimir roared again and slammed a huge fist into Lenora's chest making her cough up blood.

"Still brutal, but I will beat you!" she declared, grabbing Vladimir's head as she flew at him with a knee, slamming into him with a satisfying crunch of broken bone as his nose took the force of the knee.

"Your master couldn't beat me, what hope do you have!" he roared at her in defiance.

Lenora pulled out her staff and clicked a button on the shaft, a small blade appeared at the end of her weapon. Swinging it towards her attacker face the blade managed cut him across the chin as he managed to rock back almost out of range. Pulling out a big, black-headed hammer from a holder on his back, Vladimir tried to catch Lenora. But, the young master was utilizing her speed advantage as she dropped and rolled under the giant's attack.

Springing to her feet she was forced to back away as the giant continued to swing his hammer at her, one blow could be enough to end her defense.

Moving to the side, Lenora kicked Vladimir on his right side, forcing him to stop his wild blows.

"You call me weak yet I have been dominating this fight!" she shouted, rushing forward.

Vladimir sidestepped her attack and grabbed her head, slamming her onto the ground. "You're overconfident, girl," he snarled as his raised his hammer for a killing blow

Lenora still had speed on her side though as she rolled to the side, narrowly avoiding Vladimir's hammer. Springing to her feet once more she came at the goliath of a man, her staff spinning faster and faster in her hands as she landed blow after blow on her over-sized attacker. Backing him up to the edge of the tower, Lenora sent a powerful kick towards Vladimir face, toppling him over the edge as her foot connected with his chin.

Lenora dropped breathlessly to the ground. She started to relax, until movement at the edge of the tower caught her eye. Walking to the edge she found the giant still clinging to life, his fingers white at the knuckles as he attempted to prevent himself plummeting to the depths below.

"What does it take to put you down?" Lenora growled as she slammed her staff down on the man's hand. His yell echoed as he lost his purchase and fell from the tower to the rocky ground below. Master Thompson has been avenged.

Standing in the middle of the tower the dark, ominous shroud disappeared and the other towers came into view.

***

In the Shadow's temple, the Lord of Shadows waved one of his hands elaborately through the air before him, using the dark arts to form a storm of lightning and rain around his tower. "When the masters and the armies come, I will be ready." He laughed, darkly. Next to him was his own sword. On the wall, the Dark Lord had mounted both Hathaway's great sword and the sword of Master Eirik that he had taken from Alexander's home.

A soldier approached, dressed in a dark, black cloak and hood, his face obscured except for the sight of his piercing red eyes. "My Lord, I bring bad news."

"Let me guess. We have lost a general?" asked the Lord of Shadows with no worry or care evident. "Which one?"

"Vladimir has been killed by a master."

"I see no significant loss; I have other pawns. Any news from the trials?" the Lord of Shadows inquired.

"Alexander of Norway and Lenora of the United States have both passed their trials."

"Perfect; keep me posted on the situation," said the Lord of Shadows.

Yes, my Lord." The figure slunk back into the shadows, confused at how well the Dark Lord had taken the latest news.

***

Mason was following his passageway, heading to the site of his first trial. He followed the passage until he arrived at an aged, oak door. Upon opening it, he was greeted by a room lit only by several candles on a table in the corner.

"Welcome, Master of the Order of the White Rose," said a Spanish-accented voice. A man appeared, dressed in a black suit with red shoulder pads; on his arm was a red cape. "I am Alfonso, and I am the champion matador of Spain," he finished.

"My name is Mason. It is an honor to meet you, sir."

"This first test is about endurance," the matador explained. "We will fight hand to hand but we must take the attack head-on, no blocking or dodging. You have to last a minimum of an hour."

Mason went into a jiu-jitsu stance with the master getting in a boxer stance. Alfonso started the trial with a jab, hitting Mason on his left temple. Mason retaliated with a strong punch, making Alfonso grunt as it hit him in the chest.

Alfonso sent a haymaker at Mason, landing it squarely on his chest and making the teen gasp as the force of the blow sent the air from his lungs. Mason, short of breath, sent a kick towards Alfonso's head, making him stumble from the force of the kick.

"Not bad," Alfonso said, returning a kick to Mason's left side. Mason held his ribs as the pain coursed through his body. "However, the enemy won't give you a chance to recover."

Mason, continuing to fight the pain, rushed forward and slugged Alfonso across the face, bloodying his nose. The battle continued, back and forth, until Alfonso noticed the time had passed, and halted the test. "Well done. You lasted for an hour, Master Mason. You have successfully passed your first test."

Mason's pride was mixed with confusion as his injuries started to visibly heal before his eyes. "What is this?" asked the young master.

"This tower only makes it appear as though you suffered damage; it will soon all have disappeared. It is the temple's way of playing games with the mind," said Alfonso.

"Thank you, Master," said Mason as he bowed to his senior. A door appeared on the stone wall before him, and Alfonso gestured for Mason to take the door to move forward.

"I will warn you, you must not hesitate; look forward, not back. Move without fear." With his advice passed on Alfonso disappeared.

Mason nodded his head where Alfonso had stood moments before, and walked to the door.

***

Exiting the door, Mason was greeted by the sight of a large, stone labyrinth and a man wearing the uniform of the French military.

"My name is Henri, and I am Brigadier General of the French Military. This test is designed to challenge your intelligence and aptitude for solving riddles. You are tasked with making it to the other side of the maze before you, successfully answering riddles as you go to eventually access the passageway to the next room."

Mason nodded his head and went to approach the maze. However the Brigadier General put a hand on his shoulder to halt him.

"First, however, young master, you will need to read the books laid out for you," he stated, gesturing at a table to their left. "Once you have done that, we will start the test," said Henri.

Mason went across to the table and selected a book at random. Taking a seat next to table, Mason began his education.

After reading all of the books chosen for his learning, Mason rang a small bell left on the table and the Brigadier General returned to the room.

"I am ready," said Mason confidently as Henri nodded his head in agreement. A door opened before the young master, revealing the entrance to the maze.

Mason entered the labyrinth. After turning to his left and making his way through a series of ever-decreasing archways, Mason was greeted by a statue of a Sphinx in the center of a small courtyard.

The eyes of the Sphinx opened, and a deep, gravelly voice spoke to Mason, though the mouth never moved, "First riddle. For most, it is short and limited but long and unlimited: what is it?"

Mason thought for a moment before answering, "My answer is Time. It is short and limited for all living things but long and unlimited in general."

The statue's eyes glowed and the wall at the back of the small courtyard moved to the side, revealing a passage behind it. Heading into the passage, he continued down the corridor, making several turns before reaching his first dead end.

Retracing his steps, Mason took a left where he had moments before turned right and found the next riddle. The paving on the ground beneath him began to part, and a statue of a Phoenix rose from the ground. Again the eyes opened, and a similar voice, though slightly gentler, spoke, "I am flimsy and I contain knowledge but it is limited. I am a teacher of intellect: what am I?"

Mason again was forced to think. After several minutes he thought he finally might have the answer. His response though was far from confident. "The only thing that comes to mind is a book since the pages of a book could be considered flimsy." Another passageway opened before the young master, revealing a further pathway through the maze.

Taking the new path and following it around a corner, he came across a crumbling, stone wall. Hanging from a nail, high on the wall was a scroll. Taking the scroll, Mason unrolled the parchment and read its contents, only to find he had yet another riddle to solve.

"Give me food and I will live; give me water and I will die. What am I?" says Mason as he reads the riddle.

Without needing any time to think, Mason responds, "Fire." His answer correct, the scroll crumbled to dust in his hands. The wall crumbled fully to the ground, revealing a passage leading to yet another wall. Two statues of humans holding spears and covered in armor of stone stood at either end of the wall.

"This is your last riddle," confirmed one of the statues in a deep voice.

"It can run but not walk. Wherever I go it follows: what is it?" asked the other statue in a lighter voice than its partner.

Mason smiled. "That, once more, is an easy one. What is a nose? It runs when it has a cold and it goes everywhere I go."

The statue's eyes glowed as they stepped aside, revealing a corridor with a large, metal door at the end.

Using all of his strength, Mason pushed back the metal door, only to reveal the room he had left before entering the maze.

Henri appeared once more before him, "Well done on passing the test of intellect, Master Mason. Please head to your next trial." With that, the Brigadier General pointed towards a staircase that had materialized in the wall.

Mason bowed to the teacher and climbed up the stairs to his next trial.

As he reached the top of the flight of stairs and entered the next room, it morphed into a river with a log over it, suspended by thin, metal wires.

"What's happening?" he asked, shocked at the scenery before him.

A black-bearded man, dressed in dark blue overalls appeared from the other side of the river and addressed the young master.

"So you have successfully passed the first two tests!" exclaimed the man. As with the Brigadier General there was a definite French accent present in his voice.

"I am Mason of Brazil, and a master of the Order. May I have your name, Master?" he responded.

"You will have to pass my test to earn my name. We battle with staffs on the log over the river. You must knock me off to pass; this is a test of balance," said the giant, bearded man.

Mason eyed the log and grabbed a staff from the selection he found at his side, before walking onto the log. The former master also walked onto it with his own staff held out before him, ready to attack.

"Get a feel for the log and its movements before you come at me," he warned.

Mason walked forward, trying to keep his balance on the log. After several minutes getting used to the log's fluctuating position above the river, he swung the staff at the man. The bearded man easily blocked it and went low in retaliation, trying to trip Mason. The two continued the battle, with Mason trying to keep his balance and composure as he swung his staff.

Mason was hit in the chest by the man as he jabbed at him with one end of the staff, making him hunch over in pain. "Is that it?" he mocked.

Mason raised his gaze to his opponent, a defiant look in his eyes. "I have not yet begun to fight, stranger." Mason kicked the man's right leg from under him, giving Mason some room to prepare another attack. All thoughts of attacking were halted though, as he was forced to get his staff in position to block a series the strikes the man launched at him. Mason managed to parry them all, before he slammed his staff into the man's head, knocking him cleanly into the river.

The room reverted back to its original state as the man laying prostrate on the ground grunted, "Well done on passing the last trial. Andre Bear is my name, young master. Take those stairs to the top of the tower to complete your trials."

Mason bowed and the man disappeared as his previous teachers had.

Heading to the stairs, he sprinted up to the top. A brief moment to rest saved his life as a kunai whizzed by his head.

"So they did come before us." Mason concluded, as he took his spiked gloves from a pocket on the inside of his robes and put them on.

The General Kyral appeared from black smoke before him, and gave a blood-thirsty smile. "So now the student is the master. I am going to enjoy this."

Mason got into his stance as Kyral threw two more kunai at him. Mason punched them away with his spike-gloved hands. "Your tactics won't work on me!" he shouted as he rushed forward and threw a punch at Kyral who managed to block it with his kunai.

"It seems you are as strong as your master," said Kyral.

Mason sent a high kick his way, but was forced to pull out as Kyral slashed upwards with his kunai, forcing Mason to tilt his head back, avoiding the slash.

The attack evaded, Mason kneed his attacker in the chest making the assassin stumble. Kyral growled and slashed Mason's cheek with his kunai, drawing blood. "It seems I will have to try," Kyral taunted, grabbing eight throwing stars from his back and launching them at Mason, forcing him to duck and spin to avoid the stars. Getting in closer, Mason changed tactics throwing a punch which Kyral managed to avoid. Mason followed it up with a kick though and, unable to rebalance, Kyral felt the full force and was thrown backwards.

"I see you're not so strong after all," said Mason. "I wonder; how could you have killed my master? From what I have seen he should have defeated you with little effort."

Kyral got back up. "You're right. Your master would have beaten me, if it weren't for my pawns. They held him off long enough for me to finish him."

Mason ran forward and slammed Kyral into a pillar with his shoulder. Then he repeatedly punched Kyral into the pillar with his spiked gloves making it crumble from the repeated blows as Kyral's life flowed from his body in a river of red.

"Master, I have avenged you," said Mason as he breathed in. The black shroud dropped away, revealing blue sky. Turning his head, he gasped at what he saw.

Chapter 19 Guan and Yuan Trials

Guan was heading to his first trial. Exiting the passageway he found himself in a darkened room, he tried to look around as his eyes adjust, but with little success.

"Greetings, Master, and welcome to your first trial," said a feminine voice from out of the darkness.

"Why is the room dark?" responded Guan. "I can't make out anything in the room."

"This first test is in using your other senses. You will need to find me in this room to pass the test," said the voice.

Guan looked around. Still unable to see anything, Guan tried to find a wall by stretching out his arms and walking slowly.

"Feeling for the wall; no one tried that before," said the voice mockingly.

Guan sighed to himself.

"You know, you have to find me somehow." Guan turned his head to the right. "Very clever, using my voice to locate me."

Guan searched in the direction that he thought the voice had come from. He vividly remembered a lesson Sifu Shin taught him and the other Shaolin monks.

"Listen well, my young monks. Your eyes are blind all the time and should not be relied upon. I will teach you to locate my chi by utilizing your

own like sonar and will pinpoint the nearest living thing,"

His master's voice echoing clearly in his mind, Guan closed his eyes and expelled his chi. The chi almost immediately found an obstacle and Guan smiled. He walked across the room to the obstacle and grabbed it.

"Nicely done, young monk, on finding me," proclaimed the voice as the light came on and Guan found himself clutching a dark haired woman in a red kimono. "The next room will have your second test."

Guan bowed and released the woman. He headed to the door and entered the next room.

His gaze was immediately drawn to a man with a scar on his chest in front of a chalkboard. The room appeared to be set out as a classroom.

The man looked up as Guan entered. He gestured for Guan to sit as he spoke to him. "You passed the first test, young warrior, and for that I congratulate you. I am Boar and you'll need to listen carefully to my instructions if you intend on passing this second test."

"Guan, master of the order," said the monk, taking a seat.

"This test is to challenge your critical thinking. I will describe several scenarios and you will tell me how to handle each situation. Do you understand?"

Guan nodded.

"First situation: you are currently facing five enemies in a narrow alleyway. At the end of the alley is an opening. The area is deserted of pedestrians. What do you do?"

Guan ran through numerous options in his head, before choosing an appropriate response. "I will flee down the alleyway, letting them chase me. Speed and endurance are different for every person. By fleeing, I can take them out individually when each one reaches me."

Boar nodded his head as he wrote down Guan's answer.

"Next situation: You are holding a priceless artifact and taking it to a museum with a comrade. Someone attacks and surprises you. Holding your comrade hostage, he demands you hand over the item for your comrade's release. What do you do?"

Guan thinks for a moment. "The problem is that you don't know if he is going to hold up his end of the bargain.

He does not know if you can be trusted, so what you do is make it so you send the item and hostage to the middle of the standoff. The negotiators walk to their respective objects, meanwhile keeping an eye out for any sign of betrayal.

I would save a life, rather than hold a valuable artifact which can be retrieved at a later date. Lives cannot be retrieved."

Boar nodded. "Last situation," said the former master. "You are leading a platoon and are ordered to retrieve a document that determines the victor of the war. Your information is faulty. Instead of facing a small number of troops, you find yourself outnumber by a force three times the size of your own. Do you continue with this mission at the cost your platoon not making it back, or leave the information that made victory certain for your side, and retreat, giving you a higher chance of survival?"

Guan sighed. "The losses would be heavy with both choices, but I would continue. Is my platoon worth more than absolute victory or should a team be sacrificed for the greater good? In this case, I would fight to retrieve the document and send a small force back to deliver the plans to the commander. The rest of my platoon would fight a losing battle to save the lives of the whole army. I hope that situation never arises, but that is what I would do in this scenario."

"Congratulations, Guan. You have passed this test because you answer with the highest probability of survival for the main objective. In the first question, you take out your opponents individually," he explained.

"The second choice was the completion of a mission to a comrade's wellbeing. Commanders are forced to make this call constantly. I will say this: your comrade should never be sacrificed for an object," said the man.

"In the last situation it was vital for the survival of everyone, you must take the mission. Commanders are not cowards, and should be willing to go into battle with little chance of survival, if it is to attain ultimate victory," said Boar. "There will be times when it won't be as simple as I have told you, so be mindful of all factors presented, and even those not presented."

Guan bowed "Thank you for the lesson, Master Boar."

Boar nodded in response, before pointing to a door that had appeared in the corner of the classroom. "Head to your final test."

Guan entered the door in time to see the room morph into a coliseum. Standing in the middle was a red-haired woman of Asian descent wearing a battle dress with red metal plates and gold trims on the hem. On her back was a quarter staff with a cloth wrapped around the middle.

"Greetings, young master. My name is Shun."

"Guan of the Shaolin," the monk replied with a bow. "May I ask what the test is?"

"Certainly. The final tests are usually combat related; this is no different. We will fight with nothing but quarterstaffs while on the balance beam. The purpose is to test your balance in combat with limited movement." She threw him a staff. "Here, think fast."

Guan jumped on the balance beam before him as Shun did the same. The two looked at each other. Guan remained motionless allowing Shun to make the first move.

After what seemed like an age, Shun attacked, coming in low but then attempting to strike at Guan from above. Guan brought one end of his staff up, successfully blocking the blow. Raising the other end in the same motion he looked to counter as he swung the end towards Shun's head, forcing her to raise her own staff up to intercept the blow.

"Impressive," commented the female former master.

Guan stepped back and twirled his staff behind his back. "As a monk we try to not use lethal weapons in battle. I am not the strongest staff wielder but I am proficient in it. Thank you for your praise."

Swinging his staff at Shun's feet, he forced her to step over the low strike, making it seem more like a dance than a fight.

Shun put her staff behind her back, with her left hand holding it and her right knee up. Her right palm was open, facing Guan. She quickly brought her staff to Guan's foot. Guan did the unthinkable and stepped on it. Shun tried to get it loose but in doing so she lost her balance, causing her to fall off the beam. Doing a flip, she landed on her feet. Guan bowed to the female master and jumped off.

"Well done, young master, you have passed the final test," she said and bowed in respect.

"Thank you, Master Shun,"

"Now head up the stairs to finish your trials at the top of the tower."

Guan ascended the staircase. After getting to the top, a dark shroud formed and Guan saw a brown haired man with a scar on his chest standing before him. He wore two pikes strapped to his back and was dressed in green robes. "Well done, Master Guan. I am Kevin of the Wind, General of the Lord of Shadows."

Guan stood still, with no emotion on his face.

Kevin continued, "Master Shin was a worthy and honorable enemy. Let's see if his successor can equally impress me.".

Kevin eyed Guan's weaponless hand. "You don't have a weapon." He took one of his pikes and tossed it to Guan. "There is no honor in killing a defenseless man."

Guan caught it and held it in a ready position. "You're different to most generals, but I will still not hesitate to kill you today."

The two pikes clashed as Guan went for a jab with the bladed end. Kevin repeatedly dodged Guan's attacks as one of the blades tore into his cloak. Kevin swung his pike from low to high in an effort to deceive his opponent, but missed as Guan ducked under and swept his feet away sending him to the ground.

Kevin flipped back onto his feet and then the two rushed forward and clashed once more. Kevin's superior strength had finally started to push Guan off balance.

A relentless tirade of blows from Kevin sent Guan crashing to the ground. Kevin rushed at the downed monk, forcing Guan to be on the defense as repeated strikes rained down towards his head.

Blocking each blow with his own pike, Guan used one hand to swing his pike back at Kevin, making the Dark Lord's General tilt his head back to avoid it. The distraction worked, and Kevin did not see a palm heading to his chest until it connected, causing the general to stumble back from the force of the attack.

"We are getting nowhere with these weapons," growled Kevin.

Guan impaled the ground with his pike. Seeing his actions, Kevin nodded his head and threw his pike down to the side. Weaponless, Kevin dropped into his fighting stance.

Ba Shan Fan style; it will be difficult to fight this form, thought Guan.

Aware of the huge task before him, Guan threw the first punch with a hammer fist, hoping to achieve the early advantage, only for his strike to be blocked. Kevin retaliated with a palm thrust, hitting Guan high in the chest.

"First blood goes to me," said Kevin as he followed his palm thrust with a left elbow aimed towards Guan's face. Guan wasn't to be caught again though and the blow failed to connect. In evading Kevin's strike, Guan caught sight of an angle of attack and threw his own thrust at Kevin, turning him around. This was followed with a kick to the general's back, making him stumble forward.

The advantage was short lived though, as Kevin span around, backhanding Guan in the face, splitting his lip, a thick stream of blood now ran from Guan's mouth.

The two combatants jumped away again, ready to forge their next attacks. The cold wind howled as the two stared each other down. The fighters suddenly lunged at each other, unleashing a flurry of punches and kicks in an effort tyo subdue their opponent.

Kevin was again sent back by a kick to his stomach by Guan, the force of the attack sending him to the ground. He struggled to get up as Guan walked slowly towards him, ready to deliver the final blow. Kevin closed his eyes with contentment on his face.

Kevin, instead of a strike to finish him felt a hand pull him up.

"Why?" The general said confused.

"You are too honorable to die needlessly," answered Guan. "I would recommend you leave."

Kevin bowed to the superior opponent and then headed back into the tower.

Guan watched as the shroud dissipated and he found he could see the other Masters who had passed their trials.

***

Yuan was heading down the hallway of the path he had chosen, his curved sword at his waist. The room he entered was filled with flora of all types, giving it the appearance of a jungle. Glancing around he saw a man wearing a simple black robe with a white helm, and white, wooden sandals on his feet.

"So the young master to be has finally come," said the man, looking up at the new arrival.

Yuan looked at the man. "Who are you?"

"It is respectful in a situation such as this to gives one's name first, before demanding someone else's," replied the man.

"Yuan."

"You can call me The Gann. Your first test is a game of tag. To pass, you must make physical contact with me. You have two hours. You can use anything in the room including your own weapons. Ready.... Set... Go!" Gann back flipped in to the flora.

Yuan looked around as he cautiously headed into the man-made jungle. Spotting his target, he rushed forward. Once he had got close enough he grabbed at something. Yuan triumphantly looked at his hands, only to have the look of celebration wiped from his face as he saw they contained nothing.

"You'll have to do better than that to catch me," The Gann taunted, scurrying away with Yuan in hot pursuit.

The Gann grabbed a branch as he passed it and then let it fly, forcing Yuan to dodge to the side to avoid being hit.

"You know, strategy is the name of the game. You must not only rely on your skill, but also the very environment you find yourself in," said the master. "Take everything into account and use it to your advantage or it will be used against you."

Yuan ran through the foliage as The Gann's voice echoed around him with tips and advice. "Easy for you to say; strategy is not my forte," responded the young master.

"How do you hope to beat me and enemies like me? Deception is the key to winning an actual fight." Jumping down from a branch, The Gann motioned a challenge with his hand. "Is that all you have? I am disappointed."

Yuan rushed blindly forward, hoping to overpower the master. The Gann effortlessly dodged each punch with both hands behind his back rubbing more salt into Yuan's already injured pride.

"Come now, a child could beat you with the way you're fighting," goaded The Gann as he ducked under a sloppy punch. "Come on, make me sweat, at least."

Yuan jumped back, breathing heavily, sweat running down his face. In contrast, The Gann was completely relaxed. *It's proving too easy to get under his skin and have him lose focus,* thought the master.

The Gann smiled. "Maybe I should not use one of my legs to make it even," The older master illustrated his point by balancing on one foot. Yuan growled. "Don't get mad at your inability to pass the first test."

Yuan, grinding his teeth, sat down.

"Giving up already?" asked The Gann.

Yuan closed his eyes and listened to his heartbeat. Throwing his hand forward, The Gann was thrown back by a gust of wind. "You were saying?" Shouted Yuan as he jumped up.

The Gann recovered just before he got slugged in the chest with a fist.

The Gann wheezed, "You used chi energy to push me back. Not surprising considering Mistress Wu was one of the few to master chi usage completely.

Yuan composed himself. "So I passed?"

The Gann nodded his head. "With thirty minutes to spare. However, you are reckless and prone to outbursts of anger. I was able to make you lose focus rather easily. Had I been out for your life, you would have died within ten minutes of engagement. Rein in that temper and you will be stronger for it. Head to your next test and remember the lessons that were taught here today."

Yuan left for the next test and following the passageway soon came to a room with a balance beam in the center; different staffs and pole-arms adorned the walls. Hearing footsteps, Yuan turned around and saw a dark-skinned man, shorter than him by at least a foot, approaching. He was wearing a brown robe, and had two braids, one going down each side of his head.

"So you have finally arrived," said the man, his voice high with excitement. "My name is Yandi and I assume you are here to take the test?" he inquired with a Jamaican accent.

"I am. What is the test you have chosen for me, Master Yandi?"

"It is simple, young master to be; you must knock me off the balance beam barehanded. This test is a test of your balancing skills," said the shorter man.

Yuan walked to the balance beam and jumped on to the end in one movement. Yandi approached from the other end of the beam and did likewise. The two stared at each other and then rushed forward. Yandi threw the first punch which Yuan blocked. Yuan retaliated with a kick, forcing Yandi to twist his body, making the kick sail harmlessly past him.

Yuan walked forward, gingerly at first, still getting used to keeping his balance in a combat situation.

"It seems that balance is not your strong suit. What's wrong?" asked the small man, hopping around as if it was nothing.

Yuan rushed forward as the man continued to hop and managed to successfully land a punch on the Jamaican, sending him to the edge of the beam.

Hoping to get a victory, Yuan pressed his charge and threw another punch. Yandi jumped over Yuan and landed effortlessly behind him. As Yuan tried to turn, his opponent kicked him in the back making him lose his balance and fall from the beam.

Turning away, Yandi looked down as a hand grabbed his foot and threw him from the beam. Yuan dangled underneath the beam holding to the underside in a one-handed bear hug.

Yandi stood up from the mat below the beam. "Well done, using the unorthodox to overcome you own weakness is the sign of a great master."

Yuan let go of the beam and landed softly on the ground as the previous master approached him. "You have passed the second test, Yuan. I hope to see great things from you. If you exit through the door in the corner of the room and take the stairs to the next level you will find your third test."

Yuan did as Yandi commanded and followed the stairs up to a barren room, small in size, with nothing of note to catch his eye. Just as Yuan was beginning to think there had been some kind of a mistake, the empty room morphed into a meadow.

Standing in the meadow was a man with a bamboo hat and dressed in a peasant's garb. He appeared to be a dark-skinned Pacific Islander. He was digging, using a hoe, and paying no attention to the young master. Turning his head, the man stopped what he was doing and finally acknowledged Yuan's arrival.

"Welcome to the final test, young master. My name is Budi, and I was once the Master of Indonesia."

"Yuan," replied the youth, " and yes, I have come for the last test."

Budi twirled his hoe around. "The last test is a battle. You must beat me into submission, or have me concede."

"Any rules that I should be aware of?"

"No, any weapons are allowed in this instance." Budi brought his hoe up in a guard as if to signify that anything could constitute a weapon.

Yuan took out his sword and rushed forward. Bringing his sword up for a strike, he swung it only to have the retired master block the attack with the wooden handle of the hoe. Budi threw his arm up, unbalancing Yuan, before he slammed the dull end of the hoe's handle into Yuan's chest making him gasp for breath.

"Come now. Mistress Wu was able to fight me better than this," taunted Budi, twirling his hoe over his head.

Yuan growled and charged forward again. Budi sighed as he easily avoided the brash attack.

"How did you pass the first two tests with such a brash nature?" asked Budi as he kicked the back of the youngster as he went past, sending him face first into the dirt.

Yuan growled, forced himself to his feet once more and sent a palm thrust into the master, catching him off guard. However the master recovered quicker than Yuan imagined possible for a man of such years.

"Interesting use of your tactics; it would have worked against a weaker enemy. But I am different," Budi commented. As if to prove his point he slammed a foot in Yuan's chest, sending him back.

Yuan hunched over. He saw his opponent right in front of him, getting ready to strike with the metal part of the hoe. As it came down, Yuan caught the wooden shaft with his hands and growled. With one movement he slammed the handle into the master's chest making him gasp as the air was forced from his lungs.

Seizing the momentum, Yuan sent a right hook to the master's jaw, throwing his head back. Following with a strong round house kick to the side of the body, Yuan knocked the master down. Grabbing the master's hoe he pointed it at the master.

"I pass right?" asked Yuan, blood dripping from his mouth. "You concede?"

Budi smiled. "I concede. You pass!" he exclaimed, getting up. "You are now the master, well done."

Yuan bowed and turned to find himself back in the small, stone room. A voice was all that remained of the Indonisian, "Go through the door and up the stairs, young master."

Yuan arrived at the tip of the stairs as a shroud formed.

"Well, the student has become the master," said a female voice. "My blade hasn't tasted much blood since your teacher was killed."

Yuan gripped his curved sword. "Face me!" he shouted in anger as a female with metal claws attached to her hands walked out. Wearing blue battle armor made of leather, she grinned evilly at the youth.

"You are the one who murdered Mistress Wu?" he questioned, the tone of his voice doing nothing to hide his anger.

"It was a wonderful bloodbath, I was you had seen it," she mocked. "By the way, you can call me Shun Xian. It's always nice to know the name of the person who's going to kill you," she laughed.

Yuan, brandishing his sword, ran forward. The female general did the same, scraping her claws on the stone ground as she ran towards her target. Yuan, going low, tried to take her leg from under her, but jumping over the sword, Shun flipped and kicked Yuan across the chin.

"Is that it, young Master? Mistress Wu would be so disappointed in you."

Yuan looked at her with rage-filled eyes. "No more talk. You will pay for the blood on your hands!" Yuan blocked a claw with his sword and kicked her back with a round house that connected with the side of her head. Running forward, he slammed the pommel of the handle into her chest sending her back further still.

Shun got up slowly, but then rushed forward, claws behind her. Showing great speed, she came down with a swipe of her claws over Yuan's head. Yuan blocked it with his sword, but then felt himself start to lose ground as both weapons were locked together. Yuan saw the insanity in the assassin's eyes as she pushed down on the sword.

I will not lose to this madwoman, he thought as he span to the side, unlocking the weapons, and bringing his blade to Shun's back. Slowly the color drained from her face and blood ran from the corner of her mouth as she slid from on top of Yuan and fell dead to the ground.

Yuan sheathed his sword as the shroud dissipated and the sky could finally be seen. Looking around the top of the temple, he sees the other masters atop each of the other four towers, with Alexander wearing the robe of Grand Master.

"I was wondering which of us would be given that rank," he said as dropped to a knee. "I am honored to serve you, Grand Master Alexander Theodorson."

The other masters, each in turn, followed suit and declared their allegiance to the new Grand Master.

The towers one by one disappeared and the group soon found themselves on solid ground again with no trace of the temple remaining.

Bain walked up to the masters and bowed to each of them in turn. "So you five have passed. And you have passed the Grand Master's test, Alexander."

"What happened to the temple?" asked Lenora, confused by the ongoing developments.

"When the trials are over, pass or fail, the temple disappears," explained Bain.

***

The trials completed, the group headed back to the hidden cove were the Order of the White Rose were stationed.

Outside the base, Alexander was pleased to see around fifty thousand soldiers being trained by the White Rose warriors. They were currently practicing martial arts, various groups learning different fighting styles, before moving on to the next in an effort to give each soldier the best chance of survival in the upcoming battle.

"Some are also training in covert operations in order to give us an edge," Bain explained. "We will often use hit and run attacks to soften up the Dark Lord's army."

Alexander sighed. "So it has finally come to be. We are going to war. To think I would be fighting to the death at my age., before I have had the chance to truly experience all that life can offer."

"Life throws unexpected curve balls at you, Alexander. It is how you handle them that will determine your path. Come; it is time for your coronation as Grand Master," said Bain, leading the group into the base.

After a short period of preparation, Bain led Alexander into the Order's huge hall. Alexander stood speechless as he witnessed the Order's members numbering in the thousands, all standing at attention.

"Please do me the honor of following me to the altar, Alexander." Bain motioned to the altar which stood at the end of the hall, a metallic white rose adorning the top.

Bain walked up to the altar to address the waiting members, as Alexander stood respectfully to the side.

"Today is a proud day to announce the new Grand Master. It has been over one hundred years since anyone has passed the trials. Today the new Grand Master has been chosen by the temple and his name is Alexander Theodorson. Let's assist him in this war against darkness, as others have done before him," Bain said. The room responded with a roar of applause. "Now, Alexander, your audience awaits."

Alexander walked up to the altar, flanked by two masters on each side. Looking up he addressed his people. "It has been a hard battle, so far, and we have lost good people." He paused before continuing. "However, we must persevere, and as Grand Master I shall fight until we are victorious." The congregation of members cheered.

Chapter 20: Beginning of the War

In the Order of the White Rose base, Grand Master Alexander was wearing his robe as he sat at the head of a rectangular table. The other masters sat down each side of the table.

"I don't have the experience to lead such a coalition," said Alexander, he voice portraying the unease he felt at the huge responsibility he now held.

Bain was sitting to Alexander's right in a master's chair left vacant by the Grand Master's promotion. "Leadership is thrust on those who don't always want it, but have earned it. We still need to figure out a way to stop the Lord of Shadows."

Alexander sighed. "Do we know how he was beaten the first time, surely there are records?"

Bain looked down. "No one was present at the battle except one person. The Grand Master who faced him is the only one who knew the answer."

"Little good that does us," said Lenora, clearly far from impressed with this latest development. "We know he did something but he died in the process."

Bain put his hand under his chin. "There might be a way to talk to him, or his spirit, at least. However, his hut is in the Lord of Shadows' territory in Norway."

"Getting there will not be easy," Guan pointed out. "The Lord of Shadows military has grown due to his proxy governments."

Alexander stood up. "It is decided. Although it will be far from easy, we need to get to his hut and find out all we can from the late Grand Master."

"The only one who can commune with Master Eirik is the current Grand Master. Until then, we must be on our guard," finished Bain.

After the meeting, Alexander headed to his cabin. Lost in his thoughts, he startled as he felt a hand on his shoulder, and turned to see Lenora.

"Alexander, what's wrong?"

Alexander sat on the cabin stoop. "I can't do it. I always thought someone like Guan would be a better choice as a commander and Grand Master."

Lenora looked at him. "Alexander, you were the one who brought us together and fought with us. You are more than capable and we will be with you all the way. I will be with you all the way."

Lenora wrapped her arms around him and he leaned into the embrace. "Thank you, Lenora. Do you remember how we first met?"

Lenora smiled. "Yeah, we fought a bunch of thugs and I acted like a bitch to you." Alexander frowned as he saw her cry. "I just wish we could..." she started as Alexander placed a finger on her lips.

"Lenora, I have something I need you to hear. I love you."

Lenora's eyes widened and a smile lit up her face. "Alexander, I have been waiting for you to say that."

Leaning in their lips met, finally they felt able to share a private moment together. "I would love to spend my life with you. After the war will you marry me?" he asked.

Lenora smiled. "Where is the ring, and shouldn't you be down on one knee about now?" she asked.

Alexander stood and walked across the room. Opening a drawer in a cupboard he removed a small box before returning to his partner. Dropping to one knee he spoke gently, "Lenora, will you marry me?" As he spoke, Alexander opened the box. Inside was a beautiful ring made of silver with five gems set in the middle: a ruby, diamond, sapphire, emerald and amethyst.

Lenora was mesmerized by the ring as tears ran like rivers down her cheeks. "Yes, I will," she whispered.

***

The Lord of Shadows was stood in front of a fleet of ships, his sights were now firmly set on the island nations of the United Kingdom.

"Attack!" he screamed, as the ships launched. Foul magic ensured the boats made landfall under a mist created by the Lord of Shadows, but the evil Lord's army soon found themselves under attack from the waiting British Army.

***

Back at the Order's Camp, Bain approached the Grand Master. "Grand Master Alexander, The United Kingdom is under attack. The dark lord's army have set foot on the English coast."

"Can we send troops to assist them? Do we have time?" asked Alexander.

Bain shook his head. "We don't have a lot of time. They have taken over the south-east of England and have placed London under siege."

"I want a unit to go there and assess the situation. If you can help in any way possible, please do so."

***

The Lord of Shadows advance continued as his army slaughtered hundreds of soldiers in London as they tried to hold back the dark lord and his formidable army long enough to allow an evacuation of as many of the city's eight and a half million residents as possible. The commanders of the royal guard finally signaled for a full withdrawal of the remaining troops. A group of them fell back to the Tower of London for one final stand.

"These things are monsters," one frightened soldier said moments before the dark lord's army ensured they would be his final words.

The Lord of Shadows smiled under his helmet. "It's time for a test run." A goliath figure appeared beside him holding a trident. "Water golem, you know what to do."

The creature slammed his weapon into the ground, creating a torrent of water that rose and hit the tower. A British soldier's eyes widened.

"What is that thing?" asked the private, his voice trembling with pure fear as another wave slammed into the tower, shaking the building to its foundations. Cracks began to appear in the walls as now wave after wave hit the historical building.

"Yes, the might of the elements," cackled the Lord of Shadows. "The test run is successful." He turned around and walked away as the defending troops were crushed as the tower finally succumbed and fell.

As he left, the Lord of Shadows was approached by a scout. "We have found the missing general Kevin. What are our orders, my lord?"

"Send our best assassins to get rid of him," confirmed the dark lord. " He has failed me, and knows too much should he fall into our enemies' hands."

***

As London fell, several ships could be seen turning in the Thames estuary and heading back out into the English Channel. Too late to save the sacking of the city, they collected as many civilians as they could before leaving to report back to the order on the dark lord's latest devastating attack.

***

Six miles south of the German city of Cologne, Kevin walked through a heavily forested park. A noise behind him made him turn, only to be greeted by a black portal of the Lord of Shadows doing. *So it has come to this,* thought the former general. Pulling a pike from his holster he set himself as one hundred men decked in black armor walked out to meet him in combat.

"Kevin of the Wind, by order of the Lord of Shadows you are to be terminated for failure to successfully complete your mission," said a spokesman for the detachment.

Kevin growled and pulled out his second pike. "You will have to earn this victory!" he roared as he started spinning both pikes, blasting hurricane force winds at the men before him, killing many on the front line.

A soldier successfully avoided the attack and making it through his guard he lunged at Kevin with his sword, grazing his chest, Grabbing the assassin, Kevin stabbed him with a pike and threw his body away. Sensing their target distracted, the remaining soldiers decided all-out attack was their greatest opportunity for success. Kevin, quickly regained his composure, grabbed his second pike and spun it, creating a vacuum bringing the attackers closer. As one pike span the other hacked repeatedly at the approaching combatants.

One of the soldiers, deciding distance was a better option, shot an arrow into Kevin's leg. Pain seared up through his body as the arrowhead tore through tendon and ligament alike, but there was no time to suffer, Kevin's pikes continued their path of destruction.

After the battle, Kevin was on the ground, bleeding, a hundred bodies of the lifeless army were littered around him before they disappeared as one in a plume of black smoke.

A young, black-haired boy of around eight years of age was walking through the forest when he saw the ex-general at death's door. The boy grabbed a stick to poke him, unsure whether this man before him was still alive.

A voice came from behind the boy as a worried looking woman approached. "Wilhelm! There you are." She started to relax, until her gaze dropped to the downed ex-general. Rushing up to Kevin, she knelt beside him, seeing several deep wounds on his chest. "My god!" she whispered, before turning to the boy and urging, "Get my medical kit from the car!"

The boy rushed out of the forest, only to return a few minutes later, carrying a first aid kit. The woman took out bandages and gauze, and set about stemming the flow of blood from the worst of the wounds.

After applying the best care that she could, given the circumstances, she managed to help him to his feet and eventually into her car.

***

Kevin woke up, disorientated and confused. "What happened?" he wondered aloud as he tried to move his arm, but found himself in too much pain to do so. Looking around he saw a white-walled room full of sterile equipment. *A hospital?* he thought.

"I see you are up," said a feminine voice. He thought he'd looked around the room, but then this lady had been sat at his side.

"Huh?" he mumbled. "Were you the one who bandaged me?"

"Yes, and right now you are in my clinic. May I ask your name?" requested the woman.

"Kevin. But, I must go."

"Why? You are not able to walk, and as a doctor I really must request that you stay put," ordered the woman.

"I can't," replied Kevin. "I have bad guys after me and you're putting yourself in danger just by letting me stay," he warned.

"Oh, who is after you? Where are my manners." She covered her mouth, realizing she had forgotten to even give her name. "My name is Lucy. Now who is after you?"

`"I can't say for your safety. All I can say is that they are inherently evil. Really though, I must leave," he said gently but with urgency in his voice.

"I am not giving you a choice. You are staying here until you are completely healed," Lucy ordered, as she held her hands on her hips, like a mother scolding a child.

Kevin sighed in resignation. "Fine, but once I am healed I will need to leave."

The next morning, Kevin was breaking his fast when Wilhelm walked in and asked, "Mister Kevin, how did you get those cuts?"

"I was attacked by a wild animal, but I fought it off. It got me a few times though," Kevin lied.

"Wow. You must be strong," said the boy.

Kevin chuckled, "Maybe."

The boy was clearly excited. "Can I be like you when I'm older, Mister Kevin?"

A dark look spread across Kevin's face. "You don't want to be like me. Besides, you are you and no one else. What do you really want to be when you grow up?" asked the former general.

Wilhelm thought for a bit. "I would like to be a doctor and save people's lives."

"Listen to my words. A noble goal is the best goal to achieve; never lose your determination."

"Yes, Mister Kevin," said Wilhelm.

"Just Kevin, please."

The boy nodded his head rapidly.

In the doorway entrance, Lucy smiled and walked away, unseen by both Kevin and the boy.

That night, Lucy came in top the room, a serious look on her face. "Kevin, I need to know the truth about who you are and who is after you." She stated as she sat on a stool beside the bed, checking his vitals.

"Do you know of the war brewing outside?"

Lucy's eyes widened. "It is all over the news. The war with the Lord of Shadows. Kevin, were they the ones who attacked you?"

"Yes. My former master, the Lord of Shadows, wanted me out of the way because I failed to complete a mission I was given. Do you still want me around after telling you this?" he asked.

"I am a doctor and I can't with good judgment let you die from your wounds. Plus I see you are different from most of the dark soldiers," said Lucy.

Kevin looked down. "I am not so sure."

"Anyone with advice like you gave to my son can't be all bad," she said.

"I thought I heard someone eavesdropping," said Kevin with a smile.

"Are you going to kill me?" she asked with a teasing smile. "You do know I control your life at the moment."

"That you do," agreed Kevin.

"You are definitely a good person and I hope you keep that heart of yours."

"Lucy, I wanted to leave for another reason. I have killed innocent people; despite being under orders, I pulled the trigger. The stigma of helping me will hurt you in the long run," said Kevin.

"I will say it once. A doctor should never refuse help to anyone. That includes criminals. But you are different. You feel remorse for the killing. I don't associate you with being a monster.

"I am not following."

"Monsters don't feel remorse, they enjoy the killing. You feel remorse and want to protect those not involved."

Suddenly, the front door was kicked in and men in black robes flooded into the house. Kevin jumped up ignoring the pain searing through his body. Putting himself between the doctor and his attackers he shouted, "They're here! Get yourself and Wilhelm out of here!" Grabbing a scalpel from a draw in the counter, he prepared to face his assailants.

Lucy covered her mouth and rushed Wilhelm through the room and into a secondary room, one used to store supplies.

Kevin went to the staircase and counted five men down in the foyer. One looked up and met his gaze. "Kevin of Wind, surrender. If you don't we will kill the other two occupants in the house."

Kevin slipped the scalpel into his hospital gown sleeve and walked down the stairs. "All right, you win." said Kevin, putting his head down and playing the part of a defeated man.

Content that Kevin was coming quietly, the leader turned his head to the other assassins. "Kill the rest."

"You said no harm would come to them," growled Kevin.

"I said no such thing; I said they would die if you did not surrender. I said nothing about sparing them at all." The man replied, grinning.

Kevin threw a punch, revealing his weapon held between his index and forefinger. Punching towards the leader's throat the sharp blade of the scalpel ran effortlessly though skin and muscle alike killing him instantly.

"You will pay for that, General," said another soldier as they charged as one at Kevin.

Kevin evaded punch after punch as he sliced out at anyone who ventured too close. Cutting another one and moving on to a third, he slashed the scalpel across the man's neck. In cutting the fourth man down though, he was unable to see an attack in his blind spot, and was hit forcefully on the back of the head by the butt of a gun.

Kevin struggled to get back to his feet. "Say goodnight, General," said the sole remaining attacker, pointing his gun at Kevin's head. Kevin saw the man grin, and growled in frustration.

A shot was heard and the man fell to the ground in front of a shocked Kevin. Behind the body was Lucy, stood calmly with a pistol in her hand.

"Never underestimate a former soldier of Germany and never mess with a mother."

Turning her head, she saw Kevin was still on the ground. "Let's get you back to bed." Lucy flipped the safety on the gun, set it down and set about helping Kevin back up the stairway and into his bed. As she helped Kevin, the dead bodies disappeared from the hallway as though they were never there.

***

A week later, Kevin was stood in front of the clinic. "Thank you for everything, Lucy. I am forever in your debt."

Wilhelm ran up and threw his arms around Kevin's legs. "Do you have to go, Mister Kevin?"

Kevin smiled at the young boy. "I have things to do. Keep your mother safe, okay?"

Wilhelm nodded.

"Good man," said Kevin ruffling the boy's hair before he walked away.

***

Alexander sat in his room. *I am not strong, at the moment, but I need to get to that hut and learn what I can*, thought the young Grand Master.

He grabbed a backpack full of provisions. The other masters were waiting.

"Are you really going?" asked Lenora.

Alexander sighed. "We all know our chances at victory are slim at best. If there's a small chance that we can access any information that can help us, we must take it."

Yuan walked up to him and shook his hand. "I wish you the best, Grand Master Alexander."

"We will also be increasing our training to further boost our chances. Until then, may you find safe travel," said Guan.

Mason nodded his head in agreement as Lenora walked up and hugged Alexander. "Be safe and come back to me," she said, before turning away so Alexander couldn't notice the tears start to fall.

***

A factory on the outskirts of Oslo was the site of the dark lord's ammunition and weapons factory. Far from coincidently, it was also the site where the citizens of Norway who had been captured by the Lord of Shadows were being held. The dark lord had taken it upon himself to create his own slave workforce.

The prisoners were overseen by a large, heavy set man in leather armor. "The lord wants those weapons ready for his conquest of the free world." Seeing a young man fall down, he screamed, "Get back to work!"

The prisoner struggled to get up, the exhaustion and hunger were proving to be impossible to cope with. The large man stalked over to him and kicked him, sending him spiraling backwards. "No breaks for you, scum."

The prisoners looked on, despair etched across their faces.

"Get back to work!" the guard screamed again. Grabbing the fallen prisoner by his shirt neck, he dragged him towards the rear of the building. For a while the prisoner attempted kicking to break free, but the lack of food wore him down.

Unseen to anyone, a shadow moved towards the guard. "So this is what I was fighting for," said the shadow in a whisper so low no ear heard it.

The large task master was still dragging the prisoner when he saw a figure ahead blocking his path. "Get back to work!" the task master screamed again, unable to tell who it was who was obstructing his way.

The figure pulled out a pike. "I am going to enjoy making you pay for what you have done."

"Oh! The Lord of Shadows has a huge bounty on your head, Kevin. One I will take great pleasure in collecting," said the overseer as he tossed the now whimpering prisoner aside and pulled out a hammer.

Charging at Kevin, his target seemed to vanish, then, materialize again, his pike held firmly through the task master's torso.

"Normally I would be more honorable. However, you do not deserve such courtesy." Kevin unceremoniously pulled out the pike from the task master's body.

The large man's lifeless body fell and Kevin walked over to the prisoner who still had a look of fear in his eyes. Using his pike, Kevin slashed the man's shackles away. "Can you stand?" he asked, helping the prisoner up.

"Hungry," moaned the man.

Kevin took out a bag from his shoulder and gave the man bread from his supplies. "Here eat this to get some of your strength back."

The man gobbled the bread down. Reaching out and taking Kevin's hands in his own he cried, "Thank you."

"Stay here while I free the other prisoners," Kevin told him.

Kevin strode past several warriors, cutting them down without stopping. Continuing his assault, he got to the heart of factory. With attackers coming from all sides, Kevin attacked relentlessly, taking down many of the guards with his pikes as they approached.

After the battle, Kevin freed the prisoners.

" Do not squander this opportunity at freedom," he told them. "I have done all I can for you here today."

Kevin turned to leave.

"Wait," spoke the first prisoner Kevin had saved.

"Is there something else you need?"

"Allow us to help you, Kevin. The adults amongst us can form an army to fight the Lord of Shadows at your side."

"I would not usually agree to it, but…" Kevin paused and looked at the men and women around him. Seeing the state they were in, a spark of pride swelled in his heart. "I accept your proposal."

Chapter 21: The History of the Shadows

The Lord of Shadows was sitting on his throne in deep though. Reaching up he removed his helmet. *Two hundred and thirty years since I threw away my humanity*, thought the Lord. *You must be rolling around in your grave, Master Aldor.*

"You are mistaken, Gode," spoke a voice, emanating from a chain mail clad spectral form before him.

"I am impressed, Master Aldor, your spirit has survived," said the Dark Lord. "But, it is you who are wrong, Master, my name and humanity are long gone."

"Regardless, I am here to inform you that whatever you are looking to achieve in this latest war, you will ultimately be defeated, my pupil," said the spirit.

"You were beaten by me with little effort," said the Lord of Shadows with venom in his tone.

"Yes, but you used deceit and poison to get the upper hand.

The Lord of Shadows laughed, "Your prized student could not stop me, and nor can this new generation of masters. They shall fall like both you and Master Eirik did before them."

"Your arrogance is what beat you last time, and it will do so again," warned the master as he vanished once more from sight.

***

Alexander arrived in Denmark, just as the thick snow started to fall. Aware that he need to find shelter, but keen to remain out of sight he located a cave and headed inside. Grabbing some branches and leaves he insulated the cave by blocking part of the entrance.

The snow got heavier still as Alexander buckled down inside the cave, annoyed to have to slow down his journey. The snow continued long into the night as Alexander managed a fitful, cold sleep.

The next day, Alexander peered outside , only to be greeted by snow drifts taller than himself. Deciding not to wait for the snow to get worse, he started his trek slowly, careful to be on the lookout for patches of black ice.

The journey was long and arduous, but after a further couple of days travelling as incognito as he could he reached the Danish coast. From there, paying only in cash, he took the ferry to Norway.

Arriving in Norway he headed north, following the map he had been given by Bain. Dodging several Shadow scouting patrols, he arrived at the destination marked on the map.

Before him, Alexander could see a small wooden hut with a yellow straw roof. *This must be it,* he thought as he cautiously approached the ramshackle building.

Once inside found a dust covering to what little furniture was present. The hut appeared to have been abandoned long ago. *Now what am I suppose to do?* he thought.

Suddenly, the room appeared to spin, Alexander became lightheaded and reached for support. "What?" he said passing out and falling unconscious to the floor.

Alexander came round and found himself floating in a white space. His thoughts remained muggy as he struggled to understand his surroundings. Closing his eyes he struggled to get his thoughts in order.

"So this is the newest Grand Master," said a deep voice, seemingly heavy with wisdom. A man with a bald head appeared before Alexander, holding a staff a full foot in length and wearing the robe of the Grand Master. The man put his staff on the teen's head and a swirling white mist appeared. "Fully awaken, young one, let your mind and thoughts be clear."

Alexander opened his eyes once more. "His eyes widened in shock as he found himself floating above nothingness. "Where am I?" he asked.

"Please stay calm, Grand Master. You are in the void realm where the spirits are sent. I am neither amongst the living nor those who have fully passed to their final destination." The spirit motioned with his right hand and Alexander found himself upright, standing on a white, marble floor.

"Who are you though?" asked Alexander.

"I am he that you seek, Grand Master. I am Grand Master Eirik."

"It is an honor, Grand Master." Alexander bowed his head to the ground. "I need your help to win a war."

"I thought as much. Tell me what you know of the evil that you must defeat," said the elder Grand Master.

Alexander sighed. "Not much, only that it is the same evil that you managed to defeat over 200 years ago."

"I see. I am willing to train you, Grand Master. However, before I do so, we must remove any darkness that you harbor in your soul."

"What do you mean?" asked Alexander.

"To be a true Grand Master you must overcome the darkness in your soul, as I did. I had to go through the ritual during my tenure as Grand Master. I will start your training after you have beaten the darkness that lives within you."

"How do I beat this darkness?"

Eirik motioned to Alexander, "Follow me."

Further into the vastness of the void they walked. After several miles, they came upon a small altar with a gold domed roof. A golden arrow was positioned at the height of the dome, pointing to the sky.

"Inside that dome is where you will meditate and face your inner darkness," explained Eirik.

Alexander paused to control his nerves and then entered the dome. Getting to the middle,

Alexander sat down, crossed his legs and began to meditate. As swirl of blue smoke flew from his body, as he rocked gently from side to side.

"Those you call friends will betray you," said a deep, foreboding voice. "You should join the Lord of Shadows."

Alexander opened his eyes, at first believing he way looking into a mirror. An exact image of the Grand Master stood before him. That was until it opened it eyes revealing demonic yellow irises.

"So you are my darkness?" questioned Alexander, though he was sure he already knew the answer.

Ignoring his questioning the demonic vision spoke again, "What is the point of fighting when afterwards the world will go back to warring nations once more? There will never truly be peace in this world."

"That may be true," confirmed Alexander, "but the fact that the nations are willing to put aside their differences in this war against evil gives me great hope."

"If you won't take my advice, then perhaps we should settle this through combat," the demonic vision warned, before he raised his hands, two swords materializing in them as he held them above his head. Reaching for his own swords, Alexander prepared to meet his darkness in battle.

The two clashed as they both tried to overpower each other. Alexander went high for a strike from above, but it was blocked to one side by the dark entity he faced. The evil one feinted to jab with the sword he held in his right hand, before dropping his shoulder, spinning and attempting to kick Alexander back.

The two continued to battle, neither able to get the decisive hit as their styles and methods closely reflected each other.

Outside the altar, the spirit of Eirik watched as Alexander continued to sit silently on the dome's floor. "Let's see what he can do. Taming the evil spirit is a difficult task.

Let me try something else, thought Alexander, switching his style to the dragon style. Rather than mirror this change, his opponent surprised him by adopting the snake style.

"You think the world's powers will change after this war?" mocked the darkness, landing a hard punch to Alexander's chest only to receive a kick to the left side in return.

"The fact remains that they are willing to fight for the greater good. After that, it is up to them on how to proceed. Be thankful for what we can accomplish," said Alexander. "Darkness or light it makes little difference. Even the light can stray from the right path. Instead of fighting you, we should cooperate and become a completed whole instead of just pieces of a puzzle."

"The light and dark cannot coexist," warned the demonic vision.

"We will never know until we try. Without darkness, light cannot exist and vice versa," urged Alexander.

"So you say, but it cannot be possible."

"We will never know without making an attempt. What do you say, partner?" Alexander had his hand outstretched.

The yellow-eyed darkness before him sighed. "I will try."

Clasping their hands together, an energy flowed through Alexander. Closing his eyes he felt it course through his entire body. Opening his eyes, he found himself alone once more.

Eirik smiled. *So he has accepted the darkness and is going to work with it*, he thought. Now, *that is a first.*

Coming out of his meditative state, Alexander got up and walked out of the dome and over to Eirik. "Master, I have decided to work with my darkness and stay whole."

Eirik smiles at Alexander. "Well done on choosing a different path. Time will tell at how wise a choice you have made. Before we start your training though I must tell you who the Lord of Shadows really is."

"Wait. You know?"

"I told you how to be Grand Master I had to overcome my darkness?" Eirik received a nod from Alexander. "However, I was not the only person to be chosen for the honor."

"What are you saying, Master Eirik?"

"There was another student who took his training next to me. His name was Gode and he was a prodigy with the sword. Even I was unable to beat him in sparring," said Eirik. "He outclassed me in all areas."

Eirik grew silent as he recalled the summer of 1779. He had spent most of his life in the monastery training. Though he had fought hard, sparring everyday with his master, he had always felt like he was behind. That day had been no different. He had met Gode in the training hall like any other day…

***

A tall, dark haired youth fought in a sparring match against a shaven headed youth. The dark haired combatant slammed his staff into the other's chest knocking him down.

"Come on, Eirik. Is that all? I thought you would have gotten better," the dark-haired fighter said mockingly with a smug look across his face.

"Well, you train yourself into the ground. It's going to kill you," complained young Eirik.

"Enough," said a deep voice. Another man walked into the room, dressed in the robe of a monk, but with chain mail underneath.

"Master Aldor," acknowledged both fighters, bowing to their teacher.

"Gode, do not gloat in your victory. It shows a lot about what kind of character you have," said Aldor, looking at the taller of the two fighters.

Gode scoffed at the advice. "Well, Master Aldor, what do you say?" he responded, holding up his staff. "Let me prove what you have taught me has not been wasted."

The master faced his student and brought up his own staff. "Very well. It is time for today's lesson."

The two clashed as Gode ran straight at his master aiming to prove his superiority. Aldor though proved to be far too wise for the young student, effortlessly leaning out of the way of his initial strike, only to bring his own staff down at the midpoint of Gode's breaking his student's staff in two.

Turning away, Master Alder offered, "That is your lesson for today, my students. There will always be someone stronger and smarter than you, no matter how strong you believe your abilities to be."

"Yes, Master," said both students bowing to their teacher.

"Now come, it is time to reveal who I have chosen to be my successor," continued the Master, motioning the two students to follow him into the monastery.

Both fighters followed the aged monk into the temple and waited until Aldor sat.

With no preamble the teacher addressed the pair, "I have made my decision. It is Eirik who shall be the new Grand Master."

Gode stood up, clearly unhappy. "Master, why him? He is not stronger than me."

"True you have demonstrated great skill, but that is not the main quality I am looking for in my successor. Humility and restraint are another part of being a Grand Master. And, Gode, you have shown me neither."

"Oh and Eirik has I suppose!" shouted Gode as he shook with rage.

"He has not shown as much skill in battle, but he has shown great restraint and humility in his actions. He has never gloated when another opponent was beaten and never struck to incapacitate in sparring."

"You always did play favorites," snarled Gode as he stormed through the open door, slamming it behind him like a petulant child.

Aldor sighed. "I hope he does not do something rash. Come now, Eirik, I will show you the responsibility of the Grand Master."

***

In the Army of the Order of the White Rose, Master Yuan was garbed in full battle armor. Ten thousand troops stood behind him. Turning to address his army the Master pointed to a series of flags on the horizon and urged, "Onward to victory!"

On the horizon stood an army of soldiers of similar strength in numbers. They wore black armor and carried both swords and guns and their waist. A man wearing the emblem of a General smiled while observing his opposing force. "Destroy the rabble!" screamed the man, as he charged forward, with the rest of his army closely behind.

"Attack!" yelled Yuan as his own army advanced, brandishing their guns, and doing their best to hide their fear.

***

Eirik's head snapped up and he looked at Alexander. "I sense a battle going on."

Alexander looked back at him, evidently worried at the thought of his friends in danger.

"Fear not, Grand Master, your friends will prevail; have faith in them and you will have faith in yourself.

"The sooner I finish this training, the sooner I can help. Let us continue, Master," urged Alexander. The thought of losing those closest to him spurred him to push harder than ever.

***

Yuan saw his side taking many casualties and ran forward to join the fray. Using his curved sword, he cut down many of the dark soldiers before they even knew he was upon them.

The general of the Shadow Army ordered a full scale charge, hoping to overrun the Order's line. Head down, charging, they came upon the Order of the White Rose forces with a vengeance.

Yuan marshaled his forces to best combat the Shadow army, firing their guns at the charging attackers they scored kill after kill. Grabbing their knives and melee weapons they met the enemy that had made it through to their lines head on.

Blade to blade, both sides fought with all of their might. Yuan took out soldier after soldier with his blade. Even after becoming surrounded, Yuan closed his eyes and calmed himself as the opposing soldiers level their guns at the Master. Opening his eyes, he sent them back with a powerful blast of chi energy.

The Lord of Shadows' army commander growled, seeing his forces decimated by the Master marshaling their enemy. Rushing toward Yuan, he killed any soldier unfortunate enough to be in his path, regardless of whose army they belonged to.

Charging at the master the commander tried to overpower his opponent with brute force, trying to push him back with heavy strikes. Yuan effortlessly dodged each attempt, before sidestepping the next attack, dropping low and sweeping his feet away. Spinning as his opponent fell he brought his sword down and decapitated the commander before he had even hit the ground.

The soldiers, seeing their general fall, fled the battlefield. Yuan rallied his troops and pursued the fleeing troops, killing all who failed to surrender.

***

Eirik smiled, "The first victory of this war goes to your comrades," he said as Alexander completed his latest set of pushups.

"We won the first battle?" Eirik nodded. "That is excellent news!"

"War can have turning points at any time. The real victory is the last battle. Now continue with your next set of pushups and we will move on after you complete two hundred," said the former grand master.

***

The Lord of Shadows was meditating when a messenger appeared.

"Sir, I bring news from the front lines," he stammered.

"Oh?" asked the dark lord. "Continue."

"The first battle goes to the White Rose, my lord. The commander you put in charge was killed by Master Yuan."

"This loss means little to our overall plans. However, we can't let this defeat sit without retaliating," said the Lord of Shadows.

"Orders, sir?"

"Begin Operation Snowstorm."

The messenger nodded and urgently left the room.

"All shall fall like my former comrades," the Lord of Shadows said looking from his temple to the snow falling outside.

The snow had swirled like now, that winter ten years after he had been overlooked as the Grand Master. The cold air then though had been nothing compared to the hatred in his heart. That is where one choice had changed his fate, forever.

***

Gode was walking through the forest cave when he was approached by a dark-hooded man. "It is a pity you were not picked; with your skills, you should have been chosen," said the man.

"What do I owe this second visit, Shadow?" asked Gode.

"I wish to help you, as I offered ten years ago. I did tell you then they would never accept you."

"I should have listened. I have come here today because I have decided to join you, Shadow. I wish to renounce my loyalties to the Order of the White Rose."

"That is fine news, young Gode. Let us begin your final training." Shadow motioned for Gode to follow him as he headed towards a cave.

***

In the Russian capital, President Boris was sitting with his ministers.

A swift knock at the door, was quickly followed by a soldier running in past security. "Sir, I bring urgent news! An army is approaching the capital from the South!"

The President rose from his seat and slammed his fist down on the table. "Prepare all troops and reserves. The Lord of Shadows will not take my country!" he roared in defiance.

***

Outside a small town south of the Russian capital, the Shadow Army approached, but were met by the Russian military.

"For mother Russia!" shouted the commander, as his men fired on the Shadow Army.

The Russians fought well into the evening, forcing the enemy back from the town. When it finally seemed as though they had repelled the attack they were hit from behind by a second group that had skirted the town and come in from the North.

The Russian military started to take heavy casualties as they tried to fight a two-flank battle. "Keep fighting! Give time for our military to gather the troops!" cried their leader.

The brave soldiers were boxed though, and after several hours of heavy artillery from the two Shadow Army groups the final member of the resistance succumbed.

The Shadow Army continued to the small town where they carried out their orders, to burn the now empty town to the ground, before marching on to Moscow.

The Shadow Army was hit prior to their arrival in the capital by the brunt of the Russian military, but despite heavy losses the dark lord's army eventually made it through to take Moscow.

***

The masters had taken their seats at the table in the meeting hall. Grand Master Alexander's seat at the head of table remained vacant. Guan rose first to pass on details of the bad news they had received moments before. "So Russia has fallen," said Guan. "This is troubling, I'm sure we can all agree."

"For every victory we get we lose just as much," replied Mason.

"Can't we send troops to help them retake their city?" inquired Yuan.

"If we do that we will spread our forces too thin," said Guan, glumly. "Unfortunately there seems to be nothing we can do for the terrorized citizens of Russia."

"We should take the fight to the Lord of Shadows himself," said Lenora. "Kira told us of where he can be found."

"No, right now we need Alexander to learn from Grand Master Eirik. Charging in would be suicidal without the information he needs to learn," said Mason.

Lenora slammed her hands on the table. "We can at least slow them down! Hamper their war efforts!" she said angrily.

As Lenora took her seat again, the doors to the hall opened and Bain calmly walked in taking a seat to the right of Guan. He held up a parchment and addressed the masters. "I have found something in the archives that could be of benefit to our cause."

"What did you find, Bain?" asked Guan. "We could certainly do with some good news right about now."

"The origins of the Lord of Shadows," said Bain as he locked eyes with the master. "It took me a few hours to scour the library before I found it."

Guan motioned for Bain to continue.

"He was trained by the prior Grand Master to Eirik, A Grand Master Alder. Considered a prodigy, he was denied the rank of Grand Master and left the Order. However, this parchment is the Lord of Shadows recollection of the event.

"It was the last line that caught my interest," said Bain, reading further from the parchment in his hands. "My master showed me the light within the shadows, and together with my Master, who I have come to call Lord Shadow, we shall begin the purge this world of the light. However, I digress; the Master will fall to the student."

Guan closed his eyes. "I see; to be the Lord of Shadows he must kill the master. Did you find out anything else, Bain?"

Bain closed his eyes. "I am afraid it is worse than we thought. The purging of the light is the extermination and genocide of all living things on the earth. Let me read the next part."

From anarchy, formed by victory. All life except those damned shall be destroyed as I rule a world with nothing but demon. I have prepared my troops, and the depths of hell lend me the forces necessary for victory. They shall be rewarded with the slaves and land of the conquered.

"Anything else?" asked Mason.

"I am afraid it gets worse because of the possibly of his ascension to godhood. He calls it Shaitan, which is a term for all evil including Satan, orcs and demons," replied Bain.

The masters though for a moment.

"With the orbs, and if he ascends, we will have a tough fight," said Guan. "One that I'm not sure we can survive."

***

. "You have improved greatly but I think we should stop for today," said Grand Master Eirik as they ended the spar.

Alexander sat, out of breath. "No wonder you were Grand Master. You are strong, Master Eirik."

"Strength does not always win battles. Strategy is always greater. The spoken word can stop a blade by its convictions," said the past Grand Master.

Alexander bowed. "I understand; violence should be the last resort."

Eirik nodded before continuing, "Now where was I at in the story? Ah yes. Gode, after learning from another master and being corrupted, attacked our master."

***

In the monastery, Aldor was meditating, a tea cup sat beside him.

"I never thought you would turn your blade on me, Gode," said Aldor as tried to rise to his feet, but stumbled. His every move was sluggish. "How did you poison me?" he asked. Unable to see his former student, but sure he was present.

A voice confirmed his suspicions, "I dropped poison in your tea water a few hours ago." Can you fight me, Master?" asked the voice with fake concern.

Aldor grabbed a sword. "So it has come to this." Turning, he reacted just in time to block a blade heading for his head.

Gode stood before him, wearing leather armor with spiked shoulder pads. Aiming to take advantage of his former teacher's reaction to the poison he went for a strike at the heart. Alder reacted, adrenaline working against the poison to hopefully buy him enough time to defend himself. Grabbing the blade's handle he kneed Gode in the chest. "Arrogance does not win battles. I thought I taught you better than this," said the master.

"I am no longer the student, old man," said Gode.

"Yet you made a foolish error by attacking me," said Aldor as he backhanded his former student.

Gode regained his balance swiftly and smiled.

The master's vision started to become hazy. *I have to end this fight quickly,* he thought as he blocked a series of heavy blows from Gode and was forced to his knees.

The poison had taken a stranglehold now, and the master dropped his sword and clutched at his chest. Gode smirked, crouched down before him and without a word ran his sword straight through his former teacher's heart.

As Gode turned to walk away, the door opened and Eirik walked in. Seeing Gode standing over the body of Alder he screamed, "Master Aldor!" Aware that Alder was beyond saving, Eirik unsheathed his blade, and charged at Gode. The killer expected the emotional nature of his response and within moments had disarmed Eirik.

"You aren't worth killing," Gode said as he strolled away, leaving Aldor dead and Eirik on his knees, tears streaming down his face.

***

"I was too weak to fight him, at that time, and realizing my weaknesses, I left in shame to train until I had learned all that I could," said the spirit of Eirik.

Alexander looked on. "How did you beat him in the final battle?"

"I will tell you later," said Eirik. "But for now continue your katas and I will teach you the next style you will need to master."

***

The Lord of Shadows was in his temple as reports came to him of glorious victories and damaging defeats. "So the Order has gained a few victories, however it is the last battle that will determine the victor." Summoning over a messenger, he continued, "I need the other orbs; get word out, we prepare to storm the camp of the Order."

***

A soldier stood at the far end of the table, addressing all of the masters.

"Masters, we have an emergency. Scouts report seeing a mass of troops approaching."

"What?" asked Lenora.

"This was not expected. We don't have the manpower to take on a large army," said Guan.

"What shall we do then? We can't retreat. It will show weakness," Yuan stated.

"We have to retreat. The most important thing is the survival of this order," Mason countered.

Guan sat as the two continued their debate, carefully thinking over the best course of action. "The way is to fight, but also to retreat." Stated Guan. "It will prove that we have what it takes to make the tough calls. I want five hundred men to hold the line at all cost."

"Who will be the commander?" asked Lenora.

Bain got up. "I think I should earn my keep. I will take command of this defensive unit."

"You are a master, Bain; I should not let you be on the front lines. Do you have to be the one?" asked Guan. They had all grown fond of Bain. His knowledge and experience had been a great help to them all.

"Yes, as a master I must be willing to walk towards death with no fear," said the weapons smith.

"Good luck, Bain, our hopes are that you survive," said Guan. "But, whatever happens, please know that we will be forever grateful for your sacrifice on this day.

"My survival is not the objective here. The survival of the Order is the main goal," Bain replied. Turning around, he walked out, leaving a dark, foreboding feeling in the command tent.

***

The Army of Shadows was fast approaching the small camp, as five hundred warriors stood to meet them in the valley outside the cove. Armed with knives and guns they stood fearlessly, their fate mattered less than the future of the Order, and greater still, the world. Bain was watching the approaching dark army as he thought back to his plan. *Bottle up the valley with my force and hold them off.*

"Riflemen, Attack!" he shouted, and his army began shooting into the Shadow Army's forces.

The Shadow Army commander laughed in response. "They will die, all of them. Attack!" he shouted, urging his army toward the small group of defenders.

With the terrain in the favor of the Order's forces, they managed to kills scores of shadow soldiers, however, Bain knew it was only a matter of time until they broke through.

Back at the base camp, the masters had begun to organize their retreat. Guan was at the head of the masses as they exited the camp site.

The battle had turned rather quickly as the five hundred soldiers holding the line began to falter. The sheer number of attackers was finally overwhelming them. Bain looked on, making a decision that in practice was far easier than he ever had imagined. "This is the end of the road for me." He acknowledged. Drawing a curved sword he ran down the hill, killing Shadow soldiers indiscriminately as he descended.

The commander, tired of the games and the losses his army had felt, ordered a volley of bullets, felling the remaining defenders in one swoop. The Order of White Rose had lost the last protectors of their base. "Search the camp for survivors and the orbs. Kill anyone you find."

***

Eirik was standing on a pole in front of his student. Alexander stood exactly opposite, mimicking his teacher as he stood atop a pole. Around them were various other poles of varying heights. Eirik jumped to an adjacent pole and struck out with a kick at Alexander, forcing the young master to jump away to another pole. "Remember keep your guard up at all times," he warned.

Alexander retaliated with a spin kick, but Eirik easily caught his attack and effortlessly tossed him aside. Maintaining his composure, Alexander landed on another pole. *He was not a Grand Master for nothing,* thought Alexander. *I must concentrate.*

The two stood on their respective poles. "Come now, young Alexander, is that all you have?" asked Eirik.

Alexander, with all his experience, was not easily goaded. "Well, you have yet to beat me, Master."

***

The Order was in a shambles as the forces they marshaled were forced to flee the base. Lenora looked around and then asked, "Which of you has the orbs?"

"I thought you had them," replied Yuan, panic evident in his voice.

"That's not good. That means we left the orbs. They will now be in the Lord of Shadows' possession," Guan added.

Mason looked on in silence and then said, "That might work to our advantage if we can force him to overuse them in battle."

"But will it be worth the cost of his increased power?" asked Guan.

"If their overuse weakens this monster then it will be worth it," said Mason.

"But we might lose before he is drained," worried Guan. "We will have to hit him fast and hard if we attack."

Chapter 22: The Final Conflict

Alexander was attempting to meditate as he faced Master Eirik.

"Feel the chi as it moves around you. Harness it. Use it," the master instructed as he watched the young Grand Master. Alexander was perfectly still as a light shimmered around him. "You have only just started your chi training and yet you have already called upon it. You can stop for now," he instructed, pleased with the progress his student had made in such a short space of time.

Alexander opened his eyes. "Thank you, Master." Noticing Eirik had a distant look on his face, he added "What is wrong?"

Snapping out of his daze, Eirik turned his head. "Nothing, just memories," said the former master. "Both my failings and Gode's failings."

Alexander looked on. "So how did you win the last engagement with the Lord of Shadows?" asked the young master.

"I believe now is the time to tell you. I used a technique that kills the user while, at best, imprisons the target. Are you willing to make that sacrifice, knowing you will leave your loved ones behind?" asked Eirik. Alexander frowned. "When you choose that fate, I will teach you the technique."

***

The Order of the White Rose had fled their base and gathered in a clearing, 5 mniles due west of their starting point. "Great, we lost the orbs," said Lenora with annoyance.

"We also lost our base. We need find another location," Guan reminded the group.

"I disagree. We should strike the Lord of Shadows. He thinks we are no threat, and we can use that to surprise him," Yuan said.

"But we are assuming that he is ignorant of our threat," Guan said being cautious.

"Let's take a vote," Mason suggested. "All in favor of an attack raise your hands."

Yuan raised his hand followed by Lenora. Mason raised it next with Guan doing the same.

"We'll launch our attack after gathering our forces. Then the war will end one way or another," Guan declared.

***

The Lord of Shadows was sat his throne, three figures stood close by around his altar. "Open the portal," he commanded to the three.

The figures clasped their hands together as a dark chi was shot from their fingers. Mixing together before them a black portal formed. "At last my army," said the Lord of Shadows. Thousands of demonic creatures began pouring out of the portal. Some wore armor while others wore leather clothing. The creatures wielded swords, axes and archaic weapons of destruction that even the dark lord had never laid eyes on before. "The army of hell shall descend upon the enemy. Armageddon shall start, today!" he screamed before laughing maniacally.

***

In Germany, a small group closed in on a factory outpost. "Attack!" their leader shouted as thirty men attacked, the soldiers defending it falling one by one. One started to run but was impaled by a pike thrown by the leader. As the body fell Kevin walked over to retrieve his pike. Motioning to his second in command he ordered, "Secure the area."

"Yes, Commander," replied the man, nodding to two of the men nearby to assist him.

***

"So we lost another factory?" The dark lord was pissed. He slammed his fist down on the armrest of his throne, cracking the arm in two. "This is a revolt against me and they shall be put down like the dogs they are."

A soldier walked in, seeing the state of his lord he paused momentarily before speaking, "Sir, we have reports of numerous battles being waged against us. What shall we do about this insurgency?"

The dark lord seemed to visibly relax and, to the unease of the soldier, chuckled. "We shall bide our time. After all, the real conflict will be against the Order of the White Rose."

"I see," said the soldier.

"Are our forces ready?" asked The Lord of Shadows.

"Yes, Master; the whole army is ready for battle," replied the scout.

"Good. Then the time has come for our enemies to launch their attack on the temple.

***

Kevin sat in a makeshift tent with several of his chosen commanders. "We should strike here, near the temple of the Lord of Shadows," he informed the group.

"Sir, all enemy troops are retreating from battlefronts around the world," said one of the men.

"Why would he call all units back? He would not do this unless he is getting ready to end this war against the order," said Kevin. "I want all units to head out; it is time to take the fight to the Lord of Shadows."

***

Alexander remained in the void as Eirik looked on. "There is one more thing you must do before your final battle," said Eirik. "You must create your own fighting style."

Alexander looked at his master, confused. "I am not following. How do I create a style?"

"Take your strengths and use them to formulate your new style. For example, my maneuverability is my greatest strength so I use that to out maneuver or redirect a blow from an enemy, and retaliate with my own strikes," said Eirik.

Alexander sat down. "Give me some time to figure out a way to use those skills I have acquired."

"Take all the time you time," said Eirik. "As with the temple trials, time goes slower in the void."

A few hours later, Alexander was testing out his attacking moves; jumping and flipping around the test dummy, he landed a blow on the dummy, shattering it to pieces. *My speed and attacks are strong, but my defense is non-existent,* thought the young Grand Master. *I have to put in some defensive moves or I'll need to switch my style.*

A short while later, Alexander walked out of the room and approached his teacher. "I have almost completed my own style," he confirmed.

"I see; please explain the basis of your form so far," the former Grand Master said.

"My usual style is all-out assault, keeping my opponent constantly guessing. It has some weaknesses though," admitted Alexander before continuing. "It is primarily an attacking style and very exhausting for a long battle. It has no blocking or defense capabilities other than jumping around."

"How are you going to fix this flaw?"

"I have a lot of styles to choose from, so I will change it to a more balanced style, allowing for safe defense," said Alexander.

Grand Master Eirik smiled at his student a short while later. Please that his student had returned to his room to perfect his style. "Your training is complete, young Grand Master. I could not be any prouder."

"Thank you, Master. I have a feeling the war is reaching its climax and I need to help my friends."

"Remember, young Alexander, use that technique as a last resort. Head to the Scandinavian Mountains and you will find the temple. But first you must pass my test before going," said Eirik.

"What test?" asked Alexander.

"You must beat me in a final battle and impress me sufficiently," Eirik stated, moving into his fighting stance.

Alexander did the same, before immediately attacking with a kick which Eirik caught before tossing him aside.

Eirik went for a quick finger strike forcing Alexander on the defensive. "Is that all, Alexander?" asked Eirik as he continued his assault. Alexander jumped over Eirik as his next attack came in, sending a kick to his master as he passed and forcing him back. "Not bad."

Alexander put his guard up and waited for Eirik to attack. The former Grand Master did not disappoint as he rushed the young man at a speed far greater than Alexander could ever had imagined possible, attempting a kick that would end normally the match.

Alexander caught the kick and winced as the pain shot up his arms and across his shoulders. The power of the strike gone, he launched Eirik back across to the other side of the room. Eirik flipped through the air and landed softly on his feet. Taking a moment, the elder Grand Master watched Alexander's form carefully, looking for even the smallest sign of weakness.

Alexander started jumping around the master with his newly invented style. Eirik switched to Aikido in an effort to use Alexander's own motion against him.

Alexander went for a quick kick, but was easily grabbed by the collar and tossed away. Flipping in the air he landed on his feet, effortlessly switching styles gain. This time to the dragon style, hopefully this would overpower the defensive Aikido.

Eirik rushed at Alexander in an attempt to catch him unprepared. He got within striking distance, but his initial punch was dodged as Alexander flipped on his hands, and summersault kicked Eirik in the chin. Alexander, keen to press home his advantage, punched his teacher in the chest, sending him flying back into the other side of the wall.

Eirik chuckled as he got slowly to his feet. "I haven't had to fight this hard in a hundred years." Alexander rushed his master as he continued, "A frontal assault; are you that confident?"

Eirik grabbed Alexander by the collar as he came in and tossed the young master behind him.

Alexander rose from his position on the floor and smiled. "We are both wearing ankle weights. How about we let loose completely?" said Alexander.

Eirik nodded his agreement before sitting cross-legged on the floor, pulling up his pant legs, showing metal weights on his ankles with the number one hundred carved in both of them, and then tossing them to the side. Alexander did the same, but his ankle weights had only fifty carved into them.

Eirik got into a stance as Alexander stood in a boxing stance. As if a bell rang, they launched themselves at each other in a full on flurry of punches and kicks. The battle was so fast-paced that they would change position every second, leaving after-images in their wake.

Alexander hit Eirik's arm with a devastating hammer fist when he went to block. The crack from the impact was heard clearly by both of the men. The master flinched from the pain and retaliated with a roundhouse kick, which dodged by Alexander connected with a column, breaking it in half and sending masonry to the floor.

Spinning quickly, Eirik slammed his fist into Alexander's left side, sending him to the ground. "To keep up with me for this long is impressive. No other has achieved the feat. For that reason alone, you have passed my test."

Alexander got up slowly to his feet. Every muscle in his body ached from physical exhaustion. "Thank you, Master," He bowed in respect and then dropped back breathless to the floor.

Eirik approached the young student and crouched before him, "Now you must head to the Lord of Shadows' temple to assist your comrades. Your body may feel like it's been damaged, but in reality you have been resting outside the void so you should be fine for battle, these scars will not follow you there."

The air shimmered around the youth as he struggled to remain alert. Swaying left and then right Alexander passed out.

At last my mistake will be ratified, thought Eirik. *I couldn't bring myself to finish my friend. Be careful, Grand Master Alexander.*

***

In the hut, Alexander awoke. Looking around, he began to wonder if it had all been a dream. "I should go to the temple immediately," he decided, exiting the hut and beginning his trek south for the final battle.

***

The Order of the White Rose was getting ready for their decisive battle. The four Masters stood at the front of the army. An army that now numbered close to fifty thousand troops. The plan was fairly simple: have the main army attack the front lines as the masters snuck in to defeat the Lord of Shadows in single combat.

Guan, who was given temporary command, finalized the plans.

"This battle has a lot riding on it. Are the Thorns ready for their deployment?" Guan inquired.

Kira and Kin were in the command tent with Rashid. "Yes, the Sharp Thorns are ready," Kin confirmed.

"Rashid, I want you to take command of the left wing. Kira will take command of the right wing, and Kin will be in the center. Jun, the leader of the Shaolin, will take command of the reserves," instructed Guan.

"We will have to sneak into the main temple and defeat the Lord of Shadows on his own turf. We must win this battle," Mason said with conviction.

"Supplies are ready. Despite the preparation, casualties will be high due us being outnumbered three to one," Yuan told them. "And, that's just an estimate. Who really know just how many killers he controls."

"We have no other option than to wait for the calls we have made for reinforcement to be answered, and by then it could be too late. Mobilize all troops," Guan commanded.

The Army of the White Rose marched to their final battle; a sea of white and blue robes headed to the temple on the mountain. The army stopped at the foot of mountain range, shocked to see the size of the army of darkness amassed in front of them. "Hold position! We need to take as many of them as possible!" Rashid shouted.

The Army of Darkness fired their artillery as the Army of the White Rose responded with volleys of their own. Losses were high on both sides, and were only going to get worse as both armies charged at one another, the cries of battle echoing through the mountain range and beyond.

In the temple at the summit of the tallest mountain in the range, the four masters had successfully evaded the patrols left to guard the temple and entered unnoticed. Heading through the passageways to the throne room they were surprised to find the oak double doors opening before them. "He must be excepting us. Stay on guard," Guan whispered.

Sitting on the throne, the Lord of Shadows smiled darkly, "Welcome, masters, to your death."

"Your reign ends now!" Guan declared as he brought his staff up.

Lenora got in her stance. Yuan got out his curved sword and Mason put on his spike gloves. The Lord of Shadows looked at the four and chuckled. "It seems to me that you're missing one. The Grand Master could not even be bothered to join you?"

"Enough talk!" said Yuan as he rushed forward, bringing his blade down. The Lord of Shadows caught the blade between his fingers, twisted his hand and dropped Yuan's blade to the floor.

"Weak." The Lord of Shadows threw Yuan back with the flick of his wrist.

The other masters surrounded the Lord of Shadows and prepared to fight.

"It seems like I am going to have to show you what real power looks like," the Lord of Shadows said while rising from his throne.

***

The Order of the White Rose Army inched forward but was then pushed back again. "Keep fighting!" called out Kira as she slammed her elbow into another enemy. "We shall not be beaten!"

"Rashid, we have got to take out that artillery!" shouted Kin, motioning to the encampment on the hill.

"Yes, Commander!" Rashid acknowledged. His forces split from the main line and attacked the hill, taking heavy casualties as they vainly tried to keep to the sparse cover in the rocky outcrops. Rashid slowly inched forward. After fierce fighting, their attempt to take the artillery was proving even tougher than he'd imagined.

Sensing their trouble, Kin ordered the Order's artillery away from the Army of Darkness and onto their artillery, hoping it would at least provide respite from the constant fire they had been under.

***

Sending Guan back with a powerful punch, the dark lord then grabbed Lenora by her left leg and threw her effortlessly to the other side like a ragdoll. "I am disappointed. I was expecting a little challenge," taunted the Lord of Shadows. "Your army shall be destroyed, as you will be too."

Yuan went on the offensive again, but his attack was easily blocked by the Lord of Shadow's sword. A blast of dark magic sent Yuan flying from his feet as the Lord of Shadows gazed at the four masters in front of him with contempt.

Mason tried to throw a series of lightning-fast punches at the Lord of Shadows, but as with Yuan his efforts proved futile as he was tossed aside again.

Yuan got back up and slammed his sword on the ground in frustration. "Damn it, he's making us look like amateurs," fumed the master.

Guan looked at his friend and tried to remain positive. "Stay calm, Yuan. A chance of victory will show itself eventually. His arrogance will be his undoing."

***

The battle had fast gotten out of control as a water golem appeared and joined the dark lord's army's efforts. The huge monstrosity started to cause havoc among the ranks as it threw attack after attack. Rashid, grabbing his hammer, rushed at the beast, realizing that if this continued they would soon be defeated. Swinging his hammer he threw all his might behind a killing blow, however, his hammer just passed through water and flew of his hand as he lost control.

"Did I get him?" asked Rashid, unclear as to what had happened.

A horrified expression crossed his face as the golem reformed before him. Attempting to get past the beast to retrieve his hammer for a second assault, Rashid was caught by a torrent of water that sent him crashing into the rocky wall of the valley.

The golem stalked toward Rashid, looking to finish the warrior, but his progress was halted as a pike flew from the left of Rashid and stuck in the chest of the golem.

"Leave this thing to me," said a voice, as a figure ran passed, pulled the pike from the golem's chest and set himself for a second attack.

Rashid looked at the newcomer, his savor. "Who are you?" asked Rashid.

"I am Kevin of the Wind, the former general of shadows."

"But, I don't understand," continued Rashid.

"There is no time to explain," responded Kevin, "just know that I am here to fight alongside you and stop this spread of evil. Your weapon will not work on the golem, but you can assist me if you aim for its head," he instructed his companion.

The two warriors stared down the golem and rushed it. Kevin span his pike, blasting wind at the golem, making it falter. Rashid slammed his hammer on the golem's head causing it to splatter into water.

"I have brought help to even out the odds!" Kevin shouted across as hundreds of civilians brandishing their guns charged the army of darkness.

"Now to finish this beast," Rashid declared as he rushed the water golem, only to be sent back once more by a torrent of water.

Kevin dodged an attack of water and fired a wind blast at the golem. "This thing is difficult to take down," he fumed, "but we must succeed!"

Kevin dodged a water blast as Rashid continued to pepper the golem with headshots. He slammed it one more time, and as he did so saw something shine in the beast's chest.

"Wait, I saw something in the creature's chest on last my attack," Rashid told Kevin as he returned to his side.

"What do you mean?" asked Kevin. Squinting his eyes, he could make out the faint outline of an Orb. "I see it. We have to destroy that Orb!"

Rashid and Kevin backed away as they tried to formulate a plan.

Kevin spoke first, "If you can create a distraction I'll have the opening in need. I can destroy it with wind, however I'll need you to move away so you don't get hit."

Rashid nodded and gripped his hammer before rushing the golem. The golem, turned its head toward Rashid and roared in defiance as Kevin calmed himself and prepared to throw his pike. The opportunity appeared and Kevin infused his pike with wind and threw it like a javelin. It pierced the monster's metallic Orb heart, a scream of agony followed before the Golem exploded, showering the two attackers. After a moment to ensure the creature did not reform the pair headed wearily back to the main battle.

The Army of the order was taking heavy losses as the Army of Shadows forced them back. For every soldier killed on the Lord Shadow's side, three more soldiers appear in seemingly never ending waves.

A new tactic was needed. "Block out the sun and light up the sky," shouted a voice. The Order's archers present unleashed a hail of flaming arrows at the demonic army. All hit by the fiery arrows turned black and fell to ash on the valley floor. The Shadow army faltered, and the Order of the White Rose began their counter offensive for the first time in the battle. Now they had a way to destroy their enemy without taking the huge losses the hand-to-hand combat had produced.

As the Order advanced more visitors arrived and joined in their push. Bash appeared with members of the Ugandan tribe numbering in the thousands. Seeing the result of the fire arrows he shouted, "The demons are weak to fire!"

The Ugandan warriors lit and fired their arrows as the Shadow army again got closer to their line, forced forward by their commanders at the rear. Brandishing their shields of tough hide, the tribal warriors stopped the dark army's charge. Circling the front line they forced them towards the valley walls where the archers could fire volley after volley of flaming arrows. The demons turned from the fire, panic broke out as they clawed and trampled each other in a futile attempt to get away.

The Order and its allies cheered as one as the demonic army was decimated.

The battle against the demons, however, proved to only be a brief victory. Their success was cut short as a larger army appeared around the bottom of the valley. An army made up from the governments controlled by the Lord of Shadows. Bash looked up and brought his club to his shoulder. "About face, warriors! Archer's, volley!" shouted the Ugandan warlord.

The tribal archers stalled as they prepared to loose their notched arrows. The approaching army had brought tanks, not familiar with this western weapon, the tribesmen were being taken down where they stood by the huge mortars fired from the tanks. The battle turned into chaos for the Order of the White Rose fighters, as the tribesmen that had just joined them were picked off with deadly force.

The tanks let loose round after round, taking scores of the Ugandan warriors out with their deadly shelling, turning the snow on the valley floor a deeper shade of red.

The battle quickly turned into a bloodbath as the Order and their allies struggled to combat the new threat. Quickly surrounded, they prepared for what might be their final stand.

A noise from the skies caused Bash to look up. From over the ridge of the valley walls to the east dozens of planes appeared. Hatches opened on several of the planes and groups of paratroopers jumped out, landing in proximity to the Order's army. Pulling bazookas from their shoulders, several of the new arrival started to fire on the tanks.

The battle once again had turned into slug match with neither side having the clear advantage.

***

"This has been a boring fight. It is time for you to meet your former masters." The Lord of Shadows stalked closer to his four assailants as he unsheathed his sword. "I shall show each of you true despair."

Stood in front of Lenora, the dark lord prepared to deliver the first of the masters to the afterlife. As he was about deliver the fatal strike, a knife hit the dark lord in the shoulder, piercing his armor.

"So you have finally come," he snarled, turning around to face his opponent. "Grand Master Alexander, I shall particularly enjoy killing you."

Alexander walked out of the shadows, his two short swords in his hands by his side. On his waist was a leather holster holding a series of metallic throwing knives. "This war ends now."

The two faced each other across the temple floor, the Lord of Shadows grasping his giant sword in an attack position. Alexander stayed in a relaxed but guarded stance, waiting for the Lord of Shadows to make his move.

The Lord of Shadows charged Alexander with great speed, bringing his sword down at the Grand Masters head. A strike ferocious enough to have split the young leader right down the middle, but Alexander blocked the giant blade with both swords in a cross above his head, locking the giant blade in position. Forcing the blade down he kneed the dark lord in the chest.

Stumbling back, he sneered, "Impressive boy, to actually land a blow; however, it will be the only one you will."

Back-handing Alexander, he caused the Grand Master to lose hold of one of his swords as he fell to the ground. Flipping back to his feet Alexander looked straight into his enemy's eyes, and then attacked again. The Lord of Shadows brought his arm up as he blocked a kick from the air. Even as his first strike was blocked, Alexander used his momentum to follow with a knee into the Lord of Shadows' head, making him stumble back.

"It is a pity, Gode," Alexander's use of the Lord of Shadows former name caused the dark lord to growl in anger.

"You were such a promising student of Alder and a good friend of Eirik. How could you turn on both of them?" asked Alexander in an accusing tone as he fired a chi blast at the dark lord, sending him skidding back. Alexander rushed the evil one, his speed faster than the watching masters could believe.

"They denied me my right to be the Grand Master, and so they got what was coming to them," the Lord of Shadows said, hitting Alexander with another backhand. "No one will stop me. Not you, not your comrades. No one!" The Lord of Shadows sent Alexander back with another punch. "I will burn this planet to the ground and be the ruler of an apocalyptic world."

"You have forgotten one thing," said Alexander.

"Oh, and what is that?" asked the Lord of Shadows.

"I am still breathing, and while I am I will not stop until one of us is dead." Alexander got up, his face covered in blood from the dark lord's blows. He wiped blood from around his eyes and rushed forward once more. The Lord of Shadows summoned a ball of fire and shot it at the charging Grand Master. Jumping up and spinning to his left Alexander dodged it. Landing on his feet, he then came in from the side, slamming a fist into the Lord of Shadows, cracking his armor again.

The Lord of Shadows staggered from the blow. "You continue to impress me," said the Lord of Shadows with surprise, before retaliating with a blast of wind from his hand at Alexander.

Alexander was swept up in the galeforce wind and tossed to the back wall. "I will end everyone!" cried the Dark Lord. Crossing the room in a heartbeat, he brought his blade to the downed Grand Master's throat, ready to deliver the killer blow. Instinctively, he quickly turned to intercept a curved sword heading toward his back. Yuan attacked with rapid strikes of his sword, all of them easily parried and blocked.

The Lord of Shadows backhanded Yuan away and dodged a kick from Lenora. She tried to follow with a knee thrust to the chest, but the Lord of Shadows raised the earth causing Lenora to lose her footing. "Weak and pathetic," the dark lord taunted.

Catching a punch from Mason he squeezed the master's fist, sending him to his knees in agony. Punching him in the face he sent him crashing to the floor. "Is that it, Guardians? I was excepting some kind of a challenge."

The Lord of Shadows grabbed the staff held by Guan, pulled it from his grasp, and flung him across the temple. Breaking the staff in two, he threw the two ends at Guan's feet. The four masters were all on the ground unable to recover from the punishment they had been dealt as the dark lord gathered himself once more to finish off his enemies. Using his knowledge of the dark arts he gathered chi to launch at the masters.

Alexander tried to get up slowly, his body racked with pain. Fighting through it, he got to his feet. "It is over. I will end in you in this battle," Alexander declared through his blood-soaked face. Guan rose next, followed by Mason, Yuan and Lenora as they prepared for another round.

"Just die already!" screamed the Lord of Shadows as he fired a ball of dark energy at the group. The masters, as one, dodged the attack.

"Make us," Yuan said defiantly, still flinching from his injuries.

"I have been dominating this fight. You are all weak. You are nothing compared to me and the power I control. You will all die along with your army," said the Dark Lord

"You might want to stop underestimating us," said the Grand Master as he started to wobble.

"I shall end you all," said the Lord of Shadows as he attempted to conjure another fireball, only for it to fizzle out. "What is this?"

Alexander smiled. "It is over; you have lost an edge."

"That's impossible!" screamed the Lord of Shadows with madness in his voice. "I cannot die! I am a god!"

"Pride comes before the fall. I thought your last defeat would have taught you that," said Alexander.

"You have the gall to lecture me?" shouted the Lord of Shadows. Alexander rushed forward, meeting the Lord of Shadows head-on in a clash of steel.

"Your strength is diminishing," said the Grand Master with a grin as he forced the Lord of Shadows to one knee. "You have overused the Orbs and your powers. You should have finished us when you had the chance."

"I will not be denied," the Lord of Shadows said, rising slightly from his kneeling position. He threw his sword up to break the lock and sent Alexander skidding back. He then punched Alexander, doubling him over in pain "I will end this one way or another," he assured the group. "I don't need magic to beat you all."

The Lord of Shadows stumbled as Lenora snuck up behind him, knee extended. Spinning and backhanding the female master, her body span awkwardly through the air before falling. The Lord of Shadows tried to walk forward but was held in place by Mason, holding him underneath his arms in a full-nelson.

"Fool!" he shouted, flipping Mason on to the ground, the impact cracking the floor of the temple.

Breathing inward, the Lord of Shadows looked around the floor of the temple, once more the masters were groaning in pain and trying to get up. Approaching Yuan, he crouched down next to him and unsheathed his sword, "I will give you a warrior's death."

Alert to danger, the dark lord span round in his crouch and caught a knife thrown at his back. Alexander stood motionless, preparing for a counter-attack.

"It makes little difference how strong you are. I will end your reign in this world," said the Grand Master.

"I will not let it end this way," the Lord of Shadow said, removing his helmet. The masters shared a look as they discovered his face had a red 'X' tattooed across it. "I will show you true power." The tattoo started to crawl and then spread across his face turning the rest of his skin red. Horns appeared from his head and his eyes turned a deep, murky yellow. "It took me years to find a way to perform this final ascension. I accomplished it a few days before the battle, but have the moment of completion until now. Consider yourself privileged for you are the first and will also be the last to witness this."

"You are truly no longer human," said Alexander. "What are you, are demon?"

"I am the pestilence of this world. The harbinger of death and destruction and your doom. I go by many names, but shall call me Shaitan. Now Die!" screamed the demonic lord as he unleashed a blast of dark energy, sending all of the fighters back into the wall. "I shall destroy everyone on this miserable planet, starting with you."

Alexander got back up, using his sword to bring himself to his feet. "You talk too much."

"You are hard to kill, boy, but my power is unlimited and you are only a mere mortal."

"I will fight until I can fight no more. Do you hear me, demon?" shouted Alexander.

"I admire your bravado but it is pointless. Your death awaits, boy." Shaitan slammed his foot onto the ground, cracking the floor. "Now you will bear witness to the difference in our power."

Shaitan rushed forward, carrying his blade in a reverse grip. Alexander grabbed his first blade and retrieved his second blade from the floor of the temple. A blade in each hand, he strode forward to meet the demon in their final clash.

"Corrupt power is just as useless as having none. You lose sight of your purpose and become nothing more than a rabid beast, and as it's a beast you have become. I shall put you down!" Alexander shouted with a grunt, locking the demon's giant sword with both of his weapons crossed.

Alexander was unable to match the demons strength and was thrown back as his opponent laughed mockingly. "You are no match for me, boy." The demonic villain stalked closer to the downed Grand Master.

Alexander closed his eyes as he started to breathe heavily. "You are right, I am outclassed. However, I do have the means to beat you."

Alexander dug his swords into the ground as he put his hands up before his face, forming a triangle.

"What? You can't possible know that!" shouted the Dark Lord, rushing Alexander before he could finish the ritual.

He tried to break through as the other four masters blocked his way. Desperation etched across his red, demonic face. "You fools; if you let him perform that technique, he will die along with me," the villain said. Lenora turned her head away, trying to ignore his attempt to sway their minds.

"Focus. He knows the risks of performing the ritual," Guam told her.

Alexander switched from the triangle to both fists touching on the knuckle. A glow appeared around his hands. *I am sorry, Lenora. I guess we won't be together,* thought Alexander.

Looking the demon in the eyes, Alexander focused his mind. "You are done, Shaitan. Move!" he commanded. The other masters jumped back from the demonic lord as a blast of white energy struck the former Lord of Shadows.

"What is this? This is not the same technique," he cried. What have you done to me?"

"This will wipe both of our souls out of existence with no chance of reincarnation. This is it, Gode; you will not be coming back," said Alexander.

Shaitan for the first time in his existence finally felt pure fear. He could not lose. This could not happen.

"I'm sorry. I will not let you sacrifice yourself for my mistake," spoke a voice from behind Alexander as a spectral image of Alder appeared and merged with his body. "My soul will be the price that will be paid."

The white blast vanished as the former Lord of Shadows' armor crumbled to dust. Alexander lay face down on the ground.

Lenora rushed to Alexander's side. "Alexander, wake up!" she shouted. Holding his body, she started to cry, as the other masters bowed their heads.

Finally, she felt pressure grip her hand and Alexander's eyes opened. "Did we win?" he asked weakly.

"Yes," cried Lenora as she leaned down and kissed him.

The battle was over, and with the death of the Lord of Shadows his army vanished into black smoke leaving the Order and their allies cheering.

The battle may have been a victory, but the guardians knew that they must always stay vigilant to prevent another evil from surfacing.

The End?

Made in the USA
Coppell, TX
27 July 2021